THRALL

A Tennyson Bend Novel

PT Ambler

A TENNYSON BEND NOVEL

PT AMBLER

THRALL

Jet Crane has faced a lot of tests lately. He's not looking for more. But they rush in relentless as the tide. When his life implodes, Jet finds shelter on beautiful Tallon Island, a remote weather station in the Coral Sea – population 2 – home to a bazillion sea birds, hundreds of nesting turtles, and one testy co-volunteer who thinks 'friendly' means icy indifference.

Malone Archer has one last chance to prove himself to the big names in medical science. All he needs is uninterrupted time on the coral reef to collect data and secure funding for his research. But Malone doesn't factor in variables like his annoying co-volunteer who makes ridiculous art and thinks it's reasonable to skinny dip in another man's lagoon.

All it takes is one rum-soaked, hot-as-hell night for everything to change. As the brutal storm season looms, more than the air pressure rises, and, suddenly, it's not just their hearts facing natural selection...at risk is their very survival.

AUTHOR'S NOTE

To my gorgeous friend, L.B., who wanted a character named in her honour. I hope I did you justice (and that you don't mind being dead).

To keep this novel authentic to its Aussie roots, the author has used Australian English spelling and grammar.

Enjoy :)

CHAPTER ONE

Malone

Malone lodged the cider six-pack into the nook of his elbow and slid open the glass doors to Brady's flash rooftop terrace at Tennyson Bend.

He hadn't wanted a farewell party. Without Brady's insistence, Malone would still be in the lab, tying up loose ends, making sure he'd covered every variable and prepared for every random eventuality during a summer of field research on remote Tallon Island. But once Brady got an idea in his mind, he was stubborn as fuck. He wasn't about to let Malone disappear for three months without an event to mark the occasion.

Malone was just glad Brady had restricted himself to a low-key pre-departure-slash-pre-birthday-slash-pre-Christmas barbeque with their tight group of mates. Never mind that it wasn't his birthday for another week, nor another three weeks after that till Christmas.

"The man of the hour!" Brady waved his tongs from his usual station in front of his top-tier, bells-and-whistles barbeque. "Grab us a beer, would you? Thirsty work, this gig is."

Grease spattered and hissed, and flames licked up through the iron bars, so high they came close to Brady's actual fiery-red eyebrows. Unfazed, Brady barely flinched. Beside him, Spencer reared back, his reflexes sharp from years of training on the tennis court.

Malone wasn't anywhere close to the flames, but he still fought the instinct to run a mile. He corralled his racing heart and deadpanned, "You sure you don't want a fire extinguisher instead?"

"Don't listen to him, Barb." Brady patted the barbeque knobs. "He just doesn't know you like I do."

Spencer edged closer to the table in the corner of the rooftop terrace, where Dane observed with the sort of cool detachment Malone envied, and Lachlan, ever the loyal friend, smiled indulgently at Brady's antics.

By the number of empty pistachio shells and beer bottles, the four of them had been there a while. As much as he might wish to get boozy with his mates, no way would he be able to fully relax till he and his microscope landed safely on Tallon Island. He'd hang with the guys for the evening. Enjoy a drink and one of Brady's legendary steaks. But no good time was worth having if it meant driving a thousand kilometres into the sun with a hangover.

Malone hitched his chinos to squat in front of the bar fridge in Brady's outdoor kitchen, rearranged the random selection of drinks, and slid his six-pack into the new gap. He glanced over his shoulder. "Anyone need a refill?"

Dane lifted his wineglass as a silent affirmative.

Too used to classroom rules, Lachlan raised his hand. "What did you bring, Malone?"

"Pear cider. Want one? It has a honey edge to it."

"Sweet tooth." Lachlan teased.

"Piss off. Like you don't have a sweeter tooth than me."

Lachlan laughed at the over-worn gripe. Either of them could win that contest, but Malone wasn't about to admit to the weakness. Not even amongst friends. Besides, it was *his* farewell party. He could make his own rules.

Malone pulled out Dane's half-empty bottle of Chardonnay, a couple of ciders for himself and Lachlan, and a dark ale for Brady. "What about you? Spencer? Want a drink? Or are you gearing up for a tournament?"

"I'm good, thanks. Brady already plied me with this super-special glacial water, melted, bottled, and helicoptered all the way from Antarctica, just for me." Spencer jostled his glass.

"Oi! It's from Chile," Brady corrected. "Get your glaciers right."

From the sounds of the others' sniggering, it hadn't been Spencer's first dig at Brady's latest brush with luxury. None of them knew Brady prior to landing his millions on a twenty-first-birthday lottery ticket, but the way Brady bounced between high-life and low-life tastes provided them all with a ready source of amusement.

"Ta," Brady grumbled, but he wasn't the type to stay moody long. Brady clinked his beer against Malone's cider and flashed him a grin. "Tell us about this island, mate. Don't think I could stand three months alone with no Wi-Fi."

Dane fake-coughed, "Porn."

"I appreciate adult art," Brady slashed back, quick smart. "Sue me."

Malone ignored their familiar banter. "I won't be alone."

"Oh, do tell. Will you have an *assistant*?"

Oh, God. Not this again. He loved Brady, but when the man got an idea in his head, he was like a dog with a bone. "No, I do not have a thing for research assistants. And, no, I am not going to Tallon to screw around."

"Shh...don't destroy my fantasy."

"Let it go, you perv." Lachlan did a piss-poor job of hiding a grin behind his drink.

"You have to have fun some time," Brady protested. "If you don't take advantage of opportunities like this, you'll blink, years will go by, and you'll have turned from studly catch to silver fox."

"Leave him be," Dane said. "Malone's going north to work, not play."

"Thank you, Dane." It was good to know at least one of his friends understood what it meant to put his career first. Fun, he could do. Serial dating? Sure. But emotional entanglements? He'd never achieve his goals if he let himself be distracted by men.

Not that Brady listened. "No rule says he can't both work and play."

Not likely.

"I'll have plenty of time to play once the summer's over," Malone said. "My focus will be on sea cucumbers. Not men."

He thought that was the end of the discussion until Dane piped up again. "Besides, older guys aren't really Malone's style. He's more into nerdy twinks."

"I am not." Nerd, sure. But twink? Hell, no. Too high maintenance.

So what if he liked a guy with a few billion brain cells above average. It wasn't Malone's fault that those traits typically accompanied guys who spoke in 'isms' and had the muscle definition of two-week-old celery.

Brady ignored his protest and nodded in agreement with Dane. "I can see it now. You and your research assistant get cosy in your island laboratory, have an incomprehensible discussion involving pepto-cosmos and cyto-whatsits, then you stroke your sea cucumbers to get all excitable and your nuclear-plasm shoots, and—"

"Gentlemen," Dane interrupted. "Focus."

Brady didn't let it go. "Oh, I absolutely am focused. Believe me."

Malone ground his teeth. After hearing fifty-million variants of the same erectile-slash-projectile sea cucumber joke, it was getting old.

Spencer, who'd been looking at him with the sort of floaty, dreamy speculation that made Malone shift uncomfortably, said, "I like a bit of maturity in a man. Someone who's lived a bit. Knows how to press my buttons."

Lachlan rolled his eyes. "We don't need to know about your buttons, Spencer."

"Speak for yourself." Brady affected a 'thinking man' pose, just about poking his eye out with his tongs. "Tell us all about your buttons, Spencer."

Since Malone wasn't needed for that uncomfortable discussion, he took a quiet moment for himself, leaning up against the north-facing handrail and looked out over the snake loops of the Brisbane River.

In the near distance, amongst a mauve cluster of late-flowering jacaranda trees, he could just make out the tops of the university buildings where he shared lab space in the school of marine biology. As the crow flew, it was barely a kilometre away, but his daily commute by kayak was an easy six kilometres along the winding silty river.

For years, he'd waded into the cut-throat world of academic research, seeking funding to conduct a field trial into the biomedical potential of sea cucumber exudate, to no avail. He hadn't been able to convince the university to fund a preliminary data set, let alone a weightier project. The whole situation left him in a bind—he needed preliminary data to prove his hypothesis had legs, but the only way to get the preliminary data was to find support for his vision. It was a maddening chicken and egg situation.

The simple fact was, sea cucumbers weren't sexy. He couldn't compete with the migration habits of humpback whales up and down the Eastern coastline, or the crown of thorn starfish that menaced the Great Barrier Reef. Hell, even the great southern kelp forest got higher billing than his humble sea cucumbers. So, when he heard about the opportunity to volunteer on Tallon Island, the remote weather station that just happened to be in prime sea cucumber territory, he'd leaped at it. He'd never had much interest in weather, but it wasn't hard to learn how to read the meteorological instruments and report his findings to the mainland. With twenty-four hours in each day, he'd have plenty of down-time to survey and collect specimens from the local sea cucumber population—data that, Malone hoped, would support advancement in his research.

All going to plan, in three days, by road and by sea, Malone would land on Tallon Island, a tiny cay on the eastern edge of the Great Barrier Reef. Out there, it wouldn't just be tropical heat and summer storms he'd have to contend with. Extreme isolation, deadly sea-life, and two unknown co-volunteers were just a few of the uncontrollable variables on Malone's horizon. He'd deal with them, though. He'd have to if he was going to succeed.

Stay focused, Archer. Eye on the prize. No distractions.

That was the only way to achieve his goals.

Malone hadn't always been so driven, but from the day his twin brother, Myles, spilled a vat of hot oil and French fries all over his front, causing third-degree burns to his face, neck, and chest, Malone's life became about one thing—finding a way to undo his brother's agony. Even when Myles moved on—graduated from high school and made a happy life for himself—Malone hadn't been able to adjust. Every time he looked into the mirror, he saw the face his twin had lost, and the pain was rekindled. His need to help his brother became a determination to lessen the suffering for all future burn victims—an obsession that hadn't waned in over a decade. Nothing came between him and that goal.

No. It was best if he dated guys who didn't expect too much of him—who understood that he wasn't interested in competing priorities. His research would always come out on top. End of story.

"Grub's up," Brady called, drawing Malone's attention back across the terrace to his friends.

"Yum." Lachlan rubbed hands together as Brady slid a platter of thick rib-eye steaks, barbeque-seared veggies, and a basket of crusty rolls onto the table. "Thanks, man."

"Welcome." Brady beamed, ever the host.

"Need any help to get your gear loaded?" Dane asked as Malone slid into a seat.

"Thanks, but I'm good. I've already loaded my SUV with my lab equipment. All I have left to do is throw a few things into a suitcase and be on the road by dawn."

"Speaking of twinks—" Brady started.

"Which we weren't." Malone tried, again, to sideswipe that conversation.

"—don't forget your Speedos." Brady shoved a mouthful of steak in his mouth and chomped. Nothing could disguise his shit-eating grin.

Malone groaned. Would he never live that down? "It was a perfectly normal, perfectly fine swim suit."

"Uh-huh. Perfectly perfect for a twink. But you, my friend, aren't built like a twink." Brady tilted his head sideways. "Your physique's more in the realm of the superhero. You'd look good with a cape. Turquoise. Like your eyes."

"The Speedos were Justin's. Not mine." How many times did he have to say it?

"We know," the guys chorused.

Malone pointed the sharp end of his knife at each of them. "Fuck you all. Justin was not a twink."

"His super-snug swimsuit begged to differ," Brady pushed.

"It begged for a lot of things," Dane smirked.

At Spencer's snort, Malone seriously considered pulling out his phone to record a "fuck off" auto-respond message. Instead, he grumbled a live, "Fuck off," and wondered how soon he could get away. He'd kill for some time in the lap pool. A half hour of metronomic freestyle ought to be enough to take the edge off his tension and bring on a decent night's sleep. The sooner he could get to sleep, the sooner he could get on the road.

"Talking about snug swimmers," Lachlan began.

Malone was having none of it. "Which we need not."

Lachlan pulled out a package from the bench seat between him and Spencer. "Safe travels, happy birthday, merry Christmas, and happy new year. From all of us."

"You got me a present?" They never got each other gifts.

Help, yes. The odd reciprocal favour. But no outright gifts.

Malone gave the light box a shake. Nothing budged.

Classic Lachlan, he'd used dozens of colourful stickers to hold the newspaper wrapping together, each blazed with *Well Done!*, or *Good Job!*, or *Super Effort!*

Malone grazed his thumbnail across a purple sticker and a waft of sugar-sweet grape permeated the air. The sweet smell reminded him of primary school and the scratch-and-sniff stickers given to top students. Myles, his twin brother, always got As for Awesome, but Malone just wasn't that smart. Bs was about the best he could do until senior year, when Myles had his accident and the trajectories of their lives were changed forever. Myles diverted into the arts, while Malone pursued the hard sciences. He pressed himself to toe the academic line—his eye on the prize of a career in medical research.

He scratched another sticker. Cherry. It made his gut turn over with memories of what should have been.

Unaware of Malone's trip down memory lane, Lachlan smiled goofily. "Sensory overload, I reckon. They make my eyes water, but my kids love them."

Spencer leaned forward, eager, barely holding back a grin. "Come on, Malone. Open it."

"Not sure if I want to," he half-joked as he warily peeled open the paper to find an old shoe box. Inside the box was a pile of shredded tissue. Underneath that was, "Pantyhose?"

The fuck?

"Man-sized." Brady qualified, grinning shamelessly.

"Ah..." Malone blinked. "No shade on men who wear tights, but..." He could practically feel Brady vibrating with laughter from a metre away.

"What am I missing?"

"It's a stinger suit!" Brady burst out.

"So that you can swim in jelly-infested waters," Spencer explained.

"You do *not* want to get stung by a box jellyfish," Dane added.

"Fiery depths of hell," agreed Lachlan.

Malone wasn't entirely convinced by their concern.

For one, not one of the arseholes could hide their amusement. And, for another...he held up the offending present. "They're hot pink and covered in sparkles."

CHAPTER TWO

Jet

Ding, dong.

Jet's doorbell peeled.

Fuck.

"Coming!" He stuck the strip of packing tape across the top of yet another cardboard box, then added it to the mini-mountain in the middle of his living room-slash-dining room-slash-art studio-slash-study. It was a good thing the spring semester of his art therapy program was over or he'd still be elbow-deep in research papers.

Ding, dong.

Sheesh. "I'm coming!" Jet called out as he ran his sore fingers over his near-bare scalp. The stubble had softened a bit since he'd donated his wild mop of black curls to Eloise's favourite cancer charity, but he still wasn't used to having so little to grab onto when frustration struck.

"He's such a mooch." Jet heard as he rounded the hall into the small entry and saw the shadowed visage of Richard Price—his dick of a secret blood brother—peering through the screen door, his critical gaze raking down Jet's purple tie-died sarong that Eloise always said was her favourite.

Arsehole. If anyone was mooching off of Eloise, Jet's birth mother, it was...

No. Jet stopped himself. *Don't go there. Eloise could do whatever she liked with her legacy. Even give it to a tosser like Richard.*

Standing beside Richard was a woman Jet had only ever seen in the collection of family photographs Eloise kept on her grand piano—cousin Diane, Brisbane's real estate princess, decked out in a sculpted black dress and glossy six-inch heels. Jet could appreciate her classy funeral attire, but not her pretentious expression.

Up the driveway behind them, faceless people, all cloaked in black, freely streamed into Eloise's stately old Queenslander home. Eloise's family—the Price family—God, it smarted to say that. As though he had no place in that rarefied genetic pool.

For a year, he'd lived on Eloise's property, nursed her through the agony of chemo, cared for every raw bit of her, and never gave a hint to her that he was her first-born son. Thanks to Eloise and her shame, or her embarrassment, or whatever the fuck it was that had kept her silent for the thirty-three years since she'd given him up for adoption, Jet's blood relations were all ignorant of his existence.

He was nothing to them.

The only thing Jet could hope for was that, eventually, they'd be nothing to him.

Play it cool, Jethro. Don't let them see how you're hurting. "Hello, Dick." It gave him a tiny measure of joy to see Richard wince at the nickname.

"Jethro. This is my cousin Diane."

Our cousin. Not that Dick knew they shared DNA. As far as Richard Price was concerned, Jethro Crane was nothing more than the live-in help—a convenient addition to the household while his mother was ill, but worthless since her death.

God, if only he'd had the balls to confront Eloise while she was alive. Tell her he was her son. Ask her for... Jet didn't know what.

Love?

Affection?

An explanation for why he wasn't good enough to keep?

Eloise's soul may have taken the high road, but her death left Jet alone in the dirt, caught out by the pretence of a professional relationship.

"Mr. Crane." Diane smiled a shark's smile. "Pleased to meet you."

"And you." Jet nodded. He could be polite. It wasn't Richard's fault that Eloise hadn't fessed up to giving birth to another child, or that Jet hadn't shouted the truth to the rooftops. He still couldn't bring himself to like the guy.

"We came to have a look around," said Richard.

AKA, check on Jet's tiny patch of Richard's inheritance.

Jet clenched his reddened fingers into fists, feeling the sting of the cardboard fibres that irritated every nook and cranny. He wasn't short on reasons to be pissed off at Richard, but his artist's hands were his trade, and the attack felt personal. Never mind politeness, it was time to be a hard-arse. "It hasn't even been a day since you informed me that I had precisely twenty-four hours to move out of Eloise's granny flat." He checked the time on his phone. "That gives me—" Shit. Numbers had never been his strong suit, especially when he was stressed.

"Three-and-a-half hours." Diane helped.

"Exactly. I still have three-and-a-half hours." Three-and-a-half hours left to put to rest the lost hope that his birth mother might recognise him. Might want him in her life. Might love him. Jet shook away the nagging disappointment. "After that, the place is yours. Now, if you'll excuse me. I have a lot to get on with." And no time for more aggravation.

Jet made sure the screen door was securely locked so that Dick and Diane couldn't invade his peace any more than they already had. Then he reversed course back to his mini-mountain of boxes and the still-unpacked chaos of a year spent living in the shade of Eloise's home.

What he really needed was a reminder that he still had parents who loved him. A mother and father who'd welcomed baby-Jet into their home and made him their own.

He raised his phone again and scrolled through his contacts to the 'C' section.

"Son? You'll never believe where we are."

His mum and dad had never been inclined to settle down on a quarter acre block in the suburbs. Since they'd decided to flip the retirement switch, buy an RV, and roam *wherever our whim and the weather take us, dear*, they could be anywhere in Australia. Hell, they could have even parked at any of a dozen international airports and taken off into the wide blue yonder.

"Zimbabwe?" Jet hazarded a wild guess.

"No. Better."

"Ah..."

"Tasmania! Your mum and I got an amazing deal for the ferry across the Bass Straight, and now we're at this extraordinary hydroelectric plant. It's a miracle for its time. Something like twenty megalitres of water rush through those pipes per second. Can you imagine?"

"Wow. That's incredible." Typical Dad, there wasn't a grand engineering project that didn't spin his wheels.

"Crappy timing, though. You'll never guess the opportunity that came up on the old Weather Warriors forum."

"Ah." Dare he ask? "What?"

"Tallon Island, Jethro. Tallon!"

Jet pulled the mobile from his ear and tapped the speakerphone icon. "No need to shout, Dad."

"The Bureau's desperate for a seasonal volunteer weather observer. Some woman was going, but she had to pull out at the last minute. Such a shame. I'd go, but your mother won't let me."

"For heaven's sake." Jet's mum's voice came through loud and clear. "We are not crossing back to the mainland and driving four thousand kilometres in three days."

"But..."

"No."

"Yeah, but..."

"No buts."

Jet let the silence at the other end extend. Then his dad's ever-chipper voice started up again.

"No reason you can't go, though, Jethro. Just think, no light pollution, deep blue ocean as far as your eye can see."

"Sounds like a dream, Dad." Jet could see the appeal of escaping the harsh realities of life and whiling away the summer on a tropical island. But he had way too much to do over the summer to even contemplate that indulgence. His life had imploded, and he had limited time to get it back on track.

After a year of caring for Eloise for far more hours than he'd been paid, Jet's savings were meagre. He could probably scrape together a rental bond, but he'd have to pick up more shifts at the hospital to prove he had adequate income before he could even think about applying for a new apartment lease. Worst case scenario, he could join a student share house. Plenty of students in his master's course shacked up together. But Jet had grown out of that lifestyle a decade ago when his best friend, Shane, put an engagement ring on Kristy's finger and moved out of his and Jet's bachelor pad.

Volunteering for the summer would put him in an even worse financial position.

Besides, meteorology had always been his dad's passion. Not his.

"Summer is the best time for wild weather. Between the warm South Equatorial Current and the perpetual north-easterly trade winds, the thunderstorms that whip up are incredible. Adventure on the high seas," his dad said.

"Like a pirate?" Jet teased.

"Exactly!" there was a pause on the line. "Well...not *exactly* like a pirate. An island isn't a ship. But it comes pretty damn close. After that last cyclone that hit a decade ago, all the systems were updated. The radar tower, solar array, even the sewage and desalination plant. Everything. Backups for backups. Safe as houses."

"That's great, Dad. So glad to hear the sewage system is in tip-top form." Jet circumnavigated the boxes clogging the room. If he was master of his own ship, it was rudderless, made of cardboard, sailed by a fool.

"What do you reckon, son? You up for it?"

"I don't know, Dad. Meteorology is your thing. Not mine."

"Of course. I wouldn't raise it if I didn't think you could do it, son."

"It's not a question of whether I *could* do it." Capability wasn't the issue. He'd trailed after his dad to umpteen weather observation stations across the state's far west, only those outposts were surrounded by seas of rock and sand, not reef and water. "I can probably remember how to work the instruments and read all the gauges." A man didn't forget how to launch a weather balloon in a hurry. "But..."

Wait, am I actually considering the idea?

Why he didn't just give a flat out 'no' was a mystery. Even contemplating it was ridiculous.

"You don't have any classes over the summer, do you?"

"No. The semester doesn't start till March, but..."

'No, but' what?

Jet stopped his circular pacing and peered out the age-wavered windows across the backyard to where he could see through the back windows of the big house. Inside, all the people who mattered milled about.

Eloise's friends.

Eloise's family.

But not Jet.

He wasn't invited.

If it wasn't for the principle of the matter, he'd turn away and never look back.

"It's such a great opportunity, Jet. You could—"

"God, Dad. Enough."

"Yeah, but—"

"I've got a lot going on." Far more than his adoptive father knew about.

"Three months on a beautiful island—just you, the sun, the sand, and the sea—it's a big ask. I'll give my contact a call and let her know you're not able to get away. I'm sure somebody else will be able to fill in."

"Nice guilt trip, Dad." Jet chuckled darkly at his dad's overt manipulation.

"No guilt, son. None at all." Silence again. "It's just that..."

"Ugh."

Which prospect was worse—homeless and broke, or sequestered on a remote tropical island?

The devil you know? Or...?

Fuck it.

"I'll think about it, Dad."

"Yes! You won't regret it." Excitement threaded his dad's voice.

"No promises."

"No, no. Of course not. Have to do your own homework on the place and the position."

"Exactly." Although homework was the last thing on his mind. He needed either a gut check, or a sanity check. Maybe both. "I've gotta go, Dad. Send me the details and I'll let you know."

"Not much time for indecision, son. Whoever volunteers has to get to Cairns and be on the boat by Wednesday morning."

"Ugh." Enough dreaming. What he needed was an objective, rational view—a pragmatic opinion on the best way forward.

Jet gave his farewells to his folks, hung up, and scrolled further down to Shane "Flash" Gordon.

If all else failed, he could crash at Shane's house. Shane's wife Kristy had already offered the sofa. But with two young kids and a third on the way, staying with his best friend could only ever be a short-term solution.

Shane picked up mid-conversation with his oldest child. "For frack's sake, Dillon, your brother is not a toy, and a choke hold is not a hug. Put him down. Now." Shane's voice muffled for a bit and the thud of a door shutting. "Sorry 'bout that. Hi."

"Flash. I need your help."

A long beat of silence hung in the air. "Did you get snatched by aliens? Tell me you're not being probed as we speak. And, please God, tell me you're not enjoying it."

"Ha. Ha. Funny guy."

"No. Seriously. Who is this? Jethro Crane gives help. He never asks for it."

"Fuck off."

"Ah, that's the Jet I know and love. What can I do you for? Did Rick-the-dick already throw you out on your arse? Need a place to bunk in? Dillon's about to lose his big-boy-bedroom privileges, so there's a comfy three-quarter-length, dinosaur-themed, single bed up for grabs. You can sleep in the foetal position, can't you?"

"Thanks, but no, although, maybe."

Way to be certain, Jethro.

"Perfect. I'll tell Kristy to expect a fifth for dinner."

"Just for a night or two. And the sofa will be fine." No way would he take over his honorary nephew's precious dinosaur bed. "But that's not why I called."

"You've decided you've been single for long enough and want me to go clubbing as your wingman?" Shane guessed, hope lacing his voice.

"No." Of that, Jet was one-hundred percent sure. Even if he was into the club scene, which he wasn't, life was complicated enough without adding a hook-up into the mix.

"Damn." Shane grumbled. "Could'a done with a few child-free hours."

"Sorry." *Not sorry.* "I just need to run an idea past you."

"Okay. Shoot."

"It's ridiculous and I'm crazy to even be considering it."

"Is it entering that portrait you did of my darling wife into the Archibald Prize?"

"No."

"Pity. That would've got me serious brownie points."

"Correction, as the artist, that would get *me* serious brownie points."

"Sure, and me by association. There's a reason why we're friends, mate."

"I thought it was because we were the only guys in our year studying nursing. You would've gone around the bend without me."

"That too." Shane conceded. "But I reckon that was a mutual de-round-the-bending."

"True." At a two-hundred-to-one, female-to-male disadvantage, neither he nor Shane would've survived three years of undergraduate nursing school without the other.

"So, you going to tell me what this idea is, or do I have to keep guessing?" Shane might talk his share of crap, but he had a neat way of cutting through it too.

As Jet outlined what he knew of the met bureau's volunteer position on Tallon Island, he felt a teasing fission of energy. Was it unease or excitement? He couldn't tell. "It's crazy, right? I'm a people person. How am I supposed to cope on an island with only two other people for company? What if they're crazies? Or arseholes?"

"It is a crazy idea. Wild, even." Shane agreed. "But—"

"Ugh. I hate 'but's.'"

Shane snorted. "As if."

"Be serious." Jet groaned. "This is my future we're talking about."

"Bzzt. Hyperbole alert." Shane pushed back. "Okay, so. Here's the *but*. You're homeless."

"Not quite." Technically, he had a roof over his head for another three hours and seven minutes.

"You're single."

"By choice." Why did he feel like he was being walked into a trap?

"You got that casual ward-nursing job, right?"

"Yeah." Jet's voice wavered, unsure where Shane was leading with his argument.

"Which means you can make yourself available anything from twenty-four hours a day, seven days a week, to one shift a quarter. You could leave town, and nobody would be the wiser."

That didn't sound reassuring. "You're saying I could disappear off the face of the earth, and nobody would notice? Way to make me feel loved, mate."

"No. I'm saying the choice is open. Even if your boss protests at your lack of availability, what's she going to do? Say you can't volunteer on a tiny island in the middle of the Pacific where you'll be protecting the entire country from deadly cyclones?"

"The *entire* country? Who's being hyperbolic now?"

"Okay, fine. Far North Queensland. That's still a vast coastline, where hundreds of thousands of people are at risk of wild weather. And don't tell me that's not the case. I've been up there during the wet season. Mother Nature does not hold back. Ask your dad. He'll tell you."

"He's the one who foisted this idea on me," Jet reluctantly admitted.

"Should've known." Shane chuckled. Then he sobered. "What does your gut say?"

Jet groaned. It was his gut that made him quit his full-time job, move out of his perfectly good, perfectly affordable apartment, and offer to be his secret mother's live-in nurse. Clearly, his gut couldn't be trusted.

Jet tried gave the unvarnished truth. "My gut says I'd be hiding from reality."

"And what does your gut tell you about your current reality?"

Trust Shane to ask the stickiest question. "That it's shit."

"Exactly." Shane let him stew for a minute. Then he said, "I'll miss you."

"Hmph."

"Don't *hmph* me. It's a no-brainer. You go. You chill. You recover from the whole Eloise drama."

"Drama?" That was harsh. "She was my mother, and she died."

"I didn't say it wasn't valid drama. In the spring, you come home and start fresh. It's too good an opportunity to pass up, and you know it."

"You sound like my dad."

"Thank you. I like your dad. He's a wise man."

Jet huffed. "Did you miss the bit about it being a volunteer position? It'll earn me nothing. In three months, I'll be worse off. And it sure won't get me any closer to graduating and starting a new practice."

"Not talking about financial opportunities."

"What then?"

"Life. The universe. Every—"

"—thing. Fuck you."

Shane ignored that. "Just don't forget to pack your hammock."

"I don't have a hammock."

"Not the point, mate."

What Shane's exact point was, Jet never found out.

At the sound of a child's high-pitched squeal, Jet skirted around the boxes to the long row of windows.

In their sad little black suits, Eloise's two youngest grandsons ran through the garden, past the swing set and the trampoline, and behind the cluster of banana palms. Beyond that, an old gate and steep wooden stairs led down to the swift-flowing Brisbane River. Both boys could swim, and Eloise had never babied them when it came to safety, but Jet couldn't help the instinct to rush out there—to protect them from everything bad in the world.

Wasn't that what an uncle did?

Even a secret uncle?

"Sorry, Flash. Gotta go."

"Yeah, yeah, sure. We'll see you for dinner. Let me know if you need more help."

"Thanks, mate."

Sometimes water really was thicker than blood.

Jet unhooked the brass window latch and stuck his head out, but before he could yell to the boys to be careful, he heard another clang of the gate and they came tearing back up the yard.

"Stand down, Uncle Jet." His breath frosted the glass, then faded away. As though he'd never been there at all.

Eloise's home wasn't his. He was a fool to ever think it could have been.

Jet gave the window latch another squeeze, then let go. Replaying the past never did anyone any good. Far better to look toward the future.

In the time it took him to tape together the bottom of yet another cardboard box, Jet had decided. He punched in a text to his dad and sent off the message before he could reconsider.

"I'm in."

Was he crazy to commit to a season on Tallon?

Absolutely.

But what did he have to lose?

CHAPTER THREE

Malone

Malone canted his hip against the catamaran's metal railing and glared down the length of the dock, as though that would do anything to hasten the second volunteer's arrival.

"How long are we supposed to wait?" he asked Kathy, the freckle-faced First Officer who sidled up close and eyed him like he was her next meal.

"Cap' said it won't be long. Your co-volunteer called from the airport to say he's landed. Just needs to find a taxi."

"In other words, delay." Malone grumped.

"Seems like. The other guy's a ring-in. Last-minute change." Kathy didn't sound all that concerned.

That wasn't news. He'd gotten the email update from the Bureau as he pulled into his motel on the first night of the long drive north. After fourteen hours on the road, he'd been in no mood to accept a change to the plan, but it was a relief to know there'd still be a second volunteer. If it'd been just him and Victor on the island doing all the work, he'd have struggled to find time to do his research.

Patience, Malone. We're on island time now.

He rolled his neck and checked his watch. Again.

Technically, the other volunteer wasn't late yet. The catamaran was due to head out to sea on the falling tide, just past
noon, but they were skating far too close to the line for Malone's
liking.

"Is that him?" she pointed. All Malone could see was a whip-
pet-thin woman, wearing a canary yellow hat, a safety-orange
tank top, and a purple sarong that billowed out as she strode
down the dock, one hand firm on the crown of her hat, the other
dragging a massive black suitcase.

Tourist.

Surprisingly, the closer she got, the more 'she' appeared to
be a 'he.' What the floppy hat and billowing sarong disguised
were square shoulders, narrow hips, and the tell-tale light and
shadow of masculine muscle definition. Tall. Sleek. Edging on
graceful. Like a bird-of-paradise flower—all gaudy colours and
sharp points, and, undoubtedly, all man.

For a few moments, Malone enjoyed the view. Fantasies
tripped through his mind about joining the guy on a tropical
island getaway—nothing but cocktail umbrellas and frivolous
fun.

Sweet indulgence.

The closer the man got, the higher the heat of the day slid
up Malone's neck. He forced his body to batten down anything
else that might get a rise out of the vision, but the effort wasn't
worth a damn. Never mind tropical getaways. If he had to share
a desert island with that guy, Malone's equilibrium would be
shot to shit. He'd never get anything worthwhile done.

He expected the man to stop at one of the many fancy superyachts moored on the upriver side of the dock. But he didn't stop. He kept coming, and coming, till there were no more superyachts to board, only the giant catamaran commissioned by the met bureau to ferry Malone and the other new volunteer out to Tallon Island. Which meant the distracting bird of paradise had to be Jethro Crane—fellow volunteer and close-quarters neighbour for the next three months.

"Brilliant," Malone muttered to himself.

"What was that?" The captain's voice came from his left, startling Malone. "Sorry."

"No. You're okay. I was...distracted. My mind was a million miles from here."

Liar. Your mind was twenty metres away, and closing fast.

Malone's attention gravitated back to the dock where his soon-to-be co-volunteer brought his enormous suitcase to a rumbling stop at the base of the steep gangplank, which just so happened to be directly below Malone's place at the railing.

Just brilliant.

He looked down on that ridiculous yellow hat—big as the sun, bright as a solar flare. And when Jethro Crane lifted it off...*fuck!* A midnight-black crew cut, offset by moon-glow skin. Malone had seen a solar eclipse once. The world slid into darkness till only the silvery afterimage remained, then appeared once again. He'd always thought it a wondrous magic. Seeing Jethro's face for the first time wasn't quite that magical. It was only a face, for fuck's sake. Skin and bone, hair and mucosa. But the sight of him did things to Malone's biorhythms that

would've probably taken a degree in biochemistry to understand.

Or bio-electrical engineering.

Or whatever the fuck was the scientific discipline that
explained why Malone felt like he had white-hot electric
shocks sparking from his eyeballs to his balls.

If he was mine to touch, I'd...

But he wasn't. And Malone wasn't interested in distractions. He had work to do. Conclusions to reach. Important
hypotheses to test that had nothing to do with his wayward
libido.

Captain Thompson traipsed down the steep gangplank to
meet him, his hand outstretched. "Hello, Mr. Crane. Jethro,
right? Glad you found us. Let's get you aboard. We're all
eager to be out on the open water."

"Sorry I'm late. If only I could have flapped my own
wings, I'd have been up here yesterday. And, please, call me
Jet." He smiled at the captain.

In Malone's opinion, that smile was all kinds of wrong.
He shouldn't be smiling like that at anyone. Especially not
some old guy who wasn't...

...him.

Shit.

Focus, Archer.

No, idiot, not on him. Focus on something else.

Malone wrenched his attention down to the black slab
of a suitcase. He leaned over the railing and grabbed the
telescopic handle.

"Wait!" Jet called out.

But Malone didn't wait. "Holy shit!" Had the guy packed rocks or something? The tiny wheels clunked sharp against the metal railing, and clattered hollow as they landed on the moulded fibreglass deck. "This must weigh fifty kilos. How the hell did you get it on a plane?"

Jet shrugged. "Half of my gear was in a cardboard box that fell apart in transit. The folks at Cairns airport helped me to consolidate. Friendly bunch."

"Consolidated what? Dumbbells?" Jet didn't look like the sort of guy who pumped iron. The heaviest thing Malone could imagine him lifting was a bottle of ice-cold vodka.

Don't prejudge, Archer.

Maybe Jet preferred gin.

"Weights? Gawd, no!" Jet flashed a grin that pinged Malone's biochemistry again. "It's mostly art supplies. Paints. Canvases. Crayons. Stuff like that. The bare necessities."

"Crayons?" Malone couldn't think of a single reason why a grown man might consider crayons a necessity of life.

"Hey, don't belittle the humble crayon."

"That's not what I meant." Malone didn't actually know what he'd meant. He took a swift side glance at the captain and Kathy. They both looked perplexed. Happily perplexed, but, still, Malone was glad he wasn't the only one.

Malone swayed. He could tell himself he was just correcting against the sway of the boat, but he'd never been good at telling himself lies. A good hypothesis dealt only with truth.

Fact.

Empirical evidence.

Admit that Jet looks like sex on legs, then move on, Archer.

He wasn't going to Tallon Island to play. He was going there to work—to test a hypothesis, not to test his bloody willpower. No way did he intend to sully his mind with sex or—Malone shuddered at the thought—romance. Aside from fulfilling his responsibilities to the bureau, his sole intention was to complete his data set and thus fast-track his future success.

Simple action and reaction—cause and effect.

For all of that to happen, though, he needed a calm, quiet, distraction-free zone.

Distractions like Jet Crane wouldn't be on his agenda any time soon.

Malone made a show of checking his watch. "Shall we be away?"

"Excellent plan." Captain Thompson nodded to Kathy.

Jet grabbed for his suitcase at the top of the gangplank. "You must be Mal. Thanks for the assist."

"Malone," he corrected.

Captain Thompson clapped his hands together. "Right. I'll leave you two with Kathy to get sorted. Grab what you need for the night, Jet, so we can stow your suitcase in the hold. The trip will take the bulk of twenty-four hours. Might as well be comfortable while you're aboard."

"Thanks, Captain," Jet gave a jaunty salute.

Self-preservation kept Malone on deck, not watching while Kathy took Jet's suitcase across to the cargo lift.

He breathed deep, filling his lungs with the briny air. Seagulls and herons swooped overhead, and ripples of water lapped at the hull as the crew readied the catamaran to cast off. And on his mental timer, Malone pressed 'start'—ninety days stuck on a tiny island with Jethro Crane.

Ninety days, and counting.

CHAPTER FOUR

Jet

"Thanks for the assist," Jet said as Kathy rolled his suitcase to the metal door of a dumbwaiter style lift. "I tried to fit everything in my nephew's dinosaur suitcase case, but it was a no go. Dillon was devastated." He shook his head in mock sadness. "If I was smart, I'd have gotten into micro art." Jet held his thumb and first finger a finger-width apart. "Would've been way more convenient for mad-dash trips to tropical islands. Alas, my friend Shane's beast of a suitcase was the only option that would fit my canvases."

"Don't worry about it. You're not the only one travelling heavy."

"Oh?"

She tossed a quick glance back across the deck, then leaned in and spoke low. "We had to use the winch to get Malone's precious crate on board. He'll need a logistics expert to get it across the sand at Tallon."

"Really?   So,   Mr. What-the-hell-did-you-pack-in-your-suitcase isn't such a perfect paragon of packing virtue?" That was good to know.

"If you mean he couldn't fit all his stuff in a kid's suitcase? No." Kathy chuckled, then waggled her eyebrows. "But he does have other virtues."

As one, they turned to look back at Malone, who was studiously ignoring them and staring east across the water.

Again, as one, they sighed.

No doubt at all, the man was gorgeous.

The glasses gave him a nerdy vibe, but, on first impression, Malone's unruly blond curls and gold-kissed skin gave him the appearance of a grown-up cupid. A very strong, and very sexy, cupid. Only there was nothing lovey-dovey-cute about Malone. He was no tender creature. Jet suspected his arrows were more likely to cause true-death than true-love.

"I can't quite figure him out," Jet had to concede.

"He's okay once you spend a bit of time with him. Quiet like. Intense." A flush raced up her neck.

"Mm-hmm." Jet agreed. "A few other adjectives come to mind, too." On the aesthetic appeal scale, Malone Archer was a ten.

"Yeah."

"Think he'll let me use him as a test subject for one of my art projects? Bring out his bright shiny side?" Jet tilted his head to the side, wondering at his chance of success. "A glimmer of sunshine, maybe?"

Kathy snorted. "You're an artist?"

"Not exactly. Art therapist, still in training. You know how when you go to an art gallery with a neophyte who thinks a five-year-old could paint what's hung on the wall?"

"Can't say I go to that many galleries, but okay."

"Well, my art looks a bit like that. Big messes of colour. Emphasis on the big. No gallery curator worth their salt would hang one on their walls. The point isn't to display. It's about individual expression. Not about meeting some random critic's idea of worthiness."

She took in the wild colours of his ensemble, then looked down at her own boring blue and white uniform. "Individual expression. Don't I wish." The lift arrived and Kathy rolled his beast of a suitcase inside. "That'll take it safely to the hold. Want to see the mess next, or your cabin?"

"Cabin sounds good. I'd kill for a shower."

"Right." Kathy led him down narrow stairs, along a tight corridor, and pointed inside an open cabin.

No. The word 'cabin' was far too generous.

The space was coffin-sized. No bones about it.

One step over the raised doorway, Jet's shins came up against the end of the fold-down bed. Beside it was just enough space to shuffle around it to a cubby beside the head of the bed. Above that was a round porthole, streaked with salt spray. And off to the side was a tiny, functional bathroom.

Jet pivoted, stepped into the bathroom, and caught his reflection in the mirror. It still felt weird to have such short hair. A month after he'd shaved it all off, the regrowth no longer grated like sandpaper, but he still looked all kinds of wrong. His eyes were too big for his face and his cheeks were hollow—as though he didn't fit himself any more—everything exposed and raw.

If someone had asked him the classic question, "Are you okay?" he didn't know what answer he'd give. Not if he was being honest.

It was as though the bonds that held together his atoms and cells and fibres of his heart had split apart and didn't know how to put themselves back together.

He needed space and time to collect himself. To heal.

"Buck up, Jet," he mouthed one of Eloise's favourite lines to his reflection. "Time to open new doors."

Exactly what I'm doing, Eloise.

New place.

New people.

New possibilities.

A flicker of movement in the mirror reminded him of Kathy's presence.

"Staff quarters are pretty small, but they do the job."

He had to laugh at that. "Why do they call them quarters? This isn't even a sixteenth."

She shrugged. "Be glad you're replacing a female volunteer. Normally, you two would have to share." Kathy indicated the higher drop-down bunk, still strapped up against the moulded plastic wall.

Me and Malone, sharing this infinitesimally small space? "Cosy." Jet smirked. *Not to mention fucking hot.*

"Other than sleeping, there's not much use for these cabins. The Opportune rarely goes to sea long enough for the crew to need to set up house and home."

Won't be much sleeping going on if Malone and I are on top of each other in here.

"Most people hang out in the mess," Kathy added.

"Mm-hmm." *Down boy.* "Makes sense."

Kathy turned on the spot, which was really all she could do in the infinitesimal space. "Anything else you need?"

"Um…" Dare he ask? "Where's Malone's cabin?"

"Next berth along." Kathy rapped a knuckle on the moulded wall between the two drop-down bunks.

Jet stared at the wall hard, as though his eyes had the power to see through fibreglass. No luck there, but his imagination was quite capable of filling in the blank. In a delicious flash, he saw a cupid-esque Malone Archer, lain out on his bunk, wearing nothing but a quiver of arrows and a come-hither smile.

Was Malone's room identical? Or mirror image? Were their beds fitted flush to the same wall, side-by-side?

Nice. Jet could appreciate that kind of cosy, too.

"I think that's it. Let me know if there's anything you need, okay?" Kathy asked.

"Yeah. Of course."

The grind of the engine startled them both, and Jet put a hand to the shared wall to steady himself.

"That's us away. I'd better get above. See you at lunch."

"Sure. Yeah. Thanks, Kathy."

She scooted out into the corridor, and Jet shut the cabin door, relieved to finally be able to stop.

It didn't take long for the catamaran to reach the mouth of the river, where the gentle glide of the hull turned to a full-throttle churn on the changing tide. Cairns' riverside parks and restaurants disappeared from view, and all Jet could see was wide blue ocean and a horizon that seemed to stretch into forever.

Freshly showered, Jet plonked his arse down on a seat beside Kathy in the mess just as the chef served him a mountain of chicken biryani. "Mmm. Yum." His stomach rumbled. "Smells delicious. Thank you, ah...sorry, I don't know your name."

"Hank." The chef gave a quick nod.

"Awesome. Thanks Hank." Jet proceeded to load his plate with crisp green leaves from the salad bowl in the middle of the table. He was famished.

Malone planted himself down at the other end of the table, a seat distant from anyone else, and lifted his ginger ale to his brow in an apologetic salute to the chef. From the look of him, Malone felt a little green around the gills.

Sympathy rose in Jet's heart. "You okay?" he asked.

"Just peachy," Malone shut him down.

Jet bit his tongue.

Alrighty, then. Guess there's more growly bear in there than sweet cupid.

"Speaking of peaches," Jet asked Hank. "Is there a kitchen garden on the island? I'm an omnivore, but I don't think I've ever gone a month without fresh fruit and veg. Can't imagine doing three."

"There's no soil on Tallon. Just sand," Malone said with cut-glass condescension, as if to say Jet was a ditz for not knowing every conceivable thing about the place. "Didn't you research the island?"

Jet narrowed his eyes. He had a caring soul, and he could forgive a bit of grumpiness from anyone who didn't feel well, but there were limits. "Must have missed that detail." After moving all his stuff into storage, and making sure his life wouldn't fall even further apart while he was gone from the mainland, Jet hadn't had time enough to say, "Boo!", let alone dive into research about Tallon.

"There's plenty of frozen veg in the hold." Hank weighed in. "Victor never orders any veg, besides peas, so I added a few dozen bags of cauliflower and spinach and blueberries and such. The way they snap-freeze produce these days, it's almost as good as fresh."

"Don't forget the lemon juice," added Kathy.

Captain Thompson cracked a laugh. "God help us if we *ever* forget the lemon juice."

There was a story there. "What's that about?" Jet asked.

The captain laughed. "Last year, on Vic's first tour of Tallon, he made a big deal out of the risk of scurvy. I think he imagined himself on the colonial First Fleet, sailing a tall ship from England to Australia, with only eighteenth-century technology to hand."

"Salted mutton? Ship's biscuits?" Jet guessed. He'd watched way too many hours of Eloise's much-loved *Hornblower* collection, recorded onto VCR tapes back in the early noughties. Between mainlining that series and *The Medicine Woman*, Jet reckoned he was primed for tech-free survival.

"Sounds about right." Captain Thompson chuckled. "Lucky for you two, Hank threw in a few other staples. You may be short on lettuce, but he assures me that all the food groups are represented."

"Good to know, Captain." Jet eyed Malone. If the man didn't loosen up, three months together was going to feel like an eternity. "What made you decide to volunteer on Tallon Island, Malone? Are you a weather buff, or a fully-fledged meteorological nerd?"

"Neither. I'm conducting a marine biology research project."

Interesting. "Cool. About...?"

"The regenerative properties of sea cucumber exudate and its bio-medical potential for burns treatment."

Jet blinked. "Sea cucumbers?" Was Malone screwing with him? He had to be. Jet poked his fork into one of the cucumber half-moons that topped his salad and waved it around. "As in cucumbers that grow in the sea?"

"Family Holothuroidea."

Holo-what-a? "Some kind of seaweed?" Jet guessed.

"No. It's an animal. Most species live on shallow sea floors. Like the reef around Tallon. I'll be conducting a survey and taking samples."

"Huh." Obscure marine animals were a step beyond his realm of expertise. Probably a few dozen steps, if Jet was completely honest. "I'm more of a Homo sapiens expert."

"What about you, Jet?" Captain Thompson asked. "What brings you to Tallon?"

"Just here to help. Explore the island. My best friend told me I have to spend at least a hundred hours lazing in a hammock. I'm to clock them, and report back."

"That's not all he'll be doing," Kathy protested. "Jet's an artist."

All eyes came back to Jet. "I dabble." He corrected. "I'm at the tail end of an art therapy Master's degree. Six more credits, then I can set up my practice." God, he could not wait.

"Interesting." Captain Thompson offered.

"I think so. It's about helping people find a therapeutic outlet through self-expression."

Everyone nodded with genuine interest. Everyone except Malone, who sighed into his ginger ale, making the aluminium can toot like a flute.

Rude.

Jet knew Malone wasn't feeling great, but still...

Ill or not, Malone Archer could go fuck his gorgeous self.

"Excuse me, Cap." Another crewmember poked his head through the door. "Tallon's on the long-range. Needs a quick word."

Jet perked up. Were they that close already?

The captain sighed. "Tell Vic we filled his special order."

Jet leaned toward Kathy. "Special order? Does he mean the anti-scurvy lemon?"

Kathy gave a quick shake of her head. "Special request for Christmas. 'All the rum in all the land.' Vic's probably stressing that we forgot."

"It's not Vic on the line, Cap.," the crew-member said. "It's Peta. She needs to speak to you. Says there's a problem."

Jet sat up straighter. "Problem?" he and Malone chorused the question, but the crew-member gave no answer.

"Apologies." The captain frowned as he pushed back his seat. "Hold my plate for me, would you Hank? I'll be back soon."

But the captain didn't return. Jet's trepidation grew as the engines roared louder and the hull of the catamaran surged through the waves, speeding ever east toward Tallon.

CHAPTER FIVE

Malone

Malone woke to the squawks of a million seabirds, the gentle knock and slosh of calm water against the hull of the catamaran, and light streaming through the porthole of his miniscule cabin.

They'd arrived.

Thank God.

Malone swallowed back the sour taste in his throat and groaned as he swung his legs over the side of the narrow bunk and got up. Of the many variables he'd prepared for, sea-sickness hadn't been one of them.

He'd suffered on boats before, but only in truly squally weather. The protected waters of the Great Barrier Reef, in fine weather, should've been okay. At least, that was what he'd told his roiling stomach at sunset as he'd trained his gaze on the darkening horizon, determined not to heave over the side. Eventually, the nausea settled long enough for him to get to sleep, but he'd lost the whole evening—hours he'd intended to spend analysing the island's tide times.

Three months was so little time to fulfill his goals. He ached to get started. Determined to catch up to his self-imposed schedule, Malone ignored his hollow stomach, threw on cargo shorts and a polo shirt marked with his university's emblem, then scaled the narrow stairs out into bright, unfettered sunshine.

The deck was a chaotic mix of stores from the hold, ready to offload, and the busy crew.

Off the starboard side, the wide expanse of calm, blue water spread out beyond the horizon. Off the port side sat the low, sandy rise of Tallon Island, topped by the white sphere of the radar tower. In between the boat and the island, a line of froth trailed out in the water along the natural arc of the reef front. Low tide, Malone thought. It was the perfect time to be working out in the lagoon, but he couldn't do anything while he was stuck on the catamaran. He gave the surface of the cay a quick scan, impatient to discover what lay beneath.

If he could convince the captain to put him on the first boat ferrying ashore, he might be able to take advantage of the favourable tide. Get a head start.

He sidled up close to where the captain hung over the rail near the stern, sheering off curses. "Morning," Malone said, and looked overboard.

A woman stood in a flat-bottomed tin skiff, surrounded by a Tetris of foam coolers, her feet wide for balance. It had to be Peta—the only woman in the three-person crew already on Tallon. She sported scruffy hair and a deep tan, and her salt-streaked shorts looked at least two sizes too large for her wiry limbs. She looked shipwrecked—like she'd given in to the sun and the sand and the sea.

Will I look like that in three months?

Malone found it hard to fathom looking that relaxed, let alone feeling it.

She gave the captain a one-shoulder shrug. "You know he won't come off the island. Not if he doesn't have to. Crusty bastard."

Captain Thompson shoved his hands through his hair. "Tell Vic he doesn't have a choice."

Peta cracked a laugh. "As if he'd listen to me. You know how Vic is."

"Tough," the captain said, clearly fed up.

Malone was about to ask what the problem was when another voice came from immediately behind him. "Can I help?"

"Shit!" Malone whirled around. Damn the man for sneaking up on him. Malone gave Jet a deadly stare, but Jet showed no sign that he'd noticed him or his aggravation.

"Ah, Jet. Thanks for coming up. Vic's hurt himself. Can you join Wallace? He's already ashore with his medic kit."

"Why does he get to go first?" Malone asked.

Silence descended, and the crew all turned to him as one.

Malone's words ran back through his head.

Fuck. He'd sounded like a whiny kid. But the question still stood. Why *did* Jet get to go first? What was so special about him? Obviously, Jet had a caring instinct, which was nice and all, but a degree in art therapy hardly equated with medical knowledge. Painting pretty pictures wouldn't solve anything.

"Of course." Jet broke the awkward moment. "Whatever you need, Captain." Jet leaned over the railing and called down to Peta. "What happened?"

"Vic, the stubborn git, got himself hurt. Fell off a ladder when he was cleaning the radar tower. He reckons it's just a sprain, but the swelling is like this." She hovered her hand a few inches above her forearm.

"I have some kit in my suitcase. Can you wait for me? I'll go grab it from the hold." Jet turned as if to go back down below decks, but Peta called out. "Big black thing? It's already ashore."

"Oh. Ta." Jet started down the ladder to the skiff, leaving Malone on the deck wondering what Jet could possibly find useful among a cache of art supplies.

"I'd like to go ashore too, Captain." His doctorate may have been in molluscs, not medicine, but he had studied vertebrates in his undergrad days. He could probably figure his way around a simple human injury. Muscle was muscle, and bone was bone. Surely, he'd be able to offer more help than an artist ever could.

Malone went to follow Jet down the ladder, but the captain stayed him with a hand. "Afraid not, Malone. Boat's sitting too low in the water already. Off you go, Peta. Radio us when you know what's what." The captain unhitched the skiff's tether and threw it overboard. "Why don't you go grab a bite of breakfast, Malone? We'll ferry you across with a lighter load. Maybe with your crate, when we get to it." The fait accompli left Malone stunned. He wasn't used to being discounted like that. He ran the tip of his tongue along the sharp edge of his teeth, tasting salt and bitter thoughts, unspoken.

An hour and three coffees later, Malone stood braced as Peta guided the skiff slowly away from the catamaran, over the sharp edge of the reef crest, and into the crystal-clear waters of the shallow reef lagoon.

From satellite imagery he'd used to scout the suitability of the island for his research, Malone knew that the coral cay grew in a teardrop shape an average fifty meters out from the shore.

The low-lying sand island shimmered in the early summer heat—a sliver of gold between the sea and the wide blue sky that arched overhead, where birds swooped and dove, wings spread wide in the sunshine, their caw, caw, cawing a raucous accompaniment to the relentless roar of the wild sea.

"Something wrong with the dock?" Malone asked as Peta directed the skiff past the stubby wooden mooring that jutted a short way into the lagoon.

"Tide's rising, but it's still too low for us to lift your crate up onto the dock. Not without a winch," she said. "If you, me, and Ben can't muscle this thing across the bow to the beach, we'll have to crack it open and decant."

Malone's temple throbbed. "I've got sensitive equipment in there."

"The island is full of sensitive equipment," she countered.

All Malone could do was kick himself for not considering the logistics of actually getting his gear onto the island. Splitting it into smaller, more manageable containers would have been better, and he felt like an idiot for not considering the problem earlier. "Thanks for the offer, but I'll sort it here." For lack of a better option, decanting everything sounded like the safest way to go.

The bow swung around and she gave a nod to the shore where a figure emerged on the heat-shimmered beach.

"That's Ben," said Peta. "He comes across as a layabout, but he's pretty cautious. You don't need to worry about your gear with him."

Malone shielded his eyes from the glare of the late-morning sun.

'Layabout' was an apt description. Ben looked like a quintessential surfer dude, complete with shaggy sun-streaked hair, scruffy chin, and eyes caught in a permanent squint. He leaned up against a tired-looking wheelbarrow.

Malone braced himself as the flat-bottomed skiff ran aground with a crunch on the white sand. Peta cut the engine and nimbly leaped ashore with the tether.

"Hey, man. I'm Ben." Ben reached over the bow to shake Malone's hand.

"Malone. Good to meet you."

"Is that beast all yours? Let me help. The sand makes lugging stuff a chore."

"Appreciate if you could take my suitcase, thanks, but I'll get the rest." Malone swung the bag onto the edge of the skiff for Ben to take, then turned back to unlatch the lid of the crate. He secured the long strap of his laptop bag across his chest, handed the bulky package of specimen dishes to Peta, and then excavated his encased field microscope from its nest at the bottom.

He got a solid hold on the side of the boat to clamber over. Tepid saltwater sloshed into his reef shoes, and, finally, it all felt real.

He'd truly arrived.

"Lead the way," he said, and followed the single track of the wheelbarrow up the beach to one of the myriad sandy tracks that radiated out from the compound in the middle of the island.

He didn't expect the place to look new. A decade had passed since the whole compound had been rebuilt after the ravaging winds and waves of Cyclone Yasi destroyed the old meteorological station. But the buildings showed a surprising amount of wear. "The freezer unit functions, right?" It'd better. He couldn't store his samples without it.

"Yeah, sure. No prob there." Ben guarded his mouth from view and whispered, "Good thing, too. Peta's addicted to liquorice flavoured ice cream. I do *not* get it. That shit looks like a squid pissed black ink into it and used all its tentacles to stir." He mimed gagging.

"More for her?" Malone ventured.

Ben went wide-eyed, probably just realising how he might've been had. "Shit. You think she got that flavour so the rest of us wouldn't eat it?"

"Could be. All I know is if someone stole my buttermilk macadamia praline chunk ice cream, I might see fit to stick a poker in their eye." It seemed safe to admit his sweet tooth to Ben. The guy was leaving, after all.

They entered a courtyard, surrounded by six structures set out in a rough hexagon shape.

"There used to be a massive palm tree in the middle here." Ben scuffed the edge of a paver. "But Yasi brought that down over the old mess. Bit plain now."

"You've been here for years? I thought volunteers only stayed on Tallon for a season. No more."

"Uh-huh. Staff do six months. Three months, max, for volunteers." Ben nodded. "This is only my second volley stint, but I've sailed past a bunch of times before that. You're not supposed to camp on the island, but the met rarely minds friendlies docking for a quick visit during the day."

He pointed to the left. "You and Jet are sharing the first accommodation donga. They did a great job of converting them from shipping containers. Separate doors at either end. Bathrooms back-to-back in the middle. This'll be your kingdom. Next to Jet's end is the mess, with kitchen and laundry. There's another gap through to the beach, then the cold store."

"Site of the legendary liquorice ice cream."

"Ha! Exactly."

"The radio shack is straight across. Then the generator. Then the dry store, which is airtight. The salt air is brutal, so everything metal—tools and ladders and such—get stored in there. Last is the second accommodation donga. The far end is a bunkhouse for short-term maintenance staff. They usually come for a few weeks mid-winter. Nothing for you to worry about. This end is Vic's."

Malone nodded. "Got it." He'd have a good look around later. First, he needed to stow his gear somewhere safe. Then he needed to find Jet. The man had already been on Tallon for ages. Who knew what decisions he'd made without Malone's input?

Peta poked her head out of the mess. "Ben, get your arse in here," she called, then disappeared just as fast.

"Great." Ben hefted the suitcase up the stairs and dropped it just inside Malone's donga door. "Let's go see what's got Peta all excited. She'll have the skinny on Vic. Damn fool thought he could hide a broken arm."

"It's broken?" They walked to the mess.

"According to your partner."

"Who?"

"Jet."

"He's not my…" Malone started to correct him, then stopped. Ben meant *volunteer* partner. Not the other kind.

"You're lucky. Vic's a wank. You're well rid of him." Ben scrunched his nose as he held the fly screen open for Malone to duck inside the mess.

Malone gathered the middle-aged man with the rabid red face was Vic. He stood against the far wall, his left arm held tight to his body, glaring down at Wallace.

Off to the side, Jet stood with his hand out as if Vic were a skittish stallion and not just a cranky middle-aged man doing an impression of a toddler.

"I can do the job," Vic insisted mulishly. "This is nothing but swelling. A bit more ice and I'll be right as rain in a few days. Besides, it's my left wrist I sprained, not my right. I'm right-handed. Means I can still work."

"Oh, for the love of…" Wallace, clearly fed up, shoved a blood pressure cuff back in his kit and snapped it shut. "Vic, it's not a sprain, and it's not a dislocation. It's a break. You need an x-ray, and possibly surgery."

Malone winced at the man's brutal assessment. He couldn't see the wound. It was wrapped in so much padding and tape, his forearm looked like a club. But from the way Vic was holding it protectively to his chest, it had to hurt.

"No. I'm not leaving."

The two men looked to be at a stubborn impasse. Malone understood that kind of dedication. He'd be pissed if anyone told him to get off the island before his work was done.

"Vic," Jet squeezed Vic's right shoulder. "I'm truly sorry, but you're not an insect. You're a human being. And humans don't have another joint half way up their forearm. If the bend was in the middle, then it was broken. You did a great job stabilizing it with the wooden spoons and electrical tape. Ingenious. But bones don't magically heal themselves. You need it x-rayed, repaired, and put in a cast, and we can't do any of that here."

What did Jet mean, 'we?' Who died and gave him a medical degree?

Malone stepped forward "Jet, I really think—"

Peta shushed him.

"It won't be forever, Vic," Jet continued. "They'll take a few pictures. Maybe put a pin or two through the bone to make sure it's stronger than ever. Then you'll have a few days to recover. Maybe go see some friends. Have a drink or two down the pub. Talk about the weather. Before you know it, you'll be back on Tallon, watching the clouds roll by and harassing me and Malone." While Jet spoke in that maddening singsong tone, he fussed around Vic, slipping a triangular sling under the man's arm and tying it behind his neck with such gentle care that Vic barely winced. "There we go. Let's get a few things together for the trip. You won't need much. Toothbrush, duds, maybe a spare t-shirt. Nothing to it."

"But..." Vic frowned.

"Vic, you've got nothing to worry about. This way..." Jet guided Vic to the door. Peta and Ben followed after. Malone half expected to see cartoon rainbows and sunshine skipping in their wake.

Wallace packed up the rest of his gear, muttering all the while, then left, too, leaving Malone feeling like he'd been deserted. His thoughts whizzed like a particle in the Hadron Collider while he tried to regain his bearings. Malone knew he ought to be sizing up the space in the mess for a work station, but his attention kept returning to the empty doorway and the distant voices beyond.

"Just supervise," he grumbled to himself, and headed out the door.

Peta and Ben waited with their hands in their pockets just as Vic and Jet came out of Vic's donga. Jet carried a limp duffel bag, while Vic clutched a worn-out toothbrush in his left hand, its stained bristles sprouting in all directions. With Wallace, Jet and Vic formed a sad little procession down to the beach where the skiff was tethered.

"I've never seen Vic so docile." Peta shook herself, as though spooked.

"Your guy's got some mad people skills," Ben agreed. "He's like the Vic whisperer."

He's not my *guy.*

"Nope." Peta shook her head. "More like that trickster that trapped Odysseus on that island."

"The one-eyed dude?" Ben asked.

"Nah, the woman with the snake hair. Jet doesn't have a lot of hair, but still."

"That was Circe, not Medusa," Malone corrected, but he understood what they were on about. Jet had a way about him. Malone couldn't help but wonder. If he did listen to Jet, would he lose all rational sense? If he looked, would he turn to stone? What about if he touched? Or tasted? Or inhaled Jet's scent? What might he risk then?

Low waves lapped at the gunmetal grey skiff, lifting it up off the sand, making it catch and flash silver in the sunlight.

Tide's turning, Malone thought as he hung back in the last of the shade, determined not to get caught up in the Jet show.

"Peta!" Wallace called back to them.

She tapped Ben in the gut with the back of her hand then jogged backward toward the skiff, calling, "Pack up the rest of Vic's stuff, would you? I doubt he'll be back before the end of the season. And get Malone started with the handover. I'll be back with Jet before the ten o'clock measures."

"Can do." Ben pointed his thumb in the direction of the compound. "Come on, mate. I'll show you the ropes. Get the jump on how it's all done."

"Sounds good." Finally, the fates were on his side. The sooner the catamaran and crew were gone, the sooner Malone could get on with his true mission on Tallon.

Chapter Six

Jet

Back on Tallon, Jet listened carefully as Peta and Ben teamed up to show him and Malone the technical and natural workings of the island.

With Vic gone, he and Malone would have to run the show on their own. The responsibility made Jet nervous. He was acutely aware that the crash course he'd received via video chat hadn't come close to making him an expert in reading meteorological instruments. He'd be fine with the easy stuff, but what if they had to troubleshoot the hardware? What if a storm hit? It wasn't Jet's fault he'd been pulled in at the last minute, but his ignorance did pose a significant risk.

Jet sincerely hoped that a few days of routine measures would prove him capable. In the meantime, he paid attention to every tip the two departing volunteers could think to give.

"Can't tell you much about the radar tower above. That was Vic's baby. Readings come through on this dedicated monitor." Peta pointed to one of the two flatscreens attached to the radio shack wall. "Best not to use it for anything else. The two-way radio here is pretty user-friendly, but there's a helpful cheat sheet up there inside the bureau's manual if you get stuck." Peta pointed to the three-inch thick folder on the shelf above the bulky radio transmitter. "That covers everything on the island, actually. Scintillating bedtime reading." She winked. "If you've got a problem, radio HQ. It's nice to hear another voice every now and then. HQ can patch you through to a landline or mobile phone. Just be aware that it's not a secure and private connection." She threw a smirk Ben's way.

"I tried to get my girlfriend into radio sex. Hot as hell, right?" Ben grinned, unabashed. "But Livvy has a funny attitude to being overheard."

"Noted," Malone said.

Jet couldn't help noticing the side-eye Malone slipped his way, and, suddenly, all he could think of was radio sex with Malone. It was...disconcerting. "No radio sex," he affirmed, and he was very glad when Peta led them out of the closed space of the radio shack and into the sunshine.

"Careful of the birds' burrows. They're small, but it's easy to twist an ankle if you don't watch your step."

"Especially in the dark, when you have to use a red-filtered headlight to see your way," Ben added.

Low scrubby bushes and hardy grasses surrounded them as Peta directed them past the radio tower and along a narrow sandy path out to the Stevenson Screen on the most distant tip of the island. The simple white louvered box looked like every other weather box Jet had visited with his dad. The open-slat sides that let the air through. The cluster of weather instruments on top. It all looked so familiar, and a new spark of confidence lit warm in Jet's heart. Maybe he wouldn't be the weak link on Tallon after all.

As they came up to the simple white box, Ben hung back while Peta pointed further out to sea. "There's a buoy moored a few hundred meters out beyond the reef crest. It sends hourly recordings of wave height, wave period, and sea surface temps. It transmits directly to the mainland, so you don't have to do anything for that besides a quick notation that the receiver is functioning when you do the other measures. In this time zone, synaptic time happens at four o'clock and ten o'clock, am and pm. If you struggle to remember the times, just think 'ten-four', meaning 'got it'. Get it?"

"Got it," Jet said.

"Good. The chances of another cyclone like Yasi crossing Tallon are slim, but it could happen, so watch and follow directions. Accurate records make it possible for the bureau's modellers to recognise and respond to volatile conditions. They can make the difference between life and death."

"It's like taking a set of obs.," Jet ruminated out loud. "Only these observations are of an island, instead of a patient. Air pressure, humidity, and wind speed, instead of resp rate, pulse, and blood pressure."

Peta nodded her agreement. "Temps for both. Don't worry about intermediate synaptic time, HQ doesn't expect volunteers to do three-hourly measures. Be glad about that. It's challenge enough for three people to divvy up the measures and all the chores. You won't have much time left over when it's just the two of you sharing the load."

"Sweet." Keeping busy might stop Jet from dwelling on the recent drama that had taken over his life.

"Up top is the anemometer and pyranometer." Peta unlatched the louvered vent box. "And inside is the barometer, hygrometer, and thermometer. Easy."

"Don't forget the windsock." Ben pointed at the flag pole a few meters away. "The winds can get fierce, so you might have to replace it at some point over the summer."

"Yep. Whenever it gets ragged." Peta gave one sharp clap of her hands. "So, that's all the static instruments. Did Ben show you how to do the balloon release, Malone?"

"Yes. I'll show Jet when it's time to release it tomorrow morning."

"Thanks." Jet clamped a hand over his borrowed hat and tilted his head back. But not even a wisp of high cirrus marred the iridescent azure sky. He saw no sign of a weather balloon, but he tracked the swoop of a bird wheeling high, swerving on the invisible air currents. It looked so free. In its element.

"What kind of bird is that?"

Ben followed Jet's pointed arm. "Knobby turn. Better get used to them. There are thousands."

A larger bird swooped low, like it was coming in to land, but Malone reflexively ducked and waved an arm overhead, startling the poor bird from its path.

It squawked and swung back around, dropping on Malone's head its perfect revenge.

"Ahh!" Malone danced away. "Shit!"

"Oh my God!" Jet couldn't contain the snort that burst forth, doubling over with laughter when Malone smeared the sloppy white shit across his forehead and dragged it back into his nest of curls.

Weirdly, Malone didn't seem to see the funny. He shook his head in disgust and stomped off all the way back to the compound, giving Jet a prime opportunity to get his own revenge for Malone's snotty attitude on the voyage over.

He cupped his hands around his mouth and called out, "Didn't you research the island?"

Malone didn't seem to see the funny in that, either.

C'est la vie.

When they caught up with Malone back in the courtyard, he was already out of the mess, scrubbing at his thick hair with a wad of wet kitchen paper. His flat expression dared any of them to comment.

Which, of course, meant Jet couldn't resist. "Oh, come on, Mal. You can't be angry. You scared the bejeebers out of the poor bird."

"My name's Malone. And, I don't know what the hell bejeebers are, but that's sure as fuck not what's on my head. That's shit."

"Oh, God." Jet doubled over again.

Ben chuckled. "I reckon half the island is guano, but the bloody things do love to treat us as target practice."

"Hard to avoid." Peta agreed diplomatically.

"We ought to hang a warning sign on the dock. Nobody leaves Tallon a guano virgin. Unless you're smart like Jet and wear a hat the size of a continent. Good choice, mate." Ben clapped him on the shoulder.

"Thanks." Jet tilted the brim of his giant yellow hat and shot a silent thanks to Kristy for her bold fashion choice.

Malone ignored both him and Ben. "What's next?" he asked Peta.

Jet channelled his dad's inner engineer as Peta and Ben continued to educate them on the intricacies of the island's desalinating water plant and the hybrid solar, wind, and fuel-generator power system. Then they moved on to the safety measures necessary to secure their food from the destructive heat, humidity, sand blows, and hungry birds and bugs.

"Can you imagine being here before refrigeration? It blows my mind that Australians have been coming to Tallon since the early twentieth century. A few hundred brave souls venturing so far from civilization." It hadn't quite sunk in that he was one of them. To land on a near-desert island, surrounded by a fathomless, lonely ocean.

"A testament to science," Malone said.

"And to imagination," Jet said.

"Imagination?" Malone asked. "What do you mean?"

It seemed pretty obvious to him. "You can't do what you can't imagine."

"That's ridiculous. We can't do things just because we imagine them. Human survival depends on knowledge and ingenuity. Not on..." Malone looked out to sea, searching for something.

"Creativity?" Jet prodded.

Malone gave him a withering look. "Art."

"Oh! Fighting words." For the first time since he stepped foot on the catamaran docked in Cairns, Jet felt a spark of excitement.

Surviving the rigours of living and working in such a remote place?

It'll be difficult, but I'm up for it.

Malone's company?

That'll be the true challenge.

Jet couldn't wait for the games to begin.

What felt like a lifetime later, Jet stood beside Malone on the narrow-planked jetty, squinting into the fierce afternoon sun, and waving as the Opportune steered a return course back toward Cairns.

Peta's parting words of wisdom ran through Jet's mind. *The Coral Sea is a capricious place, and neither of you know the island well. Observe. Listen to your gut. And, take care of each other.*

"I can do a roster." Jet offered. "Sort out what needs doing, when. There's a lot for two people to do, but it's not like it's constant. If we both do twelve hours a day—"

"Fourteen," Malone interrupted.

Jet took off his hat and arched a brow.

"If we swap every fourteen hours, then night duty will rotate too." Malone explained. "Fair's fair and all that."

That made sense. "Sure. Okay. Sounds good. I'll go write it up."

"No. I'll do it."

"For fuck's sake. I am capable of counting to fourteen, you know. Even on a wacky twenty-four-hour clock." Jet simmered with impatience.

It might be relaxing to live up to Malone's ultra-low expectations. Shane would approve. But Jet was wired to be helpful. He cared. Which was a fucking awful way to be when his fellow man, *singular*, seemed to resent the air he breathed.

"Your assumption that I'm a ditz is getting old." Jet knew it was partially his own fault for not disclosing his career history, but it caught in his craw to have to display a fucking curriculum vitae in order to get any respect.

A furrow appeared between Malone's brows. "I don't think you're a ditz. I think you're a tourist. You've come to sit on the beach with your froufrou outfits, looking for a coconut cocktail and time to paint a few pretty pictures of the reef, then to tell all your city friends about your idyllic island adventure. You obviously haven't come here prepared to work. Which means I can't rely on you to do your part. And now it's just the two of us here, and I've got too much else to do to babysit your beautiful arse."

Jet blinked stupidly.

Beautiful arse?

Had those words really come out of Malone Archer's disapproving mouth?

Then the rest of his startling words filtered through.

Froufrou?

Babysit?

What the hell?

"If you really feel that way, why did you let the Opportune leave? Why not ask Peta or Ben to stay?"

Malone pursed his lips and stared out at the lowering sun—the orb's raging fire reflecting phantom heat in his ice-cold eyes.

"Huh." Somehow, Jet knew the words Malone was withholding. "You did ask. Didn't you? What was their answer?"

Malone shook his head. "It doesn't matter. Neither of them could stay a week longer, let alone twelve."

"Tell me what they said," Jet insisted.

"It doesn't matter," Malone repeated.

"It matters to me."

Malone rolled his eyes. "They seemed to think you could handle yourself."

Jet waited for the 'but'.

"But—"

There it was.

"—all they've seen you do is twist an injured man's thumb to leave the island."

Jet sucked in a breath. He was more than ready to defend himself. Again. But one look at Malone's shut-down expression stopped him. What was the point? "Fine. Judge me however you will. I can cope with low expectations. You draw up a roster, and I'll do my share. We'll barely even need to cross paths." He waited a beat before asking in as strong a voice as he could manage, "Deal?"

"Deal." Malone nodded before stalking up the dock to their hexagonal home away from home.

"Just don't expect me to make you any froufrou cock-tails!" Jet hollered, then turned back to stare after the fast-retreating stern of the Opportune.

If he screamed loud enough, would they hear him? Would they come to his rescue?

A sea breeze whipped at Jet's sarong, scratching at the sea-salt that had already crusted on his sensitive skin. The material tangled around his ankles and tugged between his legs, outlining every nook and cranny.

Beautiful arse.

The words didn't sit right. They didn't match what he knew of Malone Archer's mind. Which, admittedly, wasn't much.

Was he as guilty of judging Malone as much as Malone was guilty of judging him?

Beautiful arse.

Was Malone gay?

Was the grump routine all an act?

If it was, what was Malone trying to cover up?

Attraction?

That stray thought just about broke Jet out in hysterics. Malone was gorgeous, to be sure, but the man was clearly a judgmental arsehole, and Jet had had more than enough preconceived judgment in his life. He didn't need more. Hell, he'd practically been bought as a baby on lay-by. The value of an individual's life didn't get much more precon-ceived than that. No way was Jet going near Malone. Not in *that* way. Not if he was the last man on Earth.

"Listen to your gut," he repeated Peta's parting words.

No response came but the sound of the shallow waves rushing over rough coral sand.

"Jethro!" Malone harshly called from the shore end of the dock. "Do you need an invitation? We've got work to do."

So much for not needing to cross paths.

Jet slapped his hat back on his head, did a one-eighty, and trailed after Malone down the dock. As much as it pained him to admit it, the grump was right. They did have a lot to do. Storm season was coming, and if they didn't work together, neither of them would survive.

CHAPTER SEVEN

Malone

Jet's flip-flops slap, slap, slapped across the laminated floor, the annoying sound going directly to Malone's shoulders, which stiffened. He didn't turn around, though. He had more important things to do than pay attention to the annoyingly pretty man with the vibrant clothes and captivating smile.

"Is that a schedule?" Jet asked.

Malone didn't deign to answer. Of course, it was a schedule. Any dimwit could see that.

The squeak of the marker on the white board did a valiant job of expressing his irritation.

On the vertical axis, Malone wrote the days of the week.

On the horizontal axis, he wrote 'Synoptic Time' and headed the columns: '0400', '1000', '1600', and '2200'.

Inside the chart, he filled the first few days with red and blue lines, alternating every fourteen hours, with shift-change times written in black.

"Does this make sense to you?" Malone asked. "If you're uncomfortable with the twenty-four-hour clock, I can change it." He glanced over to check Jet's level of comprehension.

In Malone's humble opinion, a fourteen-hour rota was an elegant solution to a very real problem. He'd be able to fit his research in, they'd both get a solid break to sleep, and neither of them would be stuck on nights all the time.

Win, win.

"Am I red or blue?" Jet asked.

"Red."

"That's good. I like red."

And I like blue.

The ease of Jet's acquiescence felt suspicious, but Malone wasn't sure why.

"Red goes faster, and if I get through my chores quicker, I'll have more time to play."

There it was. It felt good to be right.

"Wouldn't want to deprive you of play time. And they're not chores."

"Right, sorry, *responsibilities*," Jet clearly enunciated.

God, he was annoying.

Malone locked his jaw and drew a square legend in the lower left corner of the board. He wrote 'Malone' in blue, and 'Jethro' in red, then proceeded to fill in the rest of the chart.

"It's a cool kind of collective action, don't you think? All the meteorologists and weather observers around the world—across the wild Siberian tundra, on the rooftops of Hong Kong's skyscrapers, high up in the Swiss Alps—all of us doing the same thing at exactly the same time, syncing our results, and forming a global, living map that will benefit everyone. Alone, and yet together. It has a beautiful kind of synchronicity. Don't you think? Keeping the world safe, one observation at a time."

"That's a romantic way of putting it." He should've guessed Jet was a tree-hugging idealist. "What we're doing for the global and atmospheric environment is important. No doubt about that. But I don't fool myself into thinking only one person, or one movement, can affect the sort of change necessary to save the entire planet. Not in one fell swoop."

"Cynical."

"Realist," Malone countered in a clipped tone intended to put the conversation to bed.

Only, Jet didn't seem to get the memo.

"You don't truly believe that. If you did, you wouldn't be here tracking sea cucumbers, or whatever you're doing with them. If one person can't affect change, what's the point?"

"It's not about the masses. You said it yourself; every little bit helps. Sure, the more people I can help, the bigger the impact. But nothing I can do will turn back time. I can't prevent the original wound. My priority is knowledge. If I can find the key to making life a little better for at least one person, I will have made a difference."

And, once I've proven myself worthy, I can relax.

Maybe.

"Huh." Jet cocked his head. "Guess we're more alike than I thought." He shuddered.

"Is that so painful to admit?"

"You don't agree?"

That stung. Was he such a bad role-model to emulate? "I'm just here to do my bit."

"So, you're on tonight, then?"

Malone pulled the marker five millimetres away from the glossy surface of the whiteboard.

Jethro Crane seemed to be a lot of things—contrary and aggravating and goddamn distracting—but he was no idiot. Which made the inane question doubly irritating.

Do not react, Archer.

"Do you see anyone else here?" Malone asked.

Dammit. You weren't supposed to react.

"Just your outsized ego," he thought he heard Jet mutter, but it was covered over by the slap of rubber soles across to the kitchen. He heard Jet yank open cupboards, then an overly enthusiastic exclamation when Jet found, "Tea!"

"Fuck me." Malone wasn't going to survive if he had to put up with Mr. Sunshine every second of every day. He had serious business to get on with.

"Want a cuppa, Mal?"

"Malone," he corrected. "No, thank you."

"Are you sure? There's some fancy shit here. Earl Grey, peppermint, camomile, and vanilla. Mmm...smells good. You seem a little wound up. A cup of that will help you to de-stress."

"I'm sure."

"Yes, but are you really, truly sure?"

Malone paused his writing again. *Do not let the man get under your skin.* "I'm as certain as the fact that the Earth spins around the sun."

"Hmm...that's pretty sure."

Malone took great momentary pride in the singular fact that he did not react. He returned his attention to the appropriate square in the schedule and took dark delight in drawing a red line through 0400. Jet could get up with the birds for the first pre-dawn reading.

"There are other suns, you know," Jet said. "And planets."

Malone snapped the lid back on the marker pen. "Are you doing anything of any import right now?"

"Import?" Jet parroted. "Did I die and wake up in a period drama? My mum loves those. My mother did, too, come to think of it. Eloise used to say, 'Jet, there's nothing that can't be fixed with a hot cup of tea and a good dousing in a pond.'"

I'll douse you *in a pond.* Malone gritted his teeth and twisted to look over his shoulder to where Jet was idly leaning up against the kitchen bench, swishing a tea bag in a steaming mug. Malone had a hard time looking away from his fingers—their movements weirdly hypnotic. "You have two mothers?" he finally asked.

Jet was pretty obviously rainbow friendly. Hearing he'd grown up with two mothers made that doubly clear. Malone thought for a second about clueing Jet in about his sexuality. But he held back.

Two gay men, alone on a desert island. What would he do if Jet invoked the 'when in Rome' clause?

How will you feel if he doesn't, Archer?

"No." Jet raised his mug to blow on the steam, and Malone transferred his attention from the man's hand to his lips. "I have one mum, and I *had* one mother."

Malone heard the words, but it took a second for the pain in Jet's eyes to register.

Had.

Past tense.

Shit.

"Sorry." That was about all he felt equipped to say. It was inadequate, he knew, and the clipped way it came out made him sound like a heartless bastard. Again, he'd fallen short, but Malone was already feeling stretched thin by their unravelling circumstances. Jet's evident distress was just one too many variables for Malone to deal with.

Do what you do best, Archer. That's all anyone can expect of you.

He re-focused on the whiteboard, erased the red line through 0400, and redrew it in blue, giving himself a sixteen-hour starter shift for his penance. Not that he'd let Jet off completely. He wasn't that soft. "When you're done with your tea, our provisions need unpacking," he said. "Best if you start with the cold stores and freezer."

He couldn't control Jet's opinion of him, so why even try?

Chapter Eight

Jet

Jet watched over the rim of his mug as Malone filled in his two-toned rotating schedule. He took a big gulp of tea, letting the scorch of the hot brew sear away any inconvenient thoughts about how well Malone fit into his pants.

Not that Jet was ever likely to get into them. Or even want to.

He wouldn't have said no to an anonymous hook up in a dark corner of a club. But on Tallon? Where they wouldn't be able to get away from each other for months?

Hell, no.

Intimacy with a colleague was always a bad idea. Intimacy with someone who clearly hated him without even knowing him? Jet had had enough rejection in his life. He didn't need to hold his hand out like some sad little Oliver and beg for it.

Besides, the man was likely as much fun in the bedroom as he was out. Which was to say—not much.

Malone was uptight as all hell. Jet had no doubt that Malone's Arctic 'sorry', had been him just saying what he thought he was supposed to—for the sake of polite professionalism. There was no warmth in his voice, or in the steel of his turned back.

As for Malone's suggestion—aka, order—for Jet to make himself useful by unpacking the groceries, Jet was loath to follow it. No, please. No, thank you. But the walk-in cold-store was probably a more welcome space to hang out than with Malone. The guy was so icy, one touch was likely to give Jet frostbite.

Jet chugged the last of his tea and hauled his arse out to the cold-store unit.

Keeping the shivers at bay as best as he could, he made quick work of shelving their fresh food supplies on one side of the cool room, and the dry stores on the other. In the last cardboard box, labelled 'medicinal', he found a bulk order of multi-vitamins, enough lemon juice to keep scurvy away from a ship-full of eighteenth-century sailors, and twelve honey-brown bottles of the state's finest rum.

"Cheers, Vic. Top shelf."

If the frost never settled between him and Malone, at least he had that to warm himself up.

By the time Jet started unloading the frozen food, packed into foam coolers filled with dry-ice, the warmth of the tea had well and truly worn off.

The four-tiered shelves were almost empty, giving Jet open season on how to organise the space. He shuttled between the cool room and freezer, stacking all the meat and veggies and bread and frozen desserts in neat, individual sections. He was just congratulating himself on a job well done when Malone barged in, took one quick look around, then started rearranging the shelves.

Rude, much.

"Uh, hello." Jet forced himself to be polite. "What are you doing?"

"I need some freezer space," Malone said.

"What are you planning to freeze in—wait, you're not thinking of freezing sea cucumbers in here, are you?" A horrible image came to mind of dead sea cucumbers lined up in jars like a display in some warped, Victorian-era, natural history museum.

"No. Not whole," said Malone.

"Not whole?" Jet shuddered. "Tell me I'm not going to see dissected sea cucumbers every time I come in here for a bag of peas."

"I'm only interested in the gut tissue that they expel when they sense a threat. My research concerns the regenerative properties of those cells."

"Ri-ight." As though seeing expelled sea cucumber guts in their freezer was any better than whole dead ones. "Is that really what you're doing? Scaring the bejeebers out of them?"

"Again with the bejeebers. It's in their nature."

"Seems barbaric. Do you really have to bully them?"

"It's not like that," Malone snapped.

Jet wasn't cowered. "Walks like a duck. Talks like a duck. Is a duck." He didn't know why he was making such a big deal out of it. They were sea cucumbers, for fuck's sake. Their brains were probably tinier than a pea. But if an animal could sense danger, it could feel stress.

Malone's blank expression told Jet he'd get nowhere protesting. The man was on a mission. Clearly, Malone would do whatever the hell he liked.

But guts in the freezer?

God. Jet shuddered, and it wasn't from the cold.

Was it a battle worth fighting? Or should he save his energy for a fight that truly mattered?

"Just keep them separate from the food. I wouldn't want to mistake cucumber guts for rice noodles and accidentally throw them into a stir fry."

Malone didn't look amused. "Cross-contamination will ruin my samples."

"Uh-huh. Just sayin'...noodles." It was a thin argument, but he couldn't let Malone win everything.

Malone stuck his hands in his pockets. "Nutritional value notwithstanding," he said with an utterly straight face.

Jet choked in surprise.

Was that a joke?

Had Malone Archer cracked a funny?

Unbelievable.

"Everyone's a comedienne." Malone got Jet's back up, for sure, but maybe he wasn't quite so much of a stick-in-the-mud as he'd first appeared.

Instead of feeling reassured by that thought, it stupidly sent blood rushing to Jet's cheeks. He eyed the pile of emptied foam coolers, fog lifting from the slowly melting dry ice. Jet was tempted to claim them to build a territorial divide in the mess—one half of the room for him, the other half for Malone. Never the twain shall meet.

Remember Jethro, you need to work together if you want to survive.

Ugh.

Survival was overrated.

Time to go, Jethro. Before you say something you'll regret.

He tapped a knuckle on the thick freezer door, and sang, "Noooodles," as he hotfooted it out into the welcome heat of the day.

White-hot sun beat down on his scalp as he crossed the compound's hexagonal courtyard and scaled the few steps to his accommodation donga. The industrial cream paint on the outside of the shipping container was streaked with rust where the corrosive power of the salt-laden air had bitten through, but the re-fabbed inside was a comfortable space.

He left the door wide open to invite airflow through from the room's one and only window, cranked the ceiling fan to full blast, and used the last bit of aggravation to muscle his ten-tonne suitcase up onto his bed.

It took all of five minutes to hang his clothes in the closet and stow his toiletries in the tiny bathroom that butted up against Malone's equal-opposite half of the donga. That done, Jet turned his attention to the far more fun task of setting up an art studio in the mess.

From the look of the laptop, notebook, and glasses case arranged equidistantly on the table closest to the kitchen, Malone had already claimed his territory.

Jet happily steered clear, making his way to the third table at the other end of the long, sun-drenched room—an ideal spot. Plenty of light. Space to create. Air-con to protect his creations from the salt and humidity. And a strategic no-man's-land between him and Malone.

"Perfect," Jet said to the empty room.

CHAPTER NINE

Malone

Before Malone went out into the lagoon for the first time, he ran through his mental to-do list, gathering all the gear he'd need to create his data grid and off-shore research station. That done, he zipped up his reef shoes, slathered his bare skin with sunscreen, and clipped the waterproof walkie talkie to his t-shirt like an epaulet on his shoulder.

Check, check, and check. You're good to go, Archer.

The moment the water hit his bare skin, all of those practicalities disappeared. He exhaled a stale breath, and fresh, briny air flooded in. His shoulders dropped, his spine loosened, and his gait slowed to a relaxed amble as Malone waded in to his waist. Tension that had held him together for years dissolved into the sea and away. He flowed with the water. No urgency. No drama. No resistance. Only freedom.

It was a calm day and at low tide the water inside the cay's lagoon barely moved. The subtle ebb and flow of the current tugged on his board shorts and at the loose tail of his holey old t-shirt, soaking half-way up his chest to leave ripples of salt crusted at the boundary of sea-wet and sun-dry.

It was such a relief to be out in the water, alone, with no distractions. All the planning, the naysayers in his department, the futile attempts to gain funding—all of that was behind him. Before him was a sheltered lagoon straight out of his dreams, edging a pristine reef crest, and the wide blue sea beyond. All of it was perfect—his exclusive domain for three whole months.

The tepid water was like old glass—crystal clear with a hint of turquoise. At just the right angle, the surface mirrored the sky—a singular shade of blue, so rich it looked painted. Fake. Occasionally, a larger wave broke over the reef crest, carrying froth and fish, stirring the placid water to bring the cool up and the warm down. Most of the time Malone had an uninhibited view of the sloped back reef, teeming with life, as he secured nine metre-square quadrats, spread out across the sea cucumber habitat.

He knew he ought to wait at least one change of tide before conducting an official count. Given the disturbance he'd made on the lagoon floor, the data was void. It was grunt work, too. The sort of task usually reserved for research assistants, but Malone couldn't help himself. Counting had a steadying effect, and he relished the time to observe the subjects of his study without hinderance.

Malone stepped carefully, doing his best not to disturb any of the sea life or even the sand. Many other creatures besides sea cucumbers lived in the reef flat zone—crustaceans and molluscs and reef fish, not to mention turtles and reef sharks and rays, though larger animals tended to stay out in the open water when the tide was low. However, his primary focus was on the many sea cucumbers that lay on the rippled sand, alone or in clusters, and the grooved trails behind them that betrayed where they'd been.

When he'd first seen a sea cucumber, he'd thought it an ugly, unassuming, slug-like thing. But after years of study, he'd learned to appreciate their individual differences—subtle variations in the texture of their skin, the unique way each one moved or stretched or curled up in a ball, how some flopped all over each other in a puppy pile, while others went rogue on their own. He couldn't help tracing the patterns they made as they grazed on the seabed, hunting for nourishment, sucking up sand like a small, slow-motion vacuum cleaner. The sea cucumbers in his data field looked more than active enough to hold Malone's attention, and it wasn't until he'd finished mentally cataloguing the entire population inside his quadrats that he looked up and discovered he'd lost the last of the day to the sea.

The blue sky had turned to dusky peach in the west and bruise blue in the east—dark enough to reveal the silver pinprick of Venus. The tide had turned too, rising from hip to rib in the space of God knew how long.

Malone checked his watch.

Shit.

So close to the equator, the days on Tallon were shorter than he was used to back home, but he still didn't know where the time had gone.

So much for your acute powers of observation, Archer.

Intense focus was beneficial, but what kind of field scientist was he if he didn't notice the greater environment?

The crest of a wave washed over the near reef. White foam rushed by, rising to his pits, a sure sign that it was time to abandon his cucumbers for the night and head in. He turned away from the reef and picked a safe path toward the bright strip of light that shone from the row of windows on the mess.

Off in the far-right corner of the room, Jet stood at the window, still as a statue. He seemed to be staring out into the gathering night...directly at Malone.

For hours, Malone had lost himself to his work.

He'd forgotten all about their predicament on the island. And about their joint responsibilities for the met bureau. Hell, he'd forgotten every responsibility except the one to himself. But, most of all, he'd forgotten Jet.

Jethro Crane.

Awareness roared back, and suddenly, it all felt so real—their isolation, their co-dependence, their extreme togetherness.

Malone paused at the edge of the lapping shore.

How long had Jet stood there in the window? Watching him?

As Malone stared back, Jet made a 'V' with two fingers, pointed the two prongs at his eyes, then turned them Malone's way.

I see you.

Malone doubted it.

Nobody saw him. Not really.

Except his brother Myles.

With his other hand, Jet brought something dark to his face.

"Jet to Malone, come in Malone." Malone's walkie talkie crackled on his shoulder.

His hands full, Malone twisted to press his chin on the chunky 'speak' button. "Yes?" He gritted out.

"You're grinning."

I am?

"It's weirding me out. Stop it."

"Did you call for a reason? Or just to complain about my face?"

"Hmm...tempting." Jet's soft laugh was a blast of white noise. "You coming in any time this century? I'll have dinner ready in ten."

"Really? You cooked?" That was a surprise.

"Everyone has to eat, Malone. Even robots like you."

The bite of sarcasm probably ought to have stung, but Malone wouldn't mind being as faultless as a robot. It'd save him a stack of time if he didn't have to check and recheck his work, and he wouldn't be burdened by wild biological cravings, such as those spurred on by—"Ten minutes, Malone." Jet's voice broke through that inconvenient thought. Thank goodness. "Make that nine."

They didn't have to eat together. Malone could take care of himself. Just because they were the only humans on the island, that wasn't a good reason to have to be in each other's company every minute of every day. But knowing he'd been on Jet's mind while cooking was remarkably tantalizing.

"Fine." He made a production of rolling his eyes.

As soon as Malone stepped foot inside the air-conditioned sanctuary, his gaze went to Jet. It was as though he had a fucking tractor beam attached to his retinas. Then the aroma hit him—a rich, earthy, spicy aroma—and his stomach rolled with a different kind of hunger.

He must have groaned or something, because Jet paused and asked, "Everything alright?"

The lack of sarcasm in Jet's voice threw Malone for a moment. "Yeah. Let me just wash my hands."

"Someone trained you well."

There it was. *Welcome back, sarcasm.*

"I'm not feral," Malone grumbled.

"Uh-huh. Prove it."

"Prove it?" Who did this guy think he was?

"Show me your opposable thumbs."

"I'm not a trained monkey." He dried his hands on the dishtowel, then opened the drawer.

Exhibit A, he thought.

Jet's lips twitched, and a tiny thrill raced down Malone.

"Smells good." What an understatement. He watched Jet spoon steaming curry over pea-speckled rice. "Did you make that?" Cooking was simply chemistry, but he'd never quite got the hang of it.

"Nah. Left-overs. Lamb saag, rice, and dill raita. Hank stashed a few servings for us in the coolers."

"Mm-hmm. After you did some major sucking up, no doubt."

Jet side-eyed him, then flashed an evil grin. "Begging, yes. Sucking, no."

"That's a relief," Malone said, then stilled.

Shit. Foot, say hello to mouth.

And, of course, Jet would have to ask, "It is? Why?"

To which Malone had no ready answer. Nothing he could say out loud, at any rate. He zipped his mouth shut and turned his back on temptation.

Make yourself useful, Archer.

The kitchen had a simple 'lowest common denominator' feel that took him back to his student-share-house days, but the standing fridge-freezer took the cake.

After years exposed to salt air, the not-so-white elephant was covered in rust streaks and enough stickers to disguise a whale. Some looked very familiar—Amsterdam's picturesque canals, Germany's Castle Neuschwanstein, and the grand arched interior of the Musée d'Orsay on Paris' Left Bank—all places he recognised from the gap year shoestring tour of Europe he'd done with his brother Myles when they'd both been young and idiotic. Other stickers were of places still on his bucket list—Iceland's spectacular Vatnajokull Glacier, Tanzania's wildlife-rich Ngorongoro Crater, Jordan's mysterious Nabataean city carved into desert stone at Petra, the radiant orange rock formations of Utah's Bryce Canyon, and the giant Mayan pyramid at Chichen Itza.

Malone traced his finger down the pyramid's famous snake-like stairs, lit for tourists in gaudy colours, and wondered why there wasn't a sticker of Tallon Island in the mix. Not that anyone would need a sticker to remind them of the natural marvel right outside the door. "You want a drink?" he asked as he yanked open the fridge door. "There's desalinated water, long-life milk, cola, and...that's it."

"And enough rum in the pantry to float a pirate ship. Yeah, we have Vic to thank for that. Water for me, thanks," said Jet.

Malone grabbed the jug from the top shelf. "This is going to get monotonous."

"Are you going to find fault with everything?"

"Constructive criticism is the path to excellence."

"I don't think the fridge cares about being excellent," Jet huffed. "Besides, there's not much point in criticising anything, constructively or not, on a remote island in the middle of the Pacific Ocean."

"Coral Sea."

Jet pursed his lips. "I stand corrected."

Malone collected a couple of clean water glasses, then joined Jet at the middle table.

Jet had placed their plates side by side, which seemed like a good idea to begin with. The last thing Malone wanted was to have to stare at Jet, hide his inconvenient attraction, and make small talk. But he hadn't factored in how the rapidly failing light would turn the windows from a picture-perfect view of the lagoon to a mirrored vision of the two of them.

With the room sealed shut, his heightened awareness was maddening. Malone listened to the hum of the air-conditioning, the tinkling and scraping of cutlery on their plates, and the satisfied sounds Jet made as he ate.

"How'd the afternoon measures go?" Jet ventured. "Any issue with the radio?"

"No problem. Do you want to come along tonight when I do the ten o'clock measures? You can introduce yourself to whoever's on the line at HQ and get a feel for the whole thing."

"Sounds good." Jet was clearly surprised by his offer. In fact, Malone was surprised, too. Since when did he want to spend more time with Jet?

After they finished the meal, Malone filled the sink with suds and washed up. It was disturbingly domestic.

In his peripheral view, he saw Jet approach the whiteboard. Malone tensed as Jet uncapped the orange marker—the only one he hadn't used—and drew a star beside each of their names.

"What's that for?"

"Positive reinforcement for good behaviour."

"I don't need gold stars to acknowledge my effort," Malone protested. Never mind that Lachlan had delighted him by doing almost the exact same thing with his scratch and sniff stickers. "I'm not a child."

Jet craned to look back over his shoulder, and his hot gaze stripped Malone bare. "No." He agreed. "Far from it."

Fuck. I'm in trouble.

As soon as Malone completed kitchen duty, he escaped to shower, then filled the evening preparing his work zone. Efficiency was key. As soon as he'd collected valid data, he wanted to be able to catalogue it and start his analysis.

On one side of his table, he set up his laptop and notebooks. On the other side, he positioned a dissection tray, a neat stack of glass dissection slides, and his microscope. Then he slipped on his reading glasses and set about labelling enough sample containers to get him through the first twenty-four hours of collection.

Meanwhile, Jet thumbed through the island's ragged collection of book-swap paperbacks, then flopped down on one of the lumpy sofas with the first book in C. S. Forester's Hornblower series. Before long, Jet fell asleep with the book's pages spread across his face, the steady shush-shush of his breath keeping Malone company.

It was nice.

Probably because he didn't have to make conversation with Jet.

Or see his face.

Or pretend that he wasn't *actually* cataloguing every detail when his eyes strayed to Jet's lithe body relaxed on the sofa.

It all went swimmingly until his watch alarm jangled at twenty-one forty-five.

"What!?" Jet jerked up, and the book dropped with a clunk to the laminate floor.

"Just my alarm." Studiously ignoring Jet's rumpled beauty, Malone powered down his laptop, removed his glasses, clipped his walkie-talking onto his belt, tested the light aperture of his red-filtered headlight on the wall, and headed out into the night.

He'd already paced out the distance from the compound to the weather box and determined the most efficient way to gather the data, so, despite the heightened challenge of working in the dark, the collection went smoothly. He logged the data, radioed it in to HQ, retreated to his quarters, and set an alarm for oh-three-forty-five.

Malone rubbed his eyes, already anticipating the grit of a long night with too little sleep.

Why the hell he'd offered to take on such a long shift to start with, he did not know.

Wait. No. He knew why...

Jet.

It wasn't till he rested his head on his pillow and closed his eyes that Malone remembered he'd promised to take Jet with him.

Fuck. He hated loose ends.

Goodbye, sleep.

Hello, torment.

It was going to be a long night.

CHAPTER TEN

Jet

The new dawn felt hopeful, unformed and untested. Like a blank canvas. Or a raw lump of clay.

Jet grabbed his sketch pad and pencil and threw on his ginormous hat before he headed out to explore. The sun was no threat, but from the racket the island's birds were making, they were already up and about. Might as well give them a bigger target to hit. Bring a little joy to their day.

The soft light was incredible. The world a mix of bleached yellows, faded blues, and grey greens. The first shards of light rimmed the low saltbush foliage with silver, like a misplaced winter frost. Jet palmed open his sketchbook and scribbled a quick line drawing before the effect disappeared, then he continued on to the beach.

It would have taken ten minutes to walk the perimeter of the island if he hadn't stopped a thousand times to sketch every discovery. He found broken shells, odd pieces of coral, clumps of seaweed, gnarled driftwood, finger-like seed pods, and frayed twists of fishing net, all brought in on the tide. Eventually, Jet found himself at the most distant point of the island, where the wind-sock filled and fell on the tangy salt breeze. He stopped there to take it all in.

Having grown up in the desert-bound far west of the state, Jet was used to vast distances. He was used to the endless horizon and the discernible curvature of the earth. But the sea was different.

Blue on blue.

Sky on sea.

The boundless water was mesmerizing.

There was something hyper-exposing about it. The opposite of cabin fever, he thought, and he couldn't wait to see a summer storm amassing on the horizon—shades of purple roiling in the atmosphere.

Alas, the only storm brewing on Tallon was the one between him and Malone.

If you were stuck on a desert island for an entire season, who would you want to be stranded with?

"Not him."

Liar! Liar!

"Nope. No pants on fire here." Not with an entire ocean at his disposal to quench those flames.

At the tail end of his circumnavigation of the island, he looked up and saw Malone well out in the lagoon. Deep enough that the water skimmed his thighs.

The man's character was about as far from sunshiny as it was possible to get, but the early morning sun didn't seem to care about that. It gilded Malone's curls, licked one shoulder and side, and cast an opposing shadow in the rippling water.

It was crystal clear that Jet's overactive imagination was to blame when Malone's shirt disappeared and a trident appeared in his hand. He lifted it, the action rippling his gold-sheened muscles. Then he and Jet were deep underwater. And there were other men. No—mermen. A dozen of them arranged in an arc on the bottom of the sea, long hair wavering like sea grass. Each merman lay languid inside individual giant oyster shells, their oyster beds pink and plush as tongues. Slighter than Poseidon, but still muscled, their rippled abs dove into deep 'v's where skin turned to scales, ranging from pearlescent pale to dragon dark. Poseidon—his scales solid gold—surveyed the masculine offerings. Including Jet, whose own scales rippled indigo to magenta.

A pulse came from somewhere. Jet's tail throbbed with it, attuned to a single heartbeat.

Him. Jet's tail thrummed.

Him.

Jet looked up, straight into Poseidon's cool, aquamarine eyes.

Him.

Poseidon, master of his domain, had made his choice.

Me.

The seas parted and Jet stepped forward, eager to embrace his fate.

A chill tickled Jet's toes, the misplaced sensation lurching him out of the dream, and, too late, Jet realised he'd stepped forward into the real sea.

Not toward Poseidon.

Toward Malone.

Fuck.

The trident disappeared. Malone's shirt reappeared. And Jet cringed at the oh-so-obvious 'fin' he was sporting under his purple sarong. Which was worse—the betrayal of his imagination, or his libido?

Jesus, Jethro. Pathetic much.

Jet spun on his heels and dashed out of the shallows, doing a terrible job of pretending that he hadn't just been drooling over the sexy bastard.

"Jet?"

Shit.

Where was a tree to hide behind? Or a hole to swallow him up?

He strategically slid his sketch pad down and slowly turned around.

"What's up?" Malone asked.

Really? What's up?

Ask a more obvious question why don't you?

"Ahh..."

"Everything okay?" Malone pressed. "Did you need something?"

"Nope. Nada. Nothing." *Kill me now.* "I'm just, ah, checking the place out. Seeing if there's any..." His mind went blank. *Shit.* Jet bit his lip and looked anywhere but at Malone. The guy was glaring at him. Intense. Like a... "Shark."

"What?" Malone rushed toward land. "Where?"

Shit.

"Sorry. My mistake." Malone might be a prick, but he didn't deserve to be bullied.

If it was possible, Malone's disapproving glare intensified.

Jet's fin pulsed. Why did his libido have to choose Malone fucking Archer, for fuck's sake? It pissed the hell out of him. "Y'know, you're really good at that."

"Good at what?"

"Glaring."

Malone's eyes narrowed.

Jet shrugged. "I like to give credit where credit's due."

Malone's mouth tightened.

It was a really gorgeous mouth. The plump bottom lip deepened with a little divot underneath when he was mad.

Yep. Just like that.

"Did you need something? Or did you come out here just to annoy me?"

It was tempting to answer 'to annoy you', but Jet refrained...just. "Nope, just, ahh..." He wracked his mind for something plausible to say. Not that he needed a plausible reason to be there. He had every right to be on Tallon.

Jet's stomach rumbled.

There's an idea. Perfect timing.

"Breakfast," Jet said.

"Breakfast?" Malone turned his wrist to check the time on his bells-and-whistles smart watch.

Sure, I could do food. Make a meal out of—

The amalgam of Malone and Poseidon returned like some hot-on-cold vision. Fuck, that was sexy.

"Scrambled eggs." *Scrambled mind, more like.* "Fifteen minutes, if you want it hot."

"I'm kind of in the middle of something."

Great. Perfect. "No problem." It wasn't as though Jet was craving company. He was just fine on his own. He was happy being a human island...on an island... *Shit. Time to stop digging holes in the sand, Jethro. Eventually, they'll collapse in on you.*

Malone looked back in the direction of his flagged research zone. "I could—"

"No. No. It's fine. You go do you your thing." Better for Jet if he didn't have to look across the table and be reminded that his idiotic imagination had turned the man into the god of the seven seas. What next? Would he offer to feed Malone prawns by hand? *Hey Malone, want to lick a mussel from my muscles? Nibble a pippin from my pecs?*

Yeah. No.

Malone turned back to face him. And those eyes. Shit. Aquamarine. Poseidon's eyes.

Look away, Jethro.

But he couldn't.

Unaware of Jet's struggle, Malone threw a casual thumb over this shoulder. "I just need to—"

"It's really okay," Jet hastened to reassure him. "It's not like we have to do everything together."

God, no.

But Malone had decided. "I'll be there."

Fuck my imaginary life.

CHAPTER ELEVEN

Malone

Who stole my brain and replaced it with sap?

Either the water supply was contaminated with together-ness juice, or Jet used his man-whisperer technique on him. Those were the only two explanations Malone could think of for why he'd hustled back to his grid, scooped into a basin the sea cucumber and its exudate sample he was midway through processing, then followed Jet back to the mess.

Perhaps he could blame it on extreme hunger.

Malone ran a quick head-to-toe.

Nope. No sign of malnutrition here.

He liked scrambled eggs, but he could make his own, on his own schedule. Jet's cooking skills weren't that much of a draw.

The only other variable was Jet himself.

The man-whisperer.

When Malone stepped into the mess, Jet greeted him with a shy smile, two generous plates of scrambled eggs on toast, and a French press full of rich, dark coffee.

I could get used to this.

His stomach growled at the aroma. "Thank God." Must've been hungry after all.

"What's that?" Jet asked.

"Nothing. Just my stomach. Hungrier than I thought."

"No, I mean that." He pointed at the basin. "You brought a sea cucumber to breakfast?"

"And its exudate."

Jet leaned closer and sniffed. "That doesn't make it any better, Mal."

"You're the one that invited me."

"I didn't invite you. I *advised* you that breakfast was on. It was more of an advisation than an invitation."

"Advisation?"

Note to self—never play Scrabble with Jet.

Malone placed the basin on the clear area of his worktable. "I'd only just made the collection when you advised me about breakfast. If I left it out there, the birds might've swooped in for a feed."

"You didn't have to come."

Yes, I did.

Malone left that awkward bit of truth unsaid.

Jet went to touch the sea cucumber.

"Don't touch."

Jet pulled his finger back. "I wasn't going to hurt her."

"Not on purpose, but the microbiota on your skin could do real harm."

Jet snapped his hands behind his back and stood up, straight. "You're right."

"I know."

Jet rolled his eyes. "Humble, much."

"There's nothing humble about ignorance." Malone could feel Jet's eyes on him as he stroked a gloved knuckle down the soft back of the sea cucumber.

"Is it a he or a she?" Jet asked.

"I don't know."

"She needs a name."

"It's a research specimen. Not a pet."

Jet ignored him. "Hilda."

"You're not naming it Hilda."

"Too late. She looks like a Hilda." Their shoulders brushed as Jet leaned in again. "So cute."

Don't ask.

Malone stroked it again. "Why Hilda?"

For fuck's sake, Archer.

"She has a Hilda vibe." Jet shrugged. "You are putting her back, aren't you? I mean, you can't do dastardly experiments on her now that she's named."

"Relax. She...I mean, it...will go back, just as soon as I've catalogued her...its exudate."

Sweet Lord.

"Good." Jet nodded. "And, those creamy squiggles floating around are its exudate?"

"Technically, they're called Cuvierian tubules."

"It looks like sperm. Are you sure it's not a he sea cucumber?"

"It's not sperm."

"Gunter the gusher."

"No."

"Hmm. Gender fluid, then."

"It's *not* sperm."

"So, you're saying I *can* call her Hilda?"

Malone gave a long-suffering sigh, wondering how it was possible to finish a conversation he'd lost control of long ago. "Can we please have our eggs while they're still hot?"

"Sperm. Eggs. Wowsers, Mal. I didn't expect to get this personal over the breaky table. Must be something in the water."

Ignoring that, Malone pulled off his gloves and washed his hands. He pumped extra soap into his palm, to be sure, rinsed, then joined Jet at the table.

"Coffee?" Jet squeezed down the French press.

"Please." Malone doctored his mug with milk, then took a sip. Mmm. Perfect. "Thank you."

"You're welcome. Enjoy the eggs while they last. After this dozen is gone, breaky will be cereal and long-life milk."

"That's alright. Food's just fuel. Fill the tank a few times a day and away you go."

"Can you cook?"

"Adequately. It's just chemistry."

"Woah. Such passion!" Jet fanned his face. "Hold on to your hat, chef Archer."

"I make a mean chili." Why he felt the need to impress, Malone did not know. But when he saw a flash of a grin around Jet's forkful of eggs, Malone felt a rise of satisfaction.

Eating in companionable silence felt nice.

So nice.

Dangerously nice.

Jet slogged the last of his coffee. "I'd better clean up. Nearly time for me to do the ten o'clock readings."

"Want some help?" Malone offered. What was wrong with him, suggesting they spend *more* time together?

"It's okay. I've got it. Besides, you've got Hilda to take care of."

"Grr."

"Did you just growl at me?"

"We are not giving the sea cucumbers names."

"You're like a growly honey bear. All those blonde curls."

"That's not happening."

"No, really. Sweet honey—"

"Jethro."

"Oooh, full-naming me. Must be serious."

It took effort, but Malone did not growl again. He scraped his chair legs hard on the linoleum floor and clattered the cutlery as he stacked up the plates. The only solution was to get rid of Jet. "I've got these. You go do the measures, or I'll have to accuse you of shirking your responsibilities."

"Wouldn't want that." Jet shuddered dramatically, then made his escape.

Blissfully alone, Malone made quick work of cleaning the kitchen, then got on with his work. Before long, he had the fresh exudate samples packed, labelled, and stored in the freezer. A quick re-slick of sunscreen, and Malone was ready to return Hilda to the safety of the lagoon.

As he shut the door on his donga, the sound of Jet giving the synoptic readings stopped him in his tracks and he winced at the garbled jumble of numbers mixed in with "umms" and "ahhs" and self-deprecating "sorrys". Clearly, Jet was unfamiliar with the process, but then, so was Malone. It wasn't as though he'd done the job perfectly the first time around.

Had he unfairly judged Jet?

Jet was flighty, and sarcastic, and annoying as hell, but he did seem to care about doing the right thing. They were both making the best of a difficult situation.

Before the thread of tension could take hold, Malone headed back out to sea. He slipped on his snorkel and face mask, returned Hilda to her sandy quadrat, then moved on to the next, losing himself in the comfortable rhythm of work. One sea cucumber at a time—dive, stroke, photograph, measure, document, sample, label, return to the seabed.

The repetitive process was simple and straightforward. It left his mind free to notice other things, like the giant ray that glided through the water, its fearsome shadow causing one of the sea cucumbers to eviscerate without a single touch. How the clouds in the sky resembled a shoal of squid, shuttling across the sky. Or how Jet meandered on the beach, face hidden beneath his ridiculous yellow hat, pausing here and there to pull out his notepad and scribble something down. Then he'd snap it shut and move on. Around and around.

Malone was annoyed with himself that he was expending so much brain power thinking about Jet. Noticing him. Especially when he had far more important work to focus on. Before long, the day would be done, and he'd have to return to shore for the start of his shift. He had work to do, and that didn't include tracking his co-volunteer's every move.

Malone lost count of how many circuits Jet did of the island, but the repetition did give him a brilliant idea for how he could blow off some steam *and* refocus his mind.

Laps.

He secured his tools in the floating research station, slipped the snorkel between his teeth, and set off around the island, swimming easily over patches of weed and colonies of sharp coral. Low waves rushed over his back and threatened to inundate his snorkel, but Malone pushed on, around and around, till he fell into the zone, his mind cleared, and he lost himself to the rhythm of his stroke.

When he felt the tug of the current shift, Malone surfaced. He was amazed to see how much time had passed. He calmly finished the day's data set, then waded to shore.

Overhead, wheeling seabirds cawed in time with his steps as he traipsed up from the beach to the compound. Between one caw and the next, he overheard Jet in the radio shack, cackling with laughter.

Jet wasn't giving the synoptic readings. Not even close. "Oh, my holy hell, Shaz. I love you so much."

All the tightness in Malone's shoulders came crashing back.

Who the hell was Shaz? And what was so lovable about him? Or her?

It had to be someone at the met bureau.

Malone gritted his teeth and swung the door open the rest of the way. "Chatting up HQ now, are we?"

"Fuck!" Jet jerked in surprise.

Malone stepped up into the radio shack and flipped open the record book, but before he could look it over, Jet snatched it back. "We're a team, Malone, not boss and subordinate. I don't need you to critique my work."

Malone knew exactly how to work as part of a team. Hell, he was *born* part of a team. His twin might be on the opposite side of the world, but he still knew exactly how it was to be in sync with another person. The team element wasn't the problem. "Work? You're the one spending half the day faffing about on the beach and goofing off on the radio."

"Jesus. Do you hear yourself? Did you accidentally land on your flag and lodge it up your arse?"

"Me?"

How am I suddenly the bad guy?

Malone drew in a sharp breath, preparing to defend himself. But Jet had pushed him out and shut the door in his face.

CHAPTER TWELVE

Jet

What the hell was Malone's problem? Jet thumped the door shut, then returned to the microphone. "Sorry, Shaz. God knows what's up with him. He seriously needs to let loose."

Malone blew hot and cold. One minute he'd be treating poor Hilda with tender, loving care. The next, he was rounding on Jet as though Jet was solely to blame for climate change and every other global failing that might've gotten in the man's way.

A bit much, don't you think, Jethro?

Okay, so maybe he was being a bit dramatic. Even so, the man was maddening.

Thank goodness their contact at HQ was a decent human being. His mum would call Sharon—or Shaz, as she'd insisted he call her—a good egg. Jet had a feeling he'd need the touchstone more and more the further they got into the long, hot summer.

"Maybe he's sensitive about tomorrow," Shaz suggested.

"Tomorrow? What's tomorrow?" As far as Jet could tell, every day blended into the next on Tallon. Not a weekend in sight.

"The big three-oh."

"Three-o-oh!" Malone was turning thirty? "Seriously?" He seemed older than that. Or maybe it was just the man's overly serious attitude to...everything.

"The years sneak up on you," Sharon said. "When I turned fifty, my Dave bought me a mountain on the moon. Said it was to give me a different perspective to being over the hill." She snorted. "Different perspective, alright."

"Really? You can do that?"

"What? Change perspective? Of course, you can."

"No. I mean, buy bits of the moon?"

"Sure. I've got many celestial objects in my name. Dave reckons he'll buy me my very own universe in the multiverse when I hit the century mark. Isn't that the sweetest thing? He's such a star."

"Sweet as pie."

"Anyhoo, Malone's probably feeling a bit long in the tooth. Bake that man of yours a cake, and all will be well."

"He's not mine."

"Not if you don't take care of him, he won't be."

Jesus. "That's not what I...you know what, you're right. Every guy ought to be treated like a prince on his birthday."

"That's the spirit."

The radio went quiet for a moment, nothing but the buzz of static while Jet's thoughts spun.

"It's probably too late to buy him a comet." Shaz's voice was all seriousness.

"Mm-hmm. Probably," Jet managed to say, without even a hint of sarcasm.

"Oh, I know. You're a creative type. Why don't you make him something? A sand sculpture. A shell necklace. Something that says 'you're special to me'."

"Hmm…" The 'to me' bit wasn't exactly accurate, but Malone sure was special. A plan started brewing in Jet's mind. "You know what? That's actually not a bad idea."

"Yes!" He could practically see her fist pump. "Wait. Which idea? Tell me."

"Nope. Can't tell. Don't want to mess with the muse." He also didn't think she'd be able to keep her mouth shut, and some secrets were best left un-spilled. "Gotta go, Shaz. Thanks for the info. And say hey to Dave for me. He married one special lady."

"Wait. Don't go!"

But Jet's finger was already pressing the disconnect button. He had work to do and very little time in which to do it.

His mind whizzed with ideas as he burst into the mess.

"Woah! Where's the fire?" Malone was at his microscope, one hand on the focus knob, his nerdy glasses perched high on his nose.

Jet pulled up short. Shit. How was he going to do this with Malone underfoot? "Nothing! I'm not doing anything!"

Shit. Can anyone say 'guilty as charged'?

Malone's frown deepened, and a shiver ran down Jet's spine as he felt those icy eyes do a down-up of his body. Then he coolly turned away.

The man's oh-so-clear scorn made Jet want to invade his space.

Crank his chain.

Poke his inner bear.

Be cool, Jethro. It'll be easier to win him over with honey.

With Malone's attention refocused on the picture-perfect postcard of the lagoon outside, Jet didn't have to worry about getting caught as he took his own sweet time doing a down-up of the man's body. As far as form went, Malone Archer was a gift from Hephaestus, the Greek god of art and sculpture.

Jet's fingers twitched with the need to sketch the line of his neck, shoulders, back, arse...

Fuck. That arse.

As Malone shifted his weight from one foot to the other, Jet's artist's eye saw through the soft cotton of Malone's worn shorts to flesh and bone. It didn't take much imagination to see blood rushing through capillaries. Muscles flexing and releasing. Nerves firing. Hairs standing to attention. He imagined himself reaching out, and—

"Take a picture. It'll last longer."

Startled, Jet jerked out of his lusty daze. How had Malone known? He was facing the sea, for fuck's sake. Did he have a third eye in the back of his head? It was then that Jet noticed their electric-lit reflections in the windows—ghostly, but discernible against the soft dusk light—clear enough for Malone to catch him perving.

Busted!

Fuck.

Play dumb, Crane.

"Sorry, I was away with the fairies."

Truth.

"Thinking about dinner."

Lie.

Malone did turn around then. "Mm-hmm. Sure."

Why did the sceptic gene have to go hand-in-hand with the bastard gene?

"No need to factor me in. I grabbed a bite already," Malone said, dismissive, then turned back to his microscope.

And that was the sum total of the attention Malone gave him that night.

Jet could only be glad for the cold shoulder, since it meant he didn't have to take supremely stealthy measures to keep the whole I-know-it's-your-birthday thing a secret. Instead, Malone completed whatever scientific mumbo-jumbo he was doing, then took off early for bed, muttering about setting his alarm for the middle of the night. Which meant Jet could create in glorious peace.

As soon as the coast was clear, Jet closed his eyes and reversed time to that moment on the beach when he'd watched Malone working in the lagoon—Malone Archer: Man in his Element. An inspiring sight, to be sure.

Jet arranged his easel to face the back wall, just in case Malone had a change of heart about sleeping. He prepped one of his precious canvases with a thin, pale blue acrylic wash and left it to dry while he considered his creative options.

Hilda aside, Jet didn't really see the appeal of sea cucumbers. He could work with their shape—anything phallic was a treat—but nothing much else about them inspired. Then, he got a brilliant idea.

Jet mixed a rainbow of paints and happily lost himself to the canvas.

The hours blurred. Night ticked away. Jet's attention was lulled by the constant roar of the waves beyond the reef. It wasn't till the island's birds began their song in the pitch-black pre-dawn, that his flow was disrupted. He took a step back, rolled his weary neck, and assessed what he'd created.

"Perfect."

Monet would be proud.

Gritty eyed, he rinsed out his brushes, tidied up his gear, and collapsed in a heap on his bed. "Arsehole better appreciate it," he mumbled into his pillow three seconds before a wave of darkness rolled in and Jet was lost to slumber.

It couldn't have been more than a few seconds later when Jet's alarm blared and he shot out of bed.

"Fuck!" He staggered to the bathroom for a piss then climbed into yesterday's clothes, commando. They smelled of sweat and salt and paint, but he didn't really give a shit. Nobody but his co-volunteer was there to care, and Malone would judge him no matter what.

So early in their stint, their maintenance list wasn't long, but Peta had warned not to let the guano deposits build up too much. So, after completing the morning measures, he spent a couple of sweaty hours in a full-body coveralls, goggles, mask, and gloves, scouring the guano from every man-made surface, cursing each and every feathery crapper that had dared to fly overhead.

By the time he was done, nothing was going to keep him from diving headfirst into the lagoon. He raced to the beach on the opposite side of Tallon to Malone's territory, stripped, and waded through the shallows to ankle, shin, knee, thigh depth. When the water hit his balls, he closed his eyes and dove in, every skin cell sighing with relief as he pulled a dozen breaststrokes, skimming the sandy seabed, till his lungs screamed for oxygen and he came up spouting.

"Good?"

"Agh!" Jet squealed. A very manly squeal, but still...

Where the hell had *he* come from? Jet clutched his invisible pearls, and, after his head caught up with his racing heart, thought to duck his bare arse below the surface. Not that it did much good since the water was clear as glass. He belatedly let go of his precious pearls, crossed his hands over his even more valuable tackle, and glared across the ten metres or so of lagoon between him and Malone. "What the fuck are you doing here?"

Malone raised a very annoying brow and tapped the snorkel mask lodged on top of his head. "Snorkelling."

Underwater.

Which meant Malone had seen him all of him.

Fuck.

Do not flash your dick at the man.

Even if he is sexy as fuck.

Despite the cool of the water, heat flooded Jet's groin.

Shit. He needed bigger hands.

"I'm just gonna..." Jet hoicked his chin beachward and started crab-walking. If nothing else, his glutes would appreciate the squat.

Malone appeared completely unruffled. He paid no attention to Jet as he tipped the residual saltwater from his snorkel and re-fitted his mask. Jet counted himself lucky to be ignored long enough to remove himself from the sea and climb back into the sweaty coveralls. Ordinarily, he'd think the insensitive jerk deserved whatever he got, but not on his birthday.

Birthdays were sacred.

Give him today.

Tomorrow, all bets are off.

CHAPTER THIRTEEN

Malone

"Malone!" His walkie-talkie burst to life just as he was inspecting the arse end of a sea cucumber. Reflex made him squeeze, shocking the poor creature, and it shot straight at him, streaking his t-shirt with ropes of sticky exudate.

"Jesus." The mess looked like he'd shot a horny load.

He dropped the saggy creature back into the water and tugged at the cotton material, plucking at it to get it away from his skin. His luck, the shit would burn through.

"Malone!" Jet's voice burst through his walkie talkie again. "Come quick! Fire!"

"Fuck!" Quick as he could, Malone hauled arse to shore. His eyes skittered across every point of the island. He couldn't see any smoke, but that didn't mean much. A fire could be isolated inside one of the cyclone-proof buildings.

Shit, it better not be the freezer. If he lost his research samples, he'd...God, he didn't know what he'd do. Throw a tantrum?

Probably.

And where was Jet? Was he okay? Was he hurt? The walkie talkie had been silent for so long. Minutes, maybe. He didn't know. "Jet!" Malone shouted into it.

Nothing.

Was the thing even working?

He shook it. "Jet! Where are you?"

Still nothing.

No word from Jet.

No sign of fire.

Heart racing, Malone ran up the sandy rise from the beach. "Jet!" he shouted. "Are you okay?"

Please be okay.

Where the fuck was he?

Attention everywhere but his feet, Malone just about tripped over a paver when he dashed out from the gap between the mess and the cold store and saw Jet on the mess deck with fire in his hands.

No, not just fire.

A forest of flaming candles on top of a cake. "Ta-da!"

What the...? Malone slapped a hand to his racing heart.

"Happy Birthday to you." Jet sang. "Happy birthday to you. Happy birthday, dear Mal-oooone. Happy birthday to yoooou."

"What the hell, Jet?"

"It's a black forest lava pirate cake." Jet beamed.

Malone would not let that grin get to him. "I thought—" He gripped the walkie talkie so tight it bit into the palm of his hand. "Fuck, Jet, I thought there was a real fire."

"Surprise! Isn't it cool?"

"No. Not cool. You made me drop a cucumber, ran all the way here from the outer reaches of the lagoon, and…and…so, not cool."

Stand down, Archer.

Everything's okay.

There's no fire.

Nothing's burning.

Nobody's hurt.

Jet's grin wobbled a bit, making Malone's gut flip. Shit.

Stupid, stupid gut.

Do not go soft.

"Look at me." Malone pointed at the slash of exudate across his chest. Not that he gave a rat's arse about his t-shirt, but still, Jet had to understand that some things were more important than bloody birthdays. But it didn't take him half a second to realise he'd made a bad miscalculation when Jet swept a heated look not just down Malone's shirt, but lower still. More than Malone's gut flipped.

"For shame, Malone. You started the party without me."

"What? No. That's not. Grr…" He shifted his feet, uncomfortable as hell.

It's okay, Archer. A hard on is a perfectly natural male response to being ogled by a gorgeous devil.

Jet's full grin reappeared. "There's my favourite growly honey bear. Now, come and blow out your candles before the flames melt the frosting. I'll have you know I put a lot of effort into this gastronomic marvel."

On sensory overload, Malone's stomach growled and his mouth watered. Those were perfectly normal mammalian responses, too, he reminded himself as he eyed both temptations.

What were his options?

Fight?

The man hadn't committed a heinous crime, for fuck's sake. All he'd done was bake a birthday cake.

Flight?

Strangely, that didn't appeal.

What, then? Surrender?

You could choose to be gracious, Archer.

True.

Head to toe, Malone worked swiftly to calm his body. If he just thanked the man and enjoyed a slice, he could be back out in his lagoon in ten minutes. Fifteen, tops.

"Thank you," Malone bit out. "It looks..." *You look... fucking divine.* "Nice." His wet reef shoes squelched as he scaled the three stairs to the wooden deck, then sucked in a deep breath to blow out the bloody candles.

"Close your eyes and make a wish."

"Grr."

"Shh, Malone. If you tell me your wish, it won't come true."

Jesus. His sigh made the flames waver, but none went out.

"Close your eyes. Say to yourself, Dear Birthday Fairy—"

"I'm not saying that."

Jet raised his voice. "Dear Birthday Fairy, I wish..."

Under sufferance, Malone closed his eyes and wished. *Dear Birthday Fairy, I wish Jethro Crane would stop being so annoying and distracting and stunning and...grr...* He opened his eyes.

The bloody birthday fairy would have to figure out the rest of his garbled wish. Any more and Malone might ask for something he couldn't handle.

"Did you make a wish?"

"Yes," his voice rumbled.

"Excellent. Now, blow…"

Again, Malone took the path of least resistance and obeyed.

"Good job."

"I'm not a toddler, you know."

"Of that, I am very well aware." Jet's tongue speared his cheek, then he shifted the cake into one hand and rat-a-tatted Malone's belly with his other knuckles. "Come on."

"Come where?" Malone rubbed at the spot. It'd been months since he'd been up so close and personal with another human being, but that was no reason to go weak at the knees over a simple brush of a knuckle. It wasn't even skin on skin, for fuck's sake.

"Are you coming?" Jet called back to him from the gap on the other side of their donga.

How on earth had Jet gotten all the way over there in the space of three-quarters of a second?

Unless Malone had spaced.

"Come on, space cadet," Jet called back to him.

Jesus. Now the guy's a mind reader? On top of everything else?

"Yeah, yeah. I'm coming."

Malone followed Jet and the cake through the gap and down the gentle slope to Tallon's west-facing beach.

On the dry sand above the high-tide mark, Jet had arranged three canvas deck chairs in an arc—one draped in a towel, tented over something square, the others bare. Inside the arc, Jet's purple and yellow tie-dyed sarong was laid out like a picnic blanket, the corners weighted down by four foam coolers.

Jet set the cake on top of the cooler closest to the chairs, dropped to his knees and spread his arms wide. "Et voila!"

Malone was practically on top of the whole set up before he saw a dug-out hole in the sand in the centre of Jet's arrangement. Inside was a pile of driftwood interspersed with shiny licks of colour that looked suspiciously like... "Is that cellophane?"

"No open fires allowed on the island, so I had to improvise." Jet reached into the pile of driftwood and clicked on a headlight, its beam catching the transparent red and orange and yellow and blue sheets and turning them to flame.

Malone pursed his lips at Jet's hokey arts and crafts project. "Seems a bit misguided to allow plastics on the island, but not fire. The destruction to the aquatic environment is—"

"Oi. None of that doomsday grumbling, Malone. It's time to celebrate. Here." Jet handed him a kitchen knife. "Cut, then you get to choose a birthday throne."

Malone thought about grumbling again, but what was the sense in that? Jet was a force of nature. So, again, Malone chose the path of least resistance and did as he was asked.

"You didn't cut all the way to the bottom, did you?" Jet sounded horrified just as the tip of the knife clonked the melamine plate.

Malone froze. "Why?"

"If the first cut touches the bottom, you have to tell us who your girlfriend-slash-boyfriend-slash-person-friend is."

Person-friend? "Stop fishing."

"Not fishing. Those are the rules. Ignore them at your peril."

Malone scanned a one-eighty of the sea, the reef, the lagoon, the beach, and Jet on his knees. "I don't see any peril." *Except right in front of me.*

"That's where you're wrong." With the blade still lodged in the cake like a murder weapon, Jet whipped the whole plate, cake, and knife away.

"Hey!"

"No name—no cake."

"That's not fair."

Jet shrugged. "Thems the rules."

"Well, I don't like your rules." How could the man be so irritating, and yet...and yet...?

Malone watched as Jet cut two thick slices and dished them up. The rich chocolate icing did look delicious, but the real wonder was the flood of maraschino cherries and rum lava that spilled from the middle. Even from three feet away, he could smell the distillery.

Malone sat forward in anticipation, but instead of handing him one of the plates, Jet stuck in a fork and took a giant bite.

"Hey!" How dare he? "That's *my* cake."

"What's that?" Jet forked a cherry and made a production of licking off the sauce, then taking it between his pearly teeth. "Mmm." He moaned, chewing as slow as humanly possible.

While Jet was occupied with his food orgasm, Malone took advantage. He grabbed for the second plate and dug in.

One taste and Malone forgot all about being irritated.

"Oh, wow." His eyeballs rolled up uncontrolled—every nerve drunk on what was surely thousand-proof sauce. It was sweet and syrupy and outrageously decadent. If someone had polled his taste buds, there wouldn't have been a bell curve, just a singular column indicating one-hundred percent of respondents answered, 'Hell, yes!'

"Yum, right?"

Yum didn't even begin to describe it. "I think I found the pirate's hoard."

"You can thank Vic and his legendary love of Bundy rum for that." Jet forked another bite, his teeth a chocolatey mess as he spoke.

"Mm-hmm." Goddamn. Malone was in heaven.

Jet swallowed his last bite, then did a terrible job of licking the chocolate off his lips, smearing it into a devil's sheen. "So..."

"So?"

"Did your wish come true yet?"

Oh, God. Not that again.

Malone shoved a forkful of rummy cherries into his mouth to give himself ten seconds' grace. While he chewed, he made out like he was searching for something out on the horizon. Problem was, his wish wasn't out there. It was staring him in the face.

So, did my wish come true?

"No," he said. Jethro Crane was still annoying, and distracting, and stunning, and...yet...

Do I still wish he'd change?

Of that, Malone was no longer sure.

"Oh well. There's time yet." Jet checked his watch. "Still six hours till you turn into a pumpkin."

"Or we could re-light the candles and I could make another wish."

"Nope. That's against the rules. And don't think I've forgotten that you haven't told me the name of your soul mate."

"Still fishing?"

"Still cagey," Jet flashed back. "Three months is a long time alone together to remain strangers."

"Fine." It wasn't like his sexuality was a secret. He'd never seen the sense in that. "I do not have a person. If I did, I'd have a him."

"Okay." Jet nodded. "Good." He nodded some more. "Excellent."

"So glad you approve."

"For that, you get a reward." Jet jumped up from the sarong. "A party isn't right without company, so I rustled some up."

"If you're talking about inviting the birds, I'd rather not." Malone shuddered at the memory of their first day on the island, and combed his fingers reflexively through his hair. The only other company they'd had so far were scuttling crabs and the shy green turtles that lumbered up the beach to lay their eggs in the dead of night.

Jet eyed his shirt and smirked. "And sea cucumbers are any better?"

"They're a lot less bother." Malone plucked his tacky shirt from his chest. "Usually."

"Glad you said that." Jet rounded the 'fire' and fingered the beach towel draped over the third chair. "Ready?"

No. "For what?"

With a flourish, Jet whipped off the towel. "Ta-da!"

Underneath was a colourful painting of…

Malone squinted. Either the rum had tainted his eyesight, or Jethro had painted a host of blue and green cocks, mixed with an occasional red, orange, yellow, or coral pink cock. He tilted his head ninety degrees, searching for an alternative interpretation, but all that did was make the flaccid cocks stand to attention.

What is the collective noun for cocks? A troop? A battalion? An erection?

"Are those…?"

"Sea cucumbers! Aren't they cute?"

"Oh."

A pickle of sea cucumbers.

Not cock.

Malone honestly didn't know if he was glad of that or not.

Jet pointed at the bottom left corner of the painting. "There's Hilda."

Whoa. *Definitely not cock.*

"It's a cuc-scape. Get it? A *cuc* scape. As in a *land*scape, except—"

"Made of sea cucumbers. Yeah. I get it. Very clever."

"Thank you. I think it's important to personalise art. Don't you?"

"Absolutely." *No. Not if it gets me a cock-scape for my birthday.* Still, it *was* clever. And weirdly beautiful. If he blurred his vision, it looked more like an impressionistic seascape than a landscape, with sea cucumbers painted in every shade of sky and seawater, blending down to the sandy sea floor. And all over it, flashes of pink and red and purple hinted at the abundant sea life.

"Thank you." Malone didn't entirely mean it because he knew he'd dream of swimming through a watery wonderland made entirely of cock, and that would be all Jet's fault.

"You're welcome."

"You and my brother would get along great. He's a designer specializing in wallpaper. His fans say he's a creative genius."

"You sound very proud of him."

"He's my brother. Of course, I'm proud."

Jet looked out to sea for a moment, his jaw tight.

What did I say?

Malone replayed their conversation in his head, but none of his words raised a red flag.

"Myles appreciates colour, too, but his influences are historical. Nothing at all like your..." Malone pointed vaguely at the painting, "Style."

"I call it modernist organic." Jet said with a straight face.

"Uh-huh." Malone tipped his head sideways again, regretting it immediately.

"I think it's a mighty fine cuc-scape."

"Humble."

"Bestest cuc-scape in the land."

"More like the only cuc-scape in the land."

"You saying you want a cuc-scape-off?"

"No." Of that, Malone was one-hundred percent sure.

"Intimidated by my creative brilliance, eh?"

"No."

"No, no. It's alright. I understand. I've been painting ever since I was five years old when I accidentally discovered that I was adopted. Spoiler—I didn't handle it too well. My mum took me to a child psychologist who taught me to, in her words, express my feelings through creativity. Her mission was to turn me into a happy soul. Now look what I can do."

Malone dutifully re-inspected the cock-slash-cuc-scape. "Ah..."

"I know. Awesome, right?"

"I detect hints of Freud." It was the only comment Malone felt equipped to give.

"Hmm." Jet did that agreeable head-nod thing people in art galleries did, then seemed to snap out of it. "Anyhoo...time for food." He opened another foam cooler and pulled out container after container of nibbles jabbed with enough toothpicks to build a fort.

"Wow. That all looks..." he had no words. Jet had gone the extra mile.

No. A dozen extra miles.

For me.

He ought to be grateful, but...

Malone surreptitiously checked his watch. Any chance of getting back to his real sea cucumbers was fast disappearing.

"None of that clock-watching, Malone. It's party-time. Here." Jet poured him a black-as-tar drink from a two-litre thermos. "Get that into you."

"What is it?"

"Vic's pirate juice. Try it."

Malone took a hesitant sip, his eyes watering at the one-to-one ratio of cola and rum. It squirrelled down his oesophagus to land like a bad influence beside the sugar-coma cake. He took another sip. Then another. And another. Before

Malone knew it, his cup was empty and his urgency to leave a distant memory.

Was this what life on Tallon could be like if he gave in to rest and relaxation? To sweet temptation? To Jet?

He licked the rich sweetness from his lips and held his cup out for more.

Chapter Fourteen

Jet

Half the thermos down, Jet was willing to admit there was a strong chance he'd underestimated Malone's need to cut loose.

He was also willing to admit he'd misjudged Malone's capacity to exhibit affection.

Not only did he look like a honey bear...

Exhibit A: all those sun-bleached curls.

...he snuggled like one, too.

Hundreds of kilometres from human light pollution, the Milky Way was so bright it looked close enough to touch. They'd been lying side by side on his sarong, staring up at the brilliantly clear night sky, for well over an hour. Every time Malone pointed at "That one," or, "No, that one," or, "No, you idiot...*that* one," he'd shuffle closer to Jet's side, grazing shoulders and elbows and knuckles. Jet couldn't decide if he ought to call the game they were playing 'how to make up the most ridiculous names for constellations', or, 'how to torture Jet slowly with electrically conductive arm hair'.

It was a close call.

Jet desperately wanted some of Vic's party juice to take the edge off and smooth out the zings that travelled through his body every time Malone moved. But he had to stay sober for the late-night measures. Possibly also the pre-dawn measures, given the way Malone had gone full-hog with Vic's choice of beverage.

Time to shift gears. "Let's play a different game."

"Nooo," Malone whined.

So cute.

Eyes still on the stars, Jet said, "I spy with my little eye, something beginning with S."

Without warning, Malone rolled sideways, half his weight landing on Jet. The full-body zing of electricity was so shocking that Jet instinctively reached out to touch the sand, grounding them both.

"Hey," Jet protested, then snapped his mouth shut.

Was Malone trying to seduce him?

Seduction wasn't the S word he'd been angling for, but who cared about that when he had a ninety-kilo wall of sexy muscle plastered to his side.

It's his birthday, Jethro. Treat him like a prince. Give him what he needs.

It was just them—Adam and Adam—alone on Tallon. What possible reason could he have to resist plucking the apple from the tree? Other than the fact that they had eighty-seven days left together on the island—an awfully long time to stretch out an awkward morning after.

Or fall for the guy and face inevitable heartbreak.

Pshaw! Said the universe. *Sexy times don't have to equal white picket fences and lifelong commitments. Live a little, Jethro. Take what you want.*

The universe was really fucking annoying.

And insightful.

What should he say to Malone?

Fuck me, or keep your distance?

Even for Jet, that was a bit too binary.

Touch me like you mean it. Please.

For the few seconds it took for Jet's psyche to catch up to his body's desires, Malone hovered there, his arm outstretched. God, he smelled delicious. Salt tang and warm man. A gift sent from the sea.

Jet breathed his scent in deep and their chests grazed.

Zing!

Malone's breath hitched.

Did that mean he felt it, too?

Your move, said the universe.

Dammit! I'm not good at games like this.

Malone's rum-sweet breath ghosted across the sensitive skin at his temple, sending a shiver through every single follicle in his body.

"Lucky we're grounded," Jet said.

Malone frowned "What?"

"Electricity," Jet explained.

Malone leaned in closer, pressing into Jet's body.

Fuck! That feels good.

Jet closed his eyes, anticipating...something. He didn't know what. But suddenly, Malone's weight disappeared, and the next thing Jet heard was the muted hiss of the thermos being opened.

Shit. Was that all Malone was reaching for? Another drink?

Well, that's a bust, the universe taunted.

Jet glared up at the starts. *I spy with my little eye, something beginning with P. Here's a hint, it ends with 'rick'.*

Time to play it safe—revert to birthday-party mode.

"Let's play two truths, one lie."

Malone groaned. "Let's not."

"Don't be a party pooper, Mal. I'll go first."

Malone blew in his ear.

"Eww, Mal. Stop trying to distract me."

"What's with the nickname? My name's Malone. Not Mal."

Jet gave in to the desire to move in close. "I think we're beyond formalities. Don't you? Besides. Mal isn't a nickname. It's not like I'm calling you…I don't know…Moose. Mal's a shortening. If you're Aussie, your name gets shortened. It's one of the absolute rules of friendship."

Malone raised an eyebrow. "Moose?"

Jet shrugged. "They're horny."

"They've got antlers. Not horns."

"Whatever," Jet waved that persnickety detail off. "If you're ree-eally dead set on me using your full name. I can do that. Ma-lone." Jet strung out. "Mal means bad in Spanish, doesn't it? Bad one."

"Original."

"Bad to the bone." Jet sang.

"No."

"You're so *baaad*."

"I'm really not."

"Sexy rebel. It's right there in your name. You've got no choice in the matter."

"Hmph."

So cute.

Jet decided to offer a free truth in return. It was the least he could do after that tease.

"My name isn't much better. On my birth certificate, it's Jebediah. Jeb for short, I guess. J. E. B." Jet spelled out. "But my dad's a massive fan of Jethro Tull. You know, that wacky British band from the seventies?" Malone looked bewildered, which was pretty standard whenever he tried to explain the origin of his name to anyone younger than fifty. "Anyhoo...after the adoption, him and Mum re-named me Jethro. Jet for short."

"That's...different."

"Super cool to be named after a flautist, even if he was a rock star. Can't tell you how much fun that was in high school." Jet mouthed 'zero'.

"I can see you as a teenager, strutting down your high school corridor. Lanky, awkward..."

"Cheers, mate."

"...the promise of future glory."

Hell, yeah. "Better. Now, back to the game."

Jet ignored Mal's groan. He thought for a second, then held up a finger. "Number one. When I was three months old, my dad tried to launch me into space in a weather balloon."

"Well, that's obviously a lie. Since you're here. On this beach. With me. And not...you know...like...up in space...or not here...or dead...or whatever."

"I said almost." It was difficult, but Jet did his best to ignore Malone's prattle, which was totally out of character and not at all cute. "Number two."

"This ought to be good." Malone blew in his ear again, then he hiccupped. "Fuck, I think I might be a bit tipsy."

Not. Cute.

"Number two. When I first met my best friend, Flash, I thought he was a porn star."

Malone pulled back. "Serious? Why did you think he was a porn *hic* star?"

"Hang on. You believe that story over the weather balloon thing?"

"Nu-uh. I'm qui-*hic*, fuck. I'm quizzing you."

"I'll have you know my dad was so traumatised by almost sending me to the moon that he made me wear one of those halters every time we went outside until I was three. Like a fucking baby horse."

"Foal."

"What?"

"A baby horse is called a foal. That's the correct term for it. In the dictionary."

"Thank you, Mr. Merriam-Webster."

"You're wel-*hic*-come. Shit, that's annoying. Grr."

"Hold your breath for as long as you can. It'll help."

A slight pause in their conversation, if it could be called that, let the majesty of starlight and the roar of the ocean back in, giving Jet a minute to wonder how it was that one tipsy arsehole with an irritating penchant for perfection could overwhelm his senses so fully.

"*Hic.*"

Oh, God.

Not cute. Not cute. Not cute.

If he said it three times, would it magically become true? Jet hoped so.

"Number three—"

Malone released his pent-up breath. "Wait. Go back to the porn star."

"Do I look like the sort of person who'd make fast friends with a porn star? Not that there's anything wrong with porn stars. So long as they're happy doing their thing. And all the people involved are happy, and healthy, and...y'know...content with their choices."

Shit. Kill me now.

Jet turned away from Malone to face the silver waves licking the shore.

Pity he didn't have the power to levitate a bucketful of ocean to pour on his heated face. Cool himself down a few degrees.

"Tell me." Malone's breath tickled the short hair at Jet's nape, sending a shiver all the way to his toes.

"Fine. His real surname is Gordon, so Flash for—"

"Flash G-*hic*-Gordon."

"Exactly. Stupid me heard *Flesh* Gordon', instead of Flash. I was eighteen and horny, and, yeah...anyway. The day we met, first day of university, he invited me back to his place for...well, *I* thought he was inviting me around for...you know..."

"Extracurricular activities?"

"Exactly. I mean, who calls themselves *Flesh* Gordon for any other reason? Am I right?"

"So right."

"Thank you." Jet liked tipsy Malone. "Ever since then, he's bought me superhero boxers for Christmas and birthday presents. The bastard. Thinks he's funny."

"Could'a been worse."

"Yeah?"

"Could'a bought you boxers with, like, cocks all over them."

"True."

"Or cucumbers."

"Hmm." That would've been novel. "Anyway, when I got to his front door, a very, and I mean *very* pregnant woman opened it. I'm talking thirteen-months gestation, at least." Jet rounded his arms around a phantom beach ball to demonstrate.

"Bzzt! Lie! The human gestation period is nine months."

"Yes. Thank you. I am aware."

Malone held his hand up, as though swearing an oath, and deepened his voice. "The truth, I am arbiter of."

"Okay, Yoda."

Malone blinked, his sun-bleached lashes silvered in the moonlight. "So, they wanted a threesome?"

"Who?"

"Your fleshy Flash and his ginormous woman."

It was Jet's turn to blink owlishly. "Did that sentence seriously just come out of your mouth?"

Malone silently mouthed his words, checking over them again. "Stranger than fiction," he concluded, which Jet took as permission to get on with the game.

"Number three." He raised three fingers in a boy-scout salute.

Malone caught them. "But I already figured out the lie."

"No, you didn't. Number three. My brother, who's a dou-ble-decker dick, by the way, doesn't know he has a brother, my father doesn't know I have a brother, and my mother didn't know I'm her son." Jet swallowed thickly at the reminder of Eloise. He did his best not to think of her too often. No more than a dozen times a day.

"Liar, liar, pants on fire," Malone sing-songed.

"What makes you say that?"

"Nature." Malone swung his arm around in a giant arc, just about taking off Jet's head. "Lots of animals eat their young, but they still recognise them. Except..." his fingertip came to rest on Jet's nose, "amoebas."

Jet shooed the finger off. "I'm not an amoeba."

"Correct. *Hic.* Shit." He leaned close and bit Jet's shoulder.

"Hey!" Jet pushed Malone's forehead back. "No cannibalism on the island."

"Hungry," Malone said, *not* eying the remains of the picnic.

For fuck's sake. If grumpy Malone was a temptation, horny Malone was proving ten times harder to resist. "If you want to eat me, I can think of far more enjoyable ways to do it."

Wait. Did I just say that out loud?

Distraction. Stat. "Your turn."

Malone's eyes flashed up to his.

"Two truths, one lie," Jet clarified.

"Hmm..."

Note to self, horizontal 'thinking man' pose is way sexier than vertical 'thinking man' pose.

Malone snapped his fingers. "Got it!"

"Great. Let's hear it, then."

"Number one. I've been married seventeen times."

Jet paused before responding, waiting for the punchline. When none was forthcoming, he waved Malone on.

"Number two. My twin is a genius, but I'm not."

"Hmm." Bound to be a trick, that one was, unless the lie was in the 'twin' claim. "Identical or fraternal?" Jet tested.

Malone wavered. "Identical, sort of."

"Ooo-kay. Ignoring for the moment the fact that there's no such thing as 'sort of' identical. Go on." Not that Jet wanted the game to be over. Once it was done, he had no more ideas up his sleeve for how they could fill the time.

Well, he had plenty of inappropriate ideas, but those were already ruled out.

Bad, Jethro!

Of course, the universe chose that moment to contradict him. *You two could always get your birthday suits on and go skinny dipping.*

Not funny, Universe. Jet glared up at the stupid stars winking down at him.

Funny wasn't what I had in mind, Jethro.

Distracted, Jet missed what Malone said. "Sorry. What was that?"

"Number three, I said. When I..." Malone wet his lower lip with the tip of his tongue.

Jet didn't even try to not trace the moonbeam gleam left behind. "When you...?"

"When I blew out my candles, I wished..."

Jet sat up—far too wired to lie still. "What did you wish for?"

"A kiss."

"Oh, now, that's..." *A lie*, Jet almost declared. Except if it was a lie, the other two had to be truths, and no way could Malone have been married seventeen times.

Could he?

CHAPTER FIFTEEN

Malone

Inches away on the sarong, Jet's knee bounced, legs crossed like a super-sexy Buddha. "You weren't married seventeen times. Nobody gets married seventeen times."

"Says you." Malone licked the sweetness off his lips. He'd never admit it, but Vic's choice of rum and coke really was delicious. It took him straight back to first year university and the rum jungle in the backyard of his college residence. Not that he indulged too often. Making the grade to pursue Honours, then his PhD, had come first, second, and third on his priority list.

"Says me. So that must be the lie." Jet searched for something in Malone's expression.

Malone wished he knew what it was. The way Jet looked at him sometimes made him feel like a puzzle—one the man couldn't figure out. It was disconcerting, being the focus of someone else's microscope.

He was used to facing scientific questions and educated guesses. But they weren't usually directed toward him. He just wasn't that interesting. Nothing like his talented, fearless, scarred-beyond-recognition twin.

Jet's eyes got squinty the more he stared. "You're too much of an idiot to be a genius, so that must be a truth."

"Oi!" It was a quantifiable fact that Myles was a genius, while he was not. Didn't mean he had to let anyone flagellate him about it. "Maybe my brother isn't a genius either."

"Hmm...true. But that'd make it two lies already, and I know you wouldn't break the rules. You're a stickler, Malone Archer. No bones about it."

It wasn't a super-attractive trait, but if Jet wanted to believe that about him, he wasn't going to argue. Rules were there for a reason.

Malone looked out to the night. The stars were a little swimmy, like a time-lapse photo taken by a shaky camera. Weird. He didn't think he'd drunk *that* much.

"What about the third? My birthday wish?" Why he was trying to convince Jet that he'd wanted a kiss, Malone didn't know. Nothing about '*I wish Jethro Crane would stop being so annoying and distracting and stunning and...grr*' amounted to wishing for a kiss.

Fact.

"Test me," Malone said. *Kiss me and see how I respond.*

"Test whether you wished for a kiss? How am I supposed to do that? Magic up a truth serum?'

"No such thing," Malone said, but the notion did give him an idea. He brandished the thermos in the air like a trophy. "Vic juice."

"Eww, don't call it that."

"It's hard to lie when you're under the influence. Cheers." He re-filled his cup, congratulating himself when he only sloshed a little overboard. "Oops, sorry." Malone brushed at the splatter, wondering why there were suddenly two wet spots instead of one. He squinted one eye. It didn't help. Jet's penchant for sarongs was a little weird, but Malone had to admit he liked them. Especially when they conformed to Jet's body. "Nice." He gulped down his third cup. Or was it his fourth? Malone couldn't remember.

What are you doing, Archer? This isn't like you.

God knew. He rarely drank to excess.

Do you want a kiss this badly?

Fuck, yes.

"The drink?" Jet asked.

"Huh?" He'd lost track of the conversation.

"What's nice?" Jet asked.

"Oh. Ah. Your sarong. Looks good on you. Clingy." He moved his hands through the air, following the imaginary curves of Jet's arse.

"Oh, um, thanks." Jet bit his bottom lip, two sets of teeth flashing pearly in the moonlight.

Malone couldn't look away. He blinked rapidly, trying to clear his vision. Never mind that he *hadn't* wished for a kiss when he blew out his candles, Malone very much wanted one then. It made sense to get close, so he leaned forward. Three inches away...two inches...one.

Jet swerved sideways at the last moment. Which was disconcerting...and disappointing...and discombobulating.

Discombobulating. Malone mouthed into Jet's warm thigh, which he'd somehow face-planted into.

Such a good word.

Something tapped his shoulder. "Y'right there, mate?"

"Mmm-hmm." So, so, so alright. "Jus' a 'lil discombob-bibulateded."

Good word. Tricky to say.

The empty cup disappeared from his hand.

"Maybe a bit too much truth juice for you."

Nu-uh. "Jus' enough."

Fingers combed through his hair. Just once. It felt so good. "Mmm."

Too good.

Malone got his hand flat on the sarong beside Jet's hip and pushed up. So close. Heart thundering in his ears, Malone placed his free hand over it to stop it from barrelling right out of his ribcage and came across the sticky sea cucumber exudate. "Ugh." He grimaced. "Gross." He rocked back and stripped off his shirt. The universe spun for a second, but Malone focused on Jet's face and everything was again a-okay.

"Better?" Jet asked with a cheeky smirk that was better than pretty much anything.

"Much." It was the absolute truth.

Jet pulled his shirt off too, and Malone's salivary glands went into overdrive. He licked his lips, checking for drool.

What did Jet taste like? Malone wondered.

Only one way to find out, Archer.

He closed the final inch between them and swiped his tongue along the dark line of mystery between Jet's lips, necessary as oxygen.

"Wait, wait!" With a breathy laugh, Jet pulled a few inches away. "We can't do this. Not if you're drunk."

"Not drunk," Malone said, but the assessment wasn't entirely accurate. "Tipsy," he qualified. "Warm-blooded." In truth, Malone didn't give a shit how much rum was circulating through his blood steam, dissolving his inhibitions—what he truly wanted hadn't changed.

Jet.

Under him.

Over him.

Inside him.

Didn't matter.

"Truth juice. Remember?"

Jet stared at him for a long moment, maintaining eye contact. Testing him.

Just as Malone felt himself start to waver, Jet gave him a subtle nod, and Malone's heart tripped into the stratosphere.

He dove back into Jet's mouth, tangling tongues, tracing teeth, tasting sea-salt and sweetness.

Delicious.

And fuck! Those hands! He'd watched those nimble fingers treat every shell and fucking feather on the island like a precious tribute from the gods. Malone felt them tease around his ribs, up his lats and traps, along every groove, over every imperfection—read him like fucking braille—sure to notice every sign that Malone was a hair trigger away from losing his goddamn rational mind.

Over Jet's shoulder, the vibrant cuc-scape caught his eye. Those clever hands had already given him so much cock. Was it pushing the limit to ask for one more?

His own cock throbbed at the thought. "Your hands."

"What about them?" Jet eased away to speak, but Malone chased after him, nipping on that plush bottom lip.

"On me."

Jet's hands disappeared from where they'd slid up Malone's back, and he mourned their loss for the half second it took for them to make landfall again. Malone jerked in surprise when Jet cupped him through the rough material of his shorts, drawing out a deep groan.

"God, you're like granite," Jet said, then he snuck his hand past Malone's waistband and curled his dextrous fingers around Malone's bare length.

"Fuck!" Malone shuddered.

"What?" Jet chuckled roughly. His voice husky low. "I thought you said you wanted my hands."

"Yeah, but..." Shit, it was one thing to want, and another thing for the object of his desire to land, quite literally, in his lap. Malone's cock pulsed, hot in Jet's grasp.

Malone tried to pay attention. He wanted to remember every sensation. Notice every detail. But then Jet's thumbnail grazed his frenulum, and there wasn't enough re-oxygenated blood getting to his brain to attempt rational thought, let alone a computational analysis of Jet's technique.

Malone's head shot back, sending the stars careening across the sky, momentum taking him till his back hit the dry sand.

Thank God for his shorts trapping Jet's hand or they might've lost the connection. But Jet was with him, one-hundred percent.

Dark as moon shadow, Malone could barely make the man's features out. The sharp jut of his shoulders, the perfect oval of his bristled scalp, and the starlit compass-point tips of his ears were just enough for Malone to find his way.

Not that he needed the help.

Hand on cock aside, all Malone needed to do was feel their tangled legs, hear the rasp of Jet's laboured breath, and smell the arousal in the air to know exactly where Jet was in the wild night.

Happy birthday to me.

Malone reached up, snagged one hand around Jet's nape, and the other at the swell of his tight arse, pulled him close, and claimed his mouth.

Jet wrestled their shorts down, just low enough for full access. Then that sweet, mercenary thumb pressed his weeping slit, and Malone no longer knew up from down, in from out. All he knew was heat and want and rough desperation. His mind swam. His gut cramped with the need to thrust, but Jet's weight held him flat to the shifting sands.

Lying slightly off centre, Jet rolled against Malone's hip bone. His slender back was a sinuous reed, velvet smooth to the touch.

It wasn't enough to be connected hip to lip. Malone pulled Jet to him and traced with his tongue the ribbed arch of Jet's hard palate. How good would it feel to slide his length inside? To feel Jet gag around his cockhead?

Imagination wasn't Malone's strong suit, but, as Jet slowed, tightened his grip, and smothered Malone's mushroom head with the flat of his thumb, Malone's imagination soared—painting Jet's tonsils with his seed.

"Ungh."

Too much.

Jet's hot breath scoured across his cheek. "Come."

"No." If he came, it'd all be over. He chased those lips, but Jet had the advantage. The fucker.

Not missing a beat, Jet slid over, capturing them together. The knuckles of his shuttling hand bruised Malone's belly. Not that he cared. It was like being inside a fucking sensory tornado, only there was no calm eye in the centre...nowhere to go except along for the wildest of rides.

"Come." Jet licked at the sensitive flesh inside Malone's lower lip.

"No." He shuddered and his whole world spun off-kilter.

That's the booze talking, Archer.

Maybe.

Maybe not.

"Come." Jet ground harder, rhythm stuttering.

Malone captured Jet's lips, tense with arousal, looped his free leg around the meat of Jet's thigh, and leveraged his superior weight to switch positions, trapping Jet beneath him and their cocks together.

No getting away now.

"Mal." Jet squirmed, breathless. The friction and heat of Jet's hand supplanted by the pressure and drive of Malone's need.

"Come," Malone panted the word out, seeing the stars in Jet's eyes. "Come for me."

CHAPTER SIXTEEN

Jet

Boneless and sweaty, Jet shivered at the sudden chill when Malone rolled off of him.

"Ugh," Malone grumbled. "Don't know what's worse—sand in my crack, or cum in my eye."

"First-world problems." Jet assessed. "Can't be worse than sea cucumber ejaculate. Or bird shit."

"Oi. Didn't happen."

Jet let that slide. If Malone wanted to rewrite history, he wasn't going to argue. Not when he was feeling all sorts of wonderful, inside and out.

"And don't call it that. It's exudate, not ejaculate." Malone snuggled back in close to Jet's side. He rested his head on one hand and smeared their combined cum around with the other, doodling squiggles in the mess on Jet's skin.

"Don't know why that bothers you. You spend all day out in the lagoon, coaxing sea cucumbers out of their shells, getting them so hot and bothered they come all over your hands."

"Do not. Besides, sea cucumbers don't have shells. They're—"

"Whatever. All I'm saying is it looks a lot like aqua-porn."

"Aqua-porn? Next thing, you'll be calling me a merman."

That shut Jet up. Mostly because it was so close to the truth, but also because he was stunned to hear Malone use the word merman. It was flat-out weird to hear a guy steeped in hard scientific fact refer to himself as a mythological creature. It left Jet wondering what other quirks were lurking beneath the surface?

The doodling finger drifted lower. "Where are you going with that digit?" Jet asked.

"Nowhere."

"Doesn't feel like nowhere." Did he have the rum to thank for the glimpse behind Malone's stoic façade?

If yes, would the man revert to his objectionable, judgmental self in the morning? Would they go back to circling each other on the island? Never seeing eye to eye? Never sharing an orgasm or any kind of intimacy ever again?

Jesus Christ, Jethro. Enough with the sad sack future forecasting. You're here now. The man's cum is still warm in your treasure trail. Enjoy it. Make the most of it. Find a way to repeat it.

While Jet pondered those possibilities, the lazy night breeze blew over them, carrying the crash and tumble of the ocean, the caws of inbound seabirds, and a thousand tiny pricks of sand that stuck to his sweaty skin, turning him into human sandpaper. He'd be raw in the morning, but it was totally worth it. Because gawd had that source of friction ever raised the pain/pleasure bar.

Still… "I'd kill for a shower," he said. The donga bathrooms were tight, but he and Malone could probably both fit in his shower at the same time if they eschewed breathing for the time it would take to soap every square inch of each other's bodies. Bare handed, of course.

Jet's balls tingled at that thought, but before he could issue an invitation, Malone pulled away, rolled to stand, and held his hand out to Jet. "Come on."

Jet's balls tingled. Had Malone read his mind?

He eyed the hand. An orgasm was one thing, but did he trust Malone to hold him up? He clenched his abs, rolled up to stand, then gripped Malone's hand. "Where are we going?"

Please say to go shower.

"For a swim."

Oh. Damn. Jet glanced at the moonlit water, then away. "At night? Isn't that kinda dangerous?"

"Only if you're not careful. Besides," Malone pulled him closer. "I can protect you."

Fuck. It's official. I'm in way over my head.

Jet tried another tack. "You've been drinking. Who's going to protect me when you drown?"

"Phtht."

"Really? That's your defence?" God, he was cute. Sexy as sin, but cute, too. "You'd make the worst lawyer."

"It's my birthday."

"True." It stung a little to hear the entitlement in Malone's voice. Birthdays were supposed to be sacred, even if your *actual* day of birth was a shitty mess of rejection and abandonment.

Especially then, Jethro.

Whatever. Point was, it *was* Malone's birthday, and Jet had vowed to treat the man like a prince. Besides, creatures always did best in their natural habitat, and where did mermen live? Not to mention Poseidon—king of the merfolk. If he could trust Malone anywhere, it was out in the deep.

If Malone wanted to swim...well...Jet guessed he was going in.

He took a half step toward the water, then wriggled his fingers as though Malone had been the one to delay the inevitable. "Coming, Poseidon? Don't want to waste all that effort you made putting on your birthday suit."

"You're an idiot." Grumbly Malone was back, but his hand was in Jet's and he showed zero signs of self-consciousness as he traipsed bare-arsed to the water's edge, following the straight, moonlit path that blitzed through the reflected Milky Way.

"Doesn't it remind you of the magical bridge thingy that goes to Thor's planet? Only not a rainbow, obviously."

"The Bifrost," Malone said. "And a rainbow is just white light split through refraction."

"Ah. There's that inner nerd I know and tolerate."

"You want me to be poetical now?" Malone couldn't have sounded more incredulous if he'd tried.

"Heaven forbid." Then he really would be irresistible.

The cool water licked at the sensitive insides of Jet's thighs as they waded deeper, hand in hand. He wasn't apprehensive. Not exactly. Jet did want to go in. If for no other reason than to wash the spunk from his skin. But the way Malone strode forward, undaunted by the dark mystery beneath the surface, was something to behold. The ripples he created sent the reflected stars into a tizzy.

Jet knew how they felt.

"This reminds me of when I caught you skinny dipping in my lagoon." Malone's teeth flashed in the darkness. A wide grin that made all the trouble he'd gone to, painting and baking and planning, worthwhile.

Warm fuzzies bloomed in Jet's gut. Clearly, dragging Malone away from his rigid data set had been the right thing to do. "What do you mean *your* lagoon? This whole place is crown land. Government owned."

Malone splashed a wide arc across Jet's chest. "Seeing you made me inhale half the ocean through my snorkel."

"*Half* the ocean?" Jet managed to get out. Although that wasn't the part of Malone's statement that truly surprised. Conceding that Jet had the power to *make* him do any-thing—that was the seismic shift in their tenuous relationship. *Is it weird that having Malone under my control is a turn on? Asking for a friend.* "Who are you, and where did you bury Robo-Malone, the precision-guidance humanoid?"

"Didn't bury him. Donated his body to the birds." Malone deadpanned, making Jet laugh so hard he lost his footing and practically inhaled the other half of the ocean. "Careful." Mal-one drew Jet to him, his front to Jet's back, arm circling Jet's chest.

It was probably some official water-safety hold, tested and approved by the Australian surf lifesaving association, but Jet didn't care. Malone was being affectionate. Showing that he cared. It was sexy as fuck, and—to use one of Malone's massacred words—discombobulating. Somehow, he needed to get them back on solid ground. He tugged on the hairs on Malone's forearm. "Maybe you just need to get more snorkel-savvy."

"Not usually an issue. I live by the water. Swim most days. Kayak to and from work."

"Wow. You live at the beach?"

"On the Brisbane River."

"Huh. Me too. Well, I *did* live right by it. For a while. Up till recently. But I mostly grew up out west in landlocked mining towns. The desert has the same vast feeling. Stretching to infinity. But it doesn't move. It can't swallow you up. Not like this."

"I can't imagine that. Life would be weird without water."

Jet scanned the string-of-pearls froth that rimmed the crest of the reef and the moon-silvered surface of the lagoon, broken occasionally by the splash of an unknown sea creature, skimming the surface. It was beautiful and terrifying all at once. "It's alien. All this water. Being at the mercy of it."

"The ocean has no concept of mercy. Its nonsentient, Jet. Its objective is neither to help nor to hinder."

"What is its job, then?"

"To be."

"Wow. That's some serious philosophical shit, Doctor Archer." Jet teased.

He felt the shrug behind him.

"I try."

"Talking about dodgy snorkels and outlandish lies—"

"Which we weren't."

"—You owe me a truth."

"What are you talking about? I gave you two already."

"Don't believe you. Seventeen marriages? Not possible."

"That's your problem. Not mine."

Something nudged Jet's arse, and it wasn't a sea cucumber. "It's your problem if you want me to reach back there, and..." Jet left that threat hanging.

"Fine," Malone caved. "One more. And that's it."

"That's all I ask for."

Jet felt the roughness of chest hair on his back as Malone took a deep, steadying breath, and Jet prepared himself for something serious, trusting that whatever came out would be the truth.

"I'm a doodler," Malone said.

The confession was...unexpected. "A doodler?" Jet waited for a follow-up, but there was nothing. Was that all?

Maybe he'd misunderstood. "As in, squiggling on scrap paper? That type of doodling?"

"I try to stop, but...." His left pointer finger traipsed around on Jet's chest. "Can't."

"That's..." Jet had no idea what to say. If an irrepressible desire to doodle was Malone's greatest challenge, the guy didn't need help. From anyone.

Don't belittle your client's worries or concerns.

His art therapy textbooks were pretty clear on the matter.

Except Malone wasn't his client.

He's my...

Colleague?

Yes, but, clearly, that's not all.

Fuck buddy?

I don't know. We haven't discussed what this all means.

One hit wonder?

Hope not.

What then?

God knows.

"That, ah, must be difficult."

The finger circled his nipple. "No discipline. It's embarrassing. My brother Myles was always able to channel his energy into real accomplishments. I can't even get through a single day's data analysis without messing up my notes. Thank God for digital."

"Why embarrassing?" Jet relaxed further into Malone's arms and let his legs drift in the water. Starfish mode.

"I don't notice I'm doing it. The worst time was when I handed in the required hardback bound copy of my doctoral thesis to the university library, not realising I'd doodled an octopus doing cartwheels in the margins."

Oh, God. Jet bit his lip, trying not to laugh.

"The student collections librarian had a fit. She called me up weeks after I'd submitted it, horrified to tell me that some reprobate had scribbled in the margins of my thesis. I had to listen to her apologise profusely when, all along, I was the culprit."

"Did you own up to it?"

"God, no. I'd never be able to go into that library again. These days, all my doodles are anatomically correct."

"Oh my God." Jet tried his best, but he couldn't contain a snort. "That is seriously the best first-world problem I've ever heard. No. Not first world. A zero-world problem."

"Are you mocking me?"

"Never." He teased at the fuzz on Malone's forearm. "God's honest truth."

"Hmm." Malone nipped at his earlobe in retaliation. "Dubious, but I'll *choose* to believe you. This time."

"Good job." Jet approved. "Your autonomy remains safely intact."

"Yeah, well..." Malone huffed in his ear.

So cute.

"Show me an octopus doing a cartwheel. Draw one on me. Right there." Jet shifted Malone's doodling finger up to his left nipple.

"No."

"Don't be shy. Can't be any more ridiculous than a cuc-scape."

"Nothing's more ridiculous than a landscape comprised of cock."

"Shut up. They're not cocks."

"If I'd known you were so interested, I'd have offered mine earlier."

"Are you still tipsy?"

"Slightly."

"So, I can't trust anything you say?"

"I thought we covered the effectiveness of booze as a truth serum."

"Are you saying I can trust everything you say *now*, but I should question your word when you're fully sober?"

"I'm a beacon of honesty at all times."

"Ping. Ping. That's the bullshit detector going off, in case you were wondering."

"I was not."

Malone's shoulders relaxed, and the doodling started up again.

The lies and truths fell away.

And all that was left were the two of them, floating together, bathed in the light of the glittering Milky Way.

It was a relatively calm night, but nothing ever stopped the whisper of the wind, the lapping of the water at their shoulders, or the roar of the mighty ocean beyond the safe harbour of the reef. It was like being serenaded by one of those yogic tranquillity soundtracks.

Jet was so relaxed that when his phone trilled on the beach he jack-knifed in the water. "Shit." *Party's over, Jethro.*

"What's the alarm for? More surprises?" Malone rumbled in his ear.

I wish. "It's a reminder alarm to go do the ten o'clock measures."

"Already?"

"Mm-hmm. No rest for the wicked." He tapped at Malone's arm around his chest. It tightened for a second, then released, and cool water rushed between them—a timely reminder to maintain some level of self-preservation. The sliver of distance was probably a good thing. Things were getting way too comfortable between them, way too fast.

Life on Tallon isn't real, Jethro. Don't get too attached.

He planted his feet on the sandy sea bed. "Come on." He didn't look back or take Malone's hand. Instead of wishing for more, he listened only for the telltale swish of movement behind him, because swimming at night was crazy dangerous—even for a merman.

Malone hovered on the edge of the sarong, dripping, as Jet puttered around, making sure that nothing would fly away if a sudden gust blew up while he was gone.

"I'll be back." Unable to resist, he pressed a quick kiss to Malone's salty lips before turning in the direction of the compound.

Would Malone be there when he returned?

Did he *want* Malone to be there when he returned?

Jet honestly did not know, but as he went through the motions—taking measures, radioing them in—all he could think of was Malone, waiting for him, warm on the night-cooled sand.

A half-hour later, Jet eyed Malone's closed donga door as he closed up the radio shack for the night. No clue there. Heart in his throat, Jet wound his way back down the shadowy path through the low native foliage to the beach, where, curled up on his side on the tie-dyed sarong, Malone slept like a baby.

Jet hesitated. Should he wake him up?

The party was over. The pumpkin hour had begun. And neither he, nor Malone, had said anything about tomorrow. But Jet couldn't bring himself to let the magical night go.

Malone twitched a little, then stilled as Jet lay down behind him, spooning the bigger man. Jet folded his left arm up under his head for a pillow, wrapped his right around Malone's middle, and blindly traced the line of Malone's lax arm from elbow to wrist. He searched for the steady thrum of Malone's radial pulse, then followed the grooves on the back of his hand. His doodling hand, Jet reminded himself as he threaded their fingers intimately together.

Jet couldn't remember the last time he'd felt such simple contentment, and all it took was one rise and fall of Malone's steady breath for Jet to drift to sleep.

CHAPTER SEVENTEEN

Malone

Malone startled awake with a jerk, immediately regretting sitting up when his gut turned over and the sharp rays of the morning sun slammed like a steel tent peg through the bridge of his nose. "Fuck!"

An amused hum alerted Malone to the fact that somebody was nearby. Since the only other somebody on Tallon was Jethro Crane—baker of cakes, painter of cocks, handler (also) of cocks—Malone didn't bother opening his eyes again. "Go away," he said.

Pitiful, Archer.

"Nice thing to say to the guy who got up at the pre-arse-crack of pre-dawn to—"

"Shit." No point even looking at his watch. The blinding sun said it was way past dawn. The oh-four-hundred measures were his responsibility, and he'd missed them. Hell, he'd slept through his watch. Unforgivable. "What time is it?"

"Half six."

"Shit." Malone slumped back down and dropped an arm across his eyes. The last thing he could remember was watching Jet's rear gradually disappear into the night. "I slept that long?"

"Like a baby. I thought about waking you earlier. I know how particular you are about the schedule. But you looked too damn cute. A big guy like you, curled up like that. Couldn't do it."

Cute?

Since when was he cute?

Malone lifted the shade from his eyes and braved a look around. Gone were the coolers, the faux-fire, the camp chairs, and the ridiculous cuc-scape painting. All that remained from the birthday party was the sandy purple sarong, and him.

"Here." Jet shook a water bottle in front of his nose.

Blessed water. "Thank you." His throat was parched and his tongue felt like the hind end of a wombat. Malone unscrewed the top and slogged half of it in one go. "The four o'clocks?"

"Done."

Oh, thank God. He dug through his memory for a quick check of the schedule. "I'll do your sixteen-hundreds."

"Nah. Consider it a final birthday present."

"No. I'll do them." It was the least he could do to make up for his lapse.

"Malone, I won't think any less of you if you accept a helping hand. Or, you know, another one." Jet snickered. "Besides, I can think of a thousand other favours I'd rather receive."

"Yeah? Like what?" He knew he shouldn't've asked the second the question left his mouth.

"Well," Jet tapped his chin. "I wouldn't say no to a morning blowjob. Just as a for instance."

"A…?" Even through the fuzz of his hangover, Malone didn't have to dig far to encounter that memory. His body knew what they'd done.

Jet's lithe weight on him. The delicious friction of his hand. Floating together, cradled by the sea. If Jet's alarm hadn't rung, he could've happily stayed out there all night. Hell, he could've stayed out there all summer.

And *that* was the realisation that gave Malone pause.

He didn't have time for midnight picnics and cosy floats and strolls on the beach hand in hand. He wasn't on Tallon to play. He had a job to do. No, not just one job. *Two* jobs to do. And in the previous twelve hours, he'd failed at both.

All because he'd let Jet in.

The only answer Malone could see was to lessen the distraction. Quell the temptation. Set adrift any thought of a repeat.

Logic.

That was the way.

Cold, hard, rational thought.

Well, what are you waiting for? Get it done, Archer.

"I'm sorry." *Not really.* "I got caught up in the moment." *Jet's fault.* "Lost my head." *In more ways than one.*

"Well, I was completely sober," Jet said. "No excuse there. Guess that makes us both idiots."

That smarted. "Speak for yourself."

"I usually do."

"Hmph."

Stalemate.

"Here's an idea," Jet broke the brutal silence. "When in Rome."

Maybe it was the hangover, but Malone couldn't make sense of that. "We're not in Rome, Jet."

"Stop being so literal."

"Then stop being so lateral. My head hurts. Say what you mean."

"I'm saying, let's shag."

Oh.

Oh!

Malone's brain stopped firing all together. "Now?" Good-bye, logic. Hello, libido.

Jet snorted. "Not that I don't appreciate your enthusiasm, but I think a shower and a vat of coffee probably ought to take priority. Good scrub of those pearly whites with a toothbrush, too."

"Ugh." Bloody wombat.

"Come on." Jet tugged at the sarong caught beneath his arse.

"Come on, where?" he whined, but he was on his feet and moving.

What happened to quelling temptation, Archer?

Who was he kidding? If Jet was offering, Malone would partake.

It wasn't like they were dealing with a real, lasting relationship. Behavioural science was full of evidence that proximity, and familiarity, and repeated exposure were baseline conditions for animal attraction. In fact, it'd be more surprising if he and Jet, stuck so close together on a tiny speck of an island, hadn't wanted to get it on since day one.

Is that your explanation for having the willpower of a hungry dung beetle on a pile of shit, Archer?

Yes. Yes, it was.

The words 'when in Rome' squirrelled through the fuzz of his mind.

Did that mean Jet felt the same?

What happens on Tallon, stays on Tallon?

Could it be that easy?

I call BS. Jet is empathy on steroids. But, okay. Believe whatever floats your boat, Archer.

Jet let his hand go so they could walk in single file as they entered the narrow path back to the compound.

"Coffee, teeth, shower," Jet proposed.

Fun.

"Then we talk."

Not fun.

Malone eyed the lagoon in his peripheral vision and mentally revised Jet's plan.

Coffee, teeth, swim.

He sped up. Hot on Jet's heels.

Coffee, teeth, swim.

Unless Jet's concept of 'talk' meant rearranging their agreed schedule to allow for sex breaks. He'd stick around for that.

The detritus from their picnic was stacked in a neat pile in front of the giant white board. Well, *almost* all of it. "Where's the cock-scape?"

"Cuc-scape. I left it just inside the door of your donga. Out of the salt air. Want me to go get it? We can find a hanging spot in here if you like." Jet did a three-sixty. "Somewhere that'll inspire you while you're working."

Inspiration? More like an impediment to getting any work done. "Never mind." He pushed the thought away and made a beeline for the espresso machine, busying himself with pods, two mugs, milk for Jet, and the sugar jar for him. He usually went without the weakness in his coffee, but his brain needed the fuel. No way was he skipping the sweet stuff that morning.

Coffee. Teeth. Swim.

A solid agenda.

Simple.

Straightforward.

Wise.

"So," Jet sidled close and hip-checked him. "Last night."

"Can we do this later?"

"Oh, ah." Colour flared in Jet's cheeks and he pulled away. "Yeah. Sure. That's okay. If you're not interested. I get it."

"It's not that." Malone interrupted. If Jet only knew how far away from uninterested he was. "Right now, my head is a fuzzy mess and I smell like a two-day-old oyster left to putrefy in the heat."

"That's...descriptive."

"Yeah, so." Malone stirred two teaspoons of the good stuff into his brew, then a third for the sake of sanity. He took a sip, closing his eyes in relief. "God, that's good."

"So, we'll talk later." It wasn't a question.

"Mm-hmm." He couldn't meet Jet's eyes. *God, Archer. Grow a pair.*

"I mean, it's not like you're...either of us...is going anywhere." Jet's laugh was brittle, and Malone felt like even more of a shithead. The man had baked him a birthday cake, for fuck's sake.

Planned a whole celebration. Even made him a present, such that it was. And what was Malone doing in return? Avoiding taking decisive action? Searching for an escape hatch?

What's so difficult, Archer? It's not like you're proposing marriage. All you have to do is say, 'thanks for the birthday bash', and 'yes, let's fuck', and 'but it goes no further'.

Easy.

But Malone was used to gathering and analysing all the facts before proceeding with a plan. And something about the situation felt off. Like he was missing a crucial element.

Jet was right—neither of them was going anywhere. He could take the time he needed to gather the pertinent data, then choose the best path forward.

Outside, the blue water beckoned.

Soon, he promised.

Coffee done, Malone rinsed his cup and loaded it into the dishwasher.

Next, teeth. A couple of aspirin wouldn't go astray either.

He still had a few hours before the ten o'clock measures were due—long enough to cure his head with a swim *and* deal with Jet.

Malone eyed the schedule on the whiteboard. Whichever way they chose to rejig the plan going forward, it had to work around his research. He wasn't going to compromise his project for a fuck. No matter how much his body clamoured for it.

"Let me just go get cleaned up, eh?"

"Sure. It can wait 'til you're feeling more human."

"Great. Thanks for the, uh, party. It was...good."

Good?

Jesus, Archer. Need to import a few IQ points? They're going cheap.

"Fuck off," Malone muttered under his breath.

"What?" Jet asked, clearly mystified.

"Nothing. Just," Malone pointed in the direction of the mess door—escape hatch identified—and beat a hasty retreat.

Malone didn't believe in anything woo-woo.

Medical science was about facts and observable data, limited only by technology and intelligence to illuminate what was real. But there was something magical about water. It never failed to soothe and revitalize.

Near the reef, the water was busy—an aquatic city at rush hour. Most days, Malone was happy to skim the edge of it and observe the fascinating ecosystem from an objective distance.

That day, though, his brain and body had different needs altogether.

With the tide a couple hours from its impending height, it was safe to skim over the reef crest, then strike out beyond the steep slope of the reef wall into the deep.

The sea was never silent, but the further he swam, the quieter it got. Shards of sunlight pierced the surface, catching on creatures so tiny they resembled dust motes in the hazy light. An occasional school of fish would flicker by, or he'd catch the cold eye of a patrolling reef shark, see the stealthy charcoal of a sting ray, the wide back of a green sea turtle, or a jellyfish, its tendrils trailing as it bobbed and swayed in the shifting current.

Eventually, though, it was just him, alone and distant enough from Tallon to feel entirely at sea. He adjusted his orientation to keep the island in his peripheral vision and powered on in a clockwise direction, arms stroking, legs kicking. With every metronomic stroke, Malone felt a tiny bit of strain drift away. His body unclenched, muscle by muscle. Detangled, nerve by nerve. Gradually, his hangover dissipated into the deep.

His strokes slowed to a stop.

He felt loose.

Floaty.

The day was calm with little chop. Face-down, Malone breathed through his snorkel as he let the power of the water hold him up, happily at the mercy of the undulating waves and the shifting currents and the ever-changing tide.

This is bliss.

Finally, ready as he'd ever be, Malone turned for home.

Habit made it impossible not to scan the sea floor as he coasted back inside the lagoon via the gap in the reef. He didn't have any quadrats set up in that less-protected zone, since the sea cucumber population was sparser, but that didn't mean observations in the area had no value. He took a mental log of the various species and estimated numbers for his secondary data set. Only then did he turn for shore and saw legs striding through the shallows toward him.

Jet.

Malone couldn't help the fission of excitement that stirred at the sight.

So much for feeling loose.

He doubled his kicking pace to close the gap and was just about to pull up when Jet grabbed him and hauled him up out of the water.

"What the fuck, Mal?!"

Malone reflexively bit down on the snorkel, trumpeting his surprise as Jet manhandled him to stand.

"I thought...God!"

Malone spat out his snorkel, pushed up his goggles, and took Jet's frantic hands in his own. "What's wrong?"

"What's wrong? *What's wrong*!?" Jet's voice scaled the heights. "Where have you been?!"

"I went for a swim."

"I know you went for a fucking swim. You've been gone forever! Out there!" Eyes wild, Jet jabbed a finger out to sea, then poked Malone in the chest. Hard. "I thought you'd drowned! Or been swept out to sea. Or stung by a jelly fish. Or bitten by a shark. Or...or, shit, anything could've happened, and you'd be dead and gone. Fish food, Malone! Fish food!"

That was blatantly ridiculous. "I'm an excellent swimmer."

"I don't care if you're an Olympian. That's not the point. I was worried, arsehole."

"About me?"

"Yes. About you. Of course I was." Jet's hands skated across every bit of skin he could reach. Not an intimate touch. Clinical. Assessing him for injury.

Jet was worried about me.

Me.

Malone's chest tightened. The thrill welled up to become a golf-ball sized nexus in his throat.

He tried swallowing it down.

Nobody ever worried about him. Not after what happened to Myles. Malone was the stress-free twin. It was Malone's job to solve problems, not create them. No drama. No worries.

But Jet *had* worried.

He'd spared a thought for Malone's safety.

Spared a thought for me.

Dumfounded, Malone couldn't think what to say. "Ah...."

"Don't you 'ah' me. We're not at the bloody dentist, Malone. We're, like, the only two people on Earth, here. Adam and Adam. Co-dependent." Jet dug his thumbs into the meat of Malone's shoulders. "You can't go out there alone. Not without telling me. Not without some kind of safeguard in place. Not...not after last night." At that, all the fight seemed to go out of him.

Malone didn't know what to say. How could he express what he didn't even understand himself? "Last night was..."

Enticing. Surprising. Overwhelming.

No way could he use any of those words. Jet would think he was an emotional basket case, and their 'when in Rome' agreement would become unnecessarily complicated.

In lieu of the right words, he caught Jet's falling hands, placed them back on his own shoulders, and stepped in as close as humanly possible.

Why tangle with words when he could take clear, decisive action?

CHAPTER EIGHTEEN

Jet

Jet hadn't meant to get all *From Here to Eternity* on the beach, but he was angry, goddammit. Wild at Malone for disappearing out beyond the relative safety of the reef. Jet's blood was running hot, and Malone was feasting on him like he was a juicy ripe mango. What was he supposed to do? Resist?

Fuck, no.

It was all he could do to drag the man to the shoreline before tackling him down.

"Oof."

They rolled to the side. The lapping water doing nothing to cool their ardour as Jet hooked a heel behind Malone's thigh, and ground into his heat.

"Mmf."

Jet agreed one-hundred percent, so he did it again.

"Fuck, Jet. Killing me."

"Mm-hmm." Little deaths were good. He'd give Malone as many little deaths as the man could take. He nipped at Malone's salty mouth, taking the remainder of his anger out on Malone's prize lower lip. A sharp nip. Almost enough to bring blood. "I'll be your shark," he said. If Malone wanted danger, he'd provide it.

Safely.

No more big deaths allowed.

Not on Jet's watch.

A hand dragged at the waistband of his wet boxers, exposing his pale bare arse to the sun and the birds that wheeled overhead. For a split second, Jet pondered the possibility of anyone looking down on them from the International Space Station at that very second. Chances were slim.

Did Jet care?

Fuck, no.

During all their wrestling, Malone had managed to get his swim shorts down low enough to hook under his balls, and the flap of Jet's boxers was no match for the mighty way his dick stood to attention.

He attacked Malone's surf rashie with the same gusto, peeling the saturated thing up his muscled back till it anchored in Malone's underarms.

Skin. He wanted skin.

Stat.

A finger found its way to Jet's core and pressed there, asking for entry. And he forgot all about stripping Malone.

Yes.

God, yes.

Jet hiked his knee as high as it'd go.

They had all the time and freedom in the world, but knowing that did nothing to assuage his urgent need. He wanted Malone's fat dick in him. Stretching him wide. But a finger would have to do.

"Ah, fuck!" *Make that two fingers.* His toes curled as Malone found his deepest pressure point, "There. Right there!" Jet tightened his ring to hold them inside as Malone devoured his mouth, sucking on his tongue like it was the world's most delicious cock, and dry-humped Jet's junk. Or, salt-water humped, as the case may be. All he knew was Malone's aquamarine eyes, heavy-lidded with desire, and the roiling heat between them.

Wish, wish, said the waves on the sand as Malone took control, driving the tempo, inside and out, and Jet lost all sense of time and place. Hell, of fucking sanity.

He didn't know what tipped him over. Truth be told, Jet didn't really care. As the kernel of heat at the base of his spine erupted in a solar flare, he clamped down on Malone's fingers and shot just as a wave licked between them, dousing them with sand and salt and a rude dose of reality.

"Holy shit." Malone's hips gave a final shuddering, involuntary jerk. "That's gonna chafe."

Chuckling, Jet let his leg drop. He didn't want to move away. Not yet. Malone's arse may have been exposed to the infinite universe, but between them was a private cave of their own making. He snuck a soft kiss, and Malone chased him back for another. And another. Not saying anything. Just being together, until the incoming tide threatened to send them both adrift.

"Next time, we're doing this on a bed." Malone groaned as he rolled to his back and tucked his softening cock back into his board shorts.

Jet followed suit, hyperaware of the growing space between them. "So, we *are* doing this?"

"Seems like."

"Wow, Malone." Jet matched Malone's droll tone. "Such passion."

"It doesn't take a genius to read the data."

He was right. Twice over, they'd succumbed to temptation, with very little prompting—a bottle of booze, a harried rescue. What next?

Don't fool yourself, Jethro. If Malone Archer sneezed, you'd probably find it sexy.

Jet didn't miss the tiny quirk of Malone's lips as he rolled to stand and held out his hand for Jet to take.

Guess that's a seal of approval.

They stared at each other for a beat too long. Just as Jet was starting to feel awkward, Malone took a step closer, closing the gap.

"Is this how it'll be? Always?" Malone asked.

His question was vague, but Jet knew exactly what he was asking. He trailed a fingertip along the strip of skin left bare between Malone's waistband and his tight rashie, making Malone shiver. "Like horny aliens have taken us over? Hell, yeah."

"Aliens?" Malone shook his head. "Where the hell do you get these ideas from?"

Jet pointed directly up.

"Jesus. Are you ever serious?"

"Too often," he said, since sarcasm was his friend, then remembered the other dubious truth offered the previous night.

"Have you really been married seventeen times? How's that even possible?"

"My brother's a fan."

"Of weddings?"

"Of getting married."

Jet struggled to compute. "*He* likes getting married, so *you* got married seventeen times?" How did that make sense?

"No. *He* likes weddings, so *we* got married seventeen times."

Jet blinked. "Isn't that, like, twincest?"

"It's not like we screwed or anything. Besides, we were five years old. Maybe six. It wasn't real."

"Oh, well. That's a relief."

"I have my limits, Jet."

"Uh-huh."

"You're the one who called us Adam and Adam."

"You and me. Not you and your twin brother."

"Either way, forbidden fruit."

Eww. "No. He's your brother. I'm...not."

"What's our forbidden fruit, then?"

A bazillion ideas came to mind that instantly reawakened the well of heat in Jet's core.

"...if we're Adam and Adam." Malone unnecessarily clarified his question, but Jet didn't answer.

That way lay treacherous, stormy waters.

He tried to be a go-with-the-flow kind of guy, but in the previous twenty-four hours, they'd gone from chilly co-workers to red-hot lovers. He needed some time to adjust.

Stalling, Jet swiped Malone's goggles and snorkel off the sand, gave them a shake, and dangled them from a finger for Malone to take.

"Thanks."

"You're welcome." His watch chimed an alarm. Jet pressed the button to switch it off, not bothering to look. He knew exactly what it meant. "Time for the ten o'clocks."

"Saved by the bell."

"Yeah. You did want to do them, right?"

"Of course. They're my responsibility." It was a relief to hear the surly bear in Malone's gruff voice.

"Of course," Jet echoed.

Hot didn't have to mean heavy. So long as they kept things casual, he could keep his needy heart safe. But as he turned toward the compound, more than ready for another shower, Malone caught his hand, threaded their fingers together, and tugged him back.

Fuck. I'm so screwed.

So what if the waters were treacherous?

Bring on the storm.

CHAPTER NINETEEN

Malone

Malone was at full stretch to hang his cuc-scape above his bed when Jet came up from behind and wrapped his arms around Malone's ribs.

Ridiculous how good it felt.

"Reminds me of staying in a country pub," Jet said. "How they always have a painting hanging above the head of the bed. Only, it's usually of Jesus, or the Queen."

"King, now."

"True."

Malone gave a little, satisfied grunt as the string he'd tacked to the back of his birthday present caught on the hook. The thought of having Charles look down on him in bed left him a little squeamish... Make that a lot squeamish, especially when he thought about what he and Jet might get up to in said bed.

Painting hung, Malone came back onto his heels, but Jet didn't step away. If anything, he tightened his hold.

He covered Jet's hands with his own. "You done with work?" Malone asked.

"Yes, thank God."

After nearly twenty-four hours of them goofing off, the station had needed some attention. They had to not only clean the ultra-corrosive guano off the roofs and surfaces, but also check every bit of tech and machinery.

Jet nipped at his earlobe. "If I never read another instruction manual, it'll be too soon."

"But necessary." They'd mucked in together to get most of it done, until Jet shooed him away to take advantage of the last of the daylight with his sea cucumbers in the lagoon.

Jet snorted softly. "Typical perfectionist."

"I'm not a perfectionist."

"Malone. You're a perfectionist. Claim it. Embrace it. Love it." Jet gave him another squeeze, then shoved him down on the bed face first.

"Hey!" Rude, Malone thought, until Jet sat on his thighs and ran the heels of his hands down either side of Malone's spine, massaging the muscles that had tightened after their long day of sweat and toil. "Mmm." So good.

The second time he did it, Jet's hands travelled lower and tugged down the waistband of his shorts. "I love your butt. It's so tight. And these dimples." He pressed his thumbs into the meat of Malone's arse cheeks.

"I do not have dimples."

"So cute."

"Grr." His grumbling stopped the minute he felt a sharp sting. "Did you just bite me?"

"Mm-hmm. Tasty." Jet licked the spot. "Roll over."

Malone complied, doing nothing to hide the tent in his shorts.

Jet's hands continued their ministrations. "Well, well. What do we have here?"

"You don't know? Here I thought all artists studied the nude form."

"I'm an art therapist. Not a true artist. They're totally different things."

Could've fooled him. "You paint. You draw. You sculpt. You mess about with shells and driftwood and...and whatnot." Malone was ashamed to admit he hadn't paid much attention to what Jet actually did with the bits and bobs he collected on the shore. Well, he had, but mostly for the perv value, not in the 'how was your day, dear' kind of way.

"Whatnot?" Jet raised a brow.

"It's a word."

"Uh-huh. Sure. What about the other cucs?"

Malone tilted his head to see his cuc-scape. The painting wasn't hung exactly straight, but he'd fix that after Jet had had his wicked way with him. A man had to have his priorities.

Jet dragged Malone's chin down. "Not those cucs. The live ones. Are Hilda and her friends all safely put to bed for the night?"

"They're not children, Jet. I don't tuck them in and tell them bedtime stories."

"Oh." Jet squirmed. "Now I want a bedtime story. There once was a perfectionist named Malone, who—" Malone's tickling fingers attacked. "Aargh! No fair." Jet pouted and wrapped his arms around his ribs.

Malone instantly realised he'd done himself a disservice when he lost Jet's touch.

He grabbed Jet's wrists and rolled groin to groin.

Better.

He opened his mouth to say something that might get them back on track. Something direct like 'touch me', or 'suck me', or 'fuck me.' What came out was, "Come with me next time."

His words might've hit a six-point-five on the dirty-talk scale, in a pinch, if his brain had meant *that* kind of coming.

It had not.

Stupid, stupid brain.

Jet looked puzzled, too.

Malone tried again. "They love it when I touch them." *Fuck, Archer. Way to make it worse.* "I mean, when I stroke them, they get all...ah, shit...kill me now."

"Horny?" Jet's chuckles so weren't sexy, but they set his body on a jerky rollercoaster ride that had them both groaning. "Fu-uuck!"

Since that was exactly what Malone wanted, he resolved to keep his mouth shut. Or, better yet, keep it full. He shimmied south—eye on the prize.

Jet gave a breathy, 'thank fuck' type of sigh.

Malone heartily agreed.

Divested of all clothing, it wasn't long before they were both at the edge.

Jet dug his heels into Malone's upper back. "Condom," he said in a rush, emphasising his wish with a sharp tug at Malone's hair and an involuntary thrust of his hips.

Condom.

The film reel of Malone's life screeched to a halt, then rewound at hyper-speed to that moment of indecision back home at Tennyson Bend, standing in front of his bathroom mirror, debating whether he ought to pack condoms for his summer on Tallon.

"Not much point," his past self said as he placed them neatly back in their spot in the bathroom cabinet.

Idiot.

The film raced forward again. "I, ah...do you have any?"

Jet's eyes widened. "You didn't bring condoms?"

"I was thinking about sea cucumbers. Not cock."

Jet's choked laughter was getting to be way too familiar.

"Well, what about you?" Malone bit out, indignant, then remembered back to his first impression of Jet—a tourist on the hunt for cock and cocktails. How wrong he'd been. He ran a soothing thumb over the thrust of Jet's hipbone. "Sorry." Apologising for it all.

A little crease appeared between Jet's brows, but the fingers in Malone's hair softened. "S'alright," Jet said. "We are screwed, though. And not in the good way."

"Does that mean...?" No condoms meant no sex. At least, not the way he wanted to give it. Or take it.

"Nope. Didn't bring any. And I don't even have your cuc excuse. Just...didn't think of it."

Didn't think of sex? Wow.

Jet untangled his fingers and tapped Malone's temple. "Guess I've had other things on my mind."

"Fair enough."

From Jet's hot gaze, he knew that no matter what might've occupied Jet's thoughts in the past, right then, Malone was front and centre.

Jet brought his fingertip up to join the fun. It trailed lightly from the scooped bow at the top to catch and tug at the fleshy middle of the bottom.

Triggered by instinct, Malone took it in and sucked.

It wasn't normal how much Malone wanted to do silly things like hold Jet's hand, kiss Jet's lips, and curl himself up in Jet's arms. He'd dated, of course. Some guys for months on end. But he wasn't used to missing them when they weren't within arm's length.

Malone briefly considered the possibility that he'd picked up some sort of personality-mutating, water-borne virus in the lagoon. Not that such a thing was likely, but it was either that or Jet had worked his man-whisperer mojo on him.

They were the only two viable options Malone could figure.

The drive to fuck was understandable. Who didn't want sex? But they'd blown right past Maslow's Hierarchy of Needs, and into seriously wacky territory. It was as though he'd adopted the personality of a sea cucumber—gravitating to Jet's caring touch.

Even worse, Malone suddenly understood his brother's desire to procreate.

It was as though one orgasm...*okay, three*...had triggered his previously silent biological drive. It was awake, running rampant, imagining a host of little Jet-lets terrorizing the world with rainbow fingerpaints. Which was completely irrational. It wasn't as though he and Jet were fucking seahorses. Well, they *were* fucking, but they weren't seahorses. Male humans didn't carry their young. It just wasn't biologically viable.

By the time they finally made it out of bed, it was well past sunset, and both of their stomachs were rumbling. They set into an easy dance, cooking dinner, then lounging on either end of the couch. Jet read the next battered *Hornblower* paperback from the island's library, and Malone catalogued the day's abridged data-set with his laptop. It was quiet, comfortable, and disarmingly easy.

The days rolled by, their schedule blending till Malone's oh-so-neat whiteboard schedule became a mere mockery of intention. Nature was full of patterns. It shouldn't have surprised him that they shared the twenty-four-hour cycle of weather observer duties as readily as they shared a bed. But it did.

He kept waiting for the weather balloon to pop on the new pattern of their co-working, co-fucking relationship. But it didn't.

The world kept turning.

The sky didn't fall in.

Hermit crabs scurried from shore to shade. Green sea turtles lumbered up the beach to dig their nests in soft sand and bury their clutches of eggs. And seabirds came and went, shearwaters and terns and noddies and boobies. Some nested. Some were on the hunt. Natural instinct lay at the heart of everything they did. It probably shouldn't have come as such a surprise that he and Jet would eventually fall into a natural rhythm, too.

But that didn't mean they always saw eye-to-eye.

For instance, Jet didn't seem to understand how important it was for Malone to be able to focus when he worked on the reef. His specimen collection was growing nicely, and he wasn't behind with his data analysis, per se, but Jet had a way of using up Malone's contingency time. How was he supposed to resist when Jet claimed a two-man siesta was in order, or Jet needed him to help to find the perfect shell to weave into his latest seaweed macrame creation, or Jet needed him to pose for a sketch, "to provide perspective on the scale of the landscape, Malone."

Yeah, right.

If anyone didn't know exactly how tiny Tallon Island was, they could Google it.

His walkie-talkie squawked. "Malone. Come in, Malone. Over."

Fuck. What now? Two more quadrats and he'd have a complete data set for the day. He pulled off his gloves and pressed the speak button. "What is it, Jet?"

"There's my surly teddy bear."

"Jethro?"

"You know how you said there aren't any snakes endemic to Tallon?"

Malone resisted the desire to turn and look for Jet. "This isn't one of your false alarms, is it?"

Fire.

Snakes.

What next?

A cyclone?

He looked up at the sky. Nope. Not a cloud in sight.

"You were wrong," said Jet.

Malone frowned. He didn't hear those words too often. "What kind of snake?"

"We-ell…"

Oh, shit.

Malone knew that tone.

It meant mischief.

CHAPTER TWENTY

Jet

"We-ell," Jet purred into the walkie-talkie. God, he'd need a face massage after holding his stupid grin for so long. "It's a kinda unusual snake." He palmed himself through the sturdy material of his grotty coveralls and grinned like a loon across the distance from the top of the radar tower to the furthest edge of the lagoon where Malone stood, back square to the shore, his posture relaxed, as though nothing had interrupted his day.

Such a tease.

"Let me guess." Malone's voice couldn't've been drier. "It's got one eye."

Jet faux-gasped. "How did you know?"

"Talented, I guess."

Malone was talented, in all sorts of things, but Jet wasn't going to concur that fact out loud. The man already had the ego the size of a hump back whale.

Actually...

A memory surfaced of Malone's story about his brother. It wasn't exactly sea cucumbers Malone was passionate about. It was helping his brother after the burns he'd suffered as a teenager. That was what drove Malone. Why he was so intent. It wasn't sea cucumbers. And it wasn't ego.

Jet was about to apologise for interrupting Malone's work when heard a click and static, followed by a low, "Is it dangerous?"

Gawd, horny Malone had come to the party. "Some might say 'yes'," Jet replied, still cautious.

"Do the people who might say 'yes' know what the hell they're talking about?"

"Yes."

"How many people are we talking about?" came Malone's fast reply.

Oh, jealousy. I like that. "Some." He relaxed into the tease.

"Grr."

Jet wobbled, precariously high. The fact that Malone had pressed his radio button to deliver his growl told Jet all he needed to know. Malone wanted Jet to hear it. Which meant Malone was up for it. One way or another, Jet's greedy, one-eyed snake would be seen to before the day was through.

Having satisfied his need to remind Malone that there was more to life than cold, hard data, Jet refitted his face mask and eye protection and moved on to the real reason why he'd scaled the radar tower. Scouring guano off the surface with a wire brush wasn't the most glamorous job, but then, neither was Jet's usual day job.

In many respects, met bureau volunteering and nursing were similar roles—taking routine observations and cleaning up shit—but he had a better view from Tallon's tower than he'd ever had from a hospital ward window. If he didn't have art therapy classes and friends to return to in Brisbane, he'd be tempted to ask the powers that be if he could stay on Tallon for ever and ever, amen. Being surrounded by water still wigged him out, but the place was glorious. Every day, he discovered something new.

Except...Jet's gaze was again drawn to the man out in the lagoon. No chance would Malone choose to stay longer. Not once his data set was complete. And Tallon wouldn't be the same without him.

No. Best to stick to the original plan. Finish their three-month stint, return to Brisbane, find a new home, get done with his degree, and jumpstart his new art therapy practice.

That decided, Jet cleaned up his gear and moved on to the next item on his agenda.

Malone would hate it, but that hadn't stopped Jet yet.

He didn't turn at the sound of the mess door opening and closing. Pushing six feet, he was a decent height, but the ceiling was far too high for Jet to reach without help, so he teetered on the top rung of the triple-tiered step ladder while he tried to pin his latest creation to the ceiling in the entryway. Seaweed wasn't exactly mistletoe, but it'd do in a pinch.

As Jet went up on his tippy-toes, warm, steady hands gripped his legs. "Thanks."

"What are you doing?" Salt must have taken up residence in Malone's throat, because he sounded gruffer than usual.

"Decorating. There's only a week till Christmas, and the place was looking bland."

"Bland?"

"Exactly. Don't worry, though, I saved you some plain paper to cut out snowflakes. Figured that'd suit your fondness for symmetry."

"Symmetry?" Malone repeated.

"Mm-hmm. There. Got it." Jet came back down onto his heels and rested a hand on the top of Malone's head, not in a rush to get down. Any chance he had to thread his fingers through Malone's springy curls was a happy chance. Besides, the step ladder created a very interesting height differential. "Hey there."

"Hey yourself."

For a second, Jet was tempted to say 'catch me', and leap. But they weren't like that. Instead, he caught Malone under the chin with a finger and tilted him up for a kiss. Nothing heavy. Just a taster for things to come. "Mmm. Nice to see it works."

"It?" Malone asked, clearly baffled.

Jet pointed above his head. "The mistletoe."

Malone's eyes followed his pointer finger. "That's not—"

"Shh. Don't confuse it, or it might not work."

"But it's seaweed."

That time, Jet used his lips more directly to shush Malone. Then Jet wrapped himself around him, monkey style, because, so what if they hadn't *been* like that? If Jet had let history dictate his life, he'd still be landlocked and fuck-less—not his favourite combo.

One thing led to another, and before Jet knew it, he was spread over the kitchen bench with coleslaw in his hair and Malone in his pants.

Winner, winner, chicken dinner.

"I've decided you're going to be my next guinea pig." Shit, he hadn't meant to tell Malone that. "Never mind."

But Malone did mind. He popped off Jet's spit-shined cock, and it wavered in the air. "For what?"

Dammit!

"I said, never mind. It doesn't matter."

Malone, the fucking tease, ran the tip of his tongue around the rosy head, then blew. "Tell me."

Fuck!

"Fine. A guinea pig to practice my art therapy skills." At Malone's frown, he rushed on. "It's not what you think."

"Is it improving mental and emotional well-being through visual and textural art, motion and sound?"

"Oh, ah…" That came pretty damn close to the definition, but Jet couldn't answer because Malone traced a finger down his taint, flattened his tongue, and took him deep enough to swallow. Then he flashed his eyes at Jet and hummed.

Vision. Texture. Motion. Sound.

With Malone getting a hefty dose of Jet's taste and aroma, they had the full sensory package.

"Shit. Fuck. I get it." Malone already had art therapy in the bag. At least, in theory. But Jet still needed to practice on someone. He'd learned his lesson by stumbling through the first week of taking meteorological observations. No way would he start his art therapy practice without having his shit together. "If I could do it for myself, I would."

Malone's brow arched.

"Fuck off. I don't mean that. Sheesh. Mind out of the gutter, Malone."

"Bit hard to do that when your cock is in my mouth."

He had a point. And Jet sure didn't want to discourage that. "I'll do you a good deal."

"Oh, yeah?" Malone licked him, root to tip. "What's the deal?"

Only one thought came to mind. "I'll trade you a therapy session for a blowjob."

The eyebrow went back up. "Given? Or, taken?"

The finger travelled further south, and around his ring.

Jet couldn't help tightening in anticipation. "Don't care. Whatever you want."

"Oh, now. There's a quotable."

Why are we still talking? Over it, Jet released his death grip on the edge of the bench and took Malone's head between his two hands, directing him exactly where he wanted him.

"Quote this, lover."

Sadly, neither of them made much headway on the paper snowflakes that night.

CHAPTER TWENTY-ONE

Malone

When an alert came through the sat phone, Malone reluctantly crawled out of bed, doing his best not to disrupt Jet, who was passed out after their noon siesta. The donga screen door squealed as he pushed it shut, then he crossed the courtyard to the radio shack and awaited HQ's call.

It wasn't his usual practice to sleep through the day, but once the green turtles started to nest overnight, he could never say no when Jet begged to watch. "Just one more, Mal."

Yeah, right.

Does it bother you to know Jet has you wrapped around his little finger?

Yes.

Going to do anything about it?

No.

Why is that, Malone?

Because.

You can do better than that, Malone.

Fuck you.

Malone...

Because he's genuine, and amusing, and surprising, and sexy as hell.

So why are you holding back?

I'm not.

Self-delusion isn't smart, Malone.

He wanted to tell his inner voice to shut up, but it was right. No matter how much sense it made to keep to their 'what happens on Tallon, stays on Tallon' agreement, he knew he was in deep water.

"Malone? Come in. Over." Sharon chided. From her long-suffering tone, it probably wasn't the first time she'd tried to gain his attention.

He sat up straighter. "Sorry, Sharon. Say again. Over."

"I said, can you get Jet on the line? I have a phone call to patch through. Some lawyer. Pushy guy. Says he's been trying to find him for weeks."

That didn't sound good.

"You want me to keep the line open? Or hook back in when he's here?"

"Stay." Sharon's sharp reply was so uncharacteristic, Malone hopped to it.

"Give me a sec." He dashed back across the courtyard and up the donga stairs. The screen door whacked his butt as it closed behind him.

"Wakey, wakey." Malone shook the bare foot that poked out from under the sheet draped across Jet's lower half. Since the day-night temperature differential was barely a few degrees, neither of them bothered with anything heavier.

"Mum?" Jet's muffled response was barely audible.

"Far from it." Malone pulled open the curtains, making Jet wince at the harsh daylight. He pulled a pillow over his head. "Nope. No poking your head in the sand. Come on. Up. Sharon needs you."

"Shaz?" Jet's abs bunched as he sat up. A sight Malone would never get tired of seeing. "What the fuck time is it? Did we miss a measure?"

"No. Nothing like that. A lawyer wants to speak to you."

Frown lines marred Jet's forehead as he shifted off the bed and wrapped a sarong around his waist, free-balling it.

"Maybe you won the lottery," Malone said, awkwardly cheerful.

Jet stared at him blankly, still half asleep.

Malone hooked a thumb in the general direction of the mess. "I'll go make some coffee. Come find me when you're done. If you need to talk. Or not. Fresh air. A walk. A swim." That's what he always did to combat stress. But he and Jet were different in so many ways. "Or, you know, whatever." *Stop rambling. This is Jet's personal business. It has nothing to do with you.* "You should go hear what the lawyer guy wants. I'll be...if you..." Malone snapped his mouth shut and pointed toward the open door. Emotional support was not his forte. Problem was, there *was* nobody else. Not for hundreds of kilometres.

"I'll come find you," Jet mumbled, knocking his bare shoulder on the doorframe on the way out.

One double espresso and the half hour it took Malone to precision-scalpel-cut one snowflake later, Jet slammed through the mess door. "My blood-brother is a double-decker dick."

"Aren't they all?" Well, Myles wasn't, but most people didn't get born with a twin for a best friend.

"I'm serious. He can go fuck himself."

"What did the lawyer want?"

"To inform me that I'm a beneficiary of my birth mother's will."

That didn't seem so unusual. "And your dickish brother has a problem with that?"

"My dickish brother doesn't know he's my dickish brother. Remember? In fact, Eloise, my birth mother, didn't know she was my mother. Or so I thought. Who knows? And, for some reason that I do not understand, the lawyer couldn't tell me what Eloise bestowed on me. Not until he's adequately ascertained my identity, or some such thing. Whatever she gave me must be big, though, because Richard—"

"The dick."

"Yes. Dick, the double-decker dick, is contesting my status as a beneficiary. The lawyer said he'd get back to me with documents he needs to ascertain my identity. It's tricky, though. It's not like I brought my birth certificate to Tallon. Not much need for it here. And everything else I own is in storage. It's possible I won't know what the deal is until the reading of the will when the details are effectively made public."

"When does that happen? Do you have to go in person?" Would Jet need to leave? Just as they'd... *This isn't about you, Archer.*

"Soon. And no, thank God. If I can figure out how to video conference through satellite, I can be there. Failing that." He spread his hands. "I'd say 'to hell with it', and let Richard have whatever he wants, but..."

"But he's a dick."

"Yeah. I don't care if all I've inherited is a bushel of Lebanese cucumbers from Eloise's kitchen garden. I'm not giving those suckers up."

"Fair enough." Malone dropped his glasses on the mess of paper cuttings and scraped his chair back from the table. "Coffee?"

"Nah. I'm too wound up for caffeine." Jet glanced out the long run of windows. "Think I'll take my gear to the beach. You must be hankering to get back out into the lagoon, too."

Was Jet trying to get rid of him? "You could join me."

What are you doing, Malone? Jet's clueless out there. He'll screw up, for sure.

But Malone didn't retract the offer. He could cope with a few errors. Science was built on trial and error. If Jet needed him, Malone would take the risk. "Hilda's been pining after you."

"Oh, yeah? How can you tell?"

"She does this funny little curl, always in your direction." Pure bullshit, but seeing Jet's sunshine smile was worth the lie.

Jet came to stand between Malone's legs, plucked a paper diamond from the fuzz on his bare chest, and planted a soft kiss on his lips. "Thanks for the sweet invite, but I know only one sure-fire cure for the grumbles."

"Oh, yeah?" Malone ran his hands under Jet's sarong and up the backs of his thighs. He had a pretty good idea what Jet was hinting at. He shifted forward in the seat and nipped at Jet's sharp jaw. "What's that?"

"Crayons."

"Uh..." Had he heard that right?

"Don't you just need to scribble sometimes? Make a mess? With no intention? No judgment? No repercussions?" Jet asked.

"No."

"I thought you said you're a doodler?"

"Well, yeah, but..." Malone put his glasses back on, pulled out his field notebook, and leafed to a random page where he'd filled the margins with scribbles. It wasn't a mess, though. There was order and reason to his chaos.

"Is that..." Jet peered closer. "Are they mitochondria?"

"Mitochondrial dysfunction is a major contributor to muscle wastage after burns." Malone explained. "What? It's part of my research," he added defensively because Jet was looking at him as though he'd grown another head.

"Nothing. I'm just impressed, is all." Jet flicked to the next page. "They're beautifully drawn. Intricate. What did you use? A point-o-five ultrafine?"

"Point-o-three, actually. Anything broader and it's impossible to demarcate the structures. Looks like it's bled. I don't like that."

"Of course, you don't." Jet ran a fingertip down the margin line, paying zero attention to the data entries to the right of it that had taken Malone hours of toil to compile. As though none of that effort mattered. "It's beautiful. You're an artist, Malone."

"No." He folded the arms of his glasses and tucked them safely away in their case.

"Yes. One-hundred percent yes."

"I just doodle. It helps me concentrate. That's all. Nothing special. Not like what my brother can do. You think this is intricate? You should see Myles' designs. They're off the charts."

"Far as I'm concerned, a doodle in the margins of a book has as much right to be called art as the Mona Lisa." Jet combed his fingers into Malone's hair, scratching gently at his scalp. It felt like heaven. And Malone suddenly realised Jet was the one comforting him, when it should have been the other way around. Was that how Jet dealt with stress? Did he give care to gain care?

Somehow, Malone had to flip that on its head—give Jet exactly what *he* needed. What he'd asked for.

Jet was all about the little things—meals together, board game marathons, evenings lazing on the sofa with a paperback, mucking about with his art...

Malone rose to his feet, pulling away from Jet's touch. "Come on. Grab your crayons, a sketchbook, and your ridiculous hat."

"Why? You gonna let me draw your portrait?"

"Better."

"Oh?"

"I'm going to draw yours."

CHAPTER TWENTY-TWO

Jet

The northeast tip of Tallon was Jet's favourite place to see the sunrise. The giant flaming arc spread across the horizon, fine as a fingernail, in glorious orange and gold. Above, the pre-dawn darkness blushed in ever-lightening shades of oyster-shell silver, pale baby pink, and soft lemon yellow. Below, the ocean reflected choppy darks and lights and all the colours that licked the sky.

He sat buddha-style on the upper rise of the beach. His sarong stretched taut across his knees, with the cotton ends fluttering in the gusty breeze. Over and over, he scooped a handful of rough coral sand and sifted it through his fingers, letting the easterly wind scatter it over the low dune.

After the four o'clock measures, he'd stayed away from his donga. Not that cozying up to Malone's warm body didn't appeal, but everything between them had happened so fast. As a plan, 'when in Rome' was all well and good, but Jet could no longer pretend his heart wasn't involved.

Eye candy? Fine.

Fab in the sack? Great.

But Malone had gone and decided to be a decent guy, with real feelings and vulnerabilities. And his artistry. Shit. That was a surprise. Even if the guy did focus on sub-cellular structures, invisible to the naked eye, Malone obviously knew beauty. It was disconcerting. Which was why Jet needed space. A chance to find some perspective. Time to remind himself of the myriad ways that Malone fell short of fabulous.

First, there was the grumpiness. Even though it was sort of, maybe, a little bit cute.

Second, there was the perfectionism. Applied to some things and some situations, that wasn't a problem, but no human being was perfect all the time. Jet sure wasn't.

Third, "Hmm." He wracked his mind. There had to be something. Some other reason Jet could latch onto to see the inevitable end as a good thing. Not that it was entirely up to him. Malone would have an opinion. Of that, Jet was sure. His thoughts circled that drain as the sun finally rose above the horizon, its piercing rays throwing plenty of heat, but not much clarity on the situation.

He sighed and dug his fingers deeper, below the dry sand, seeking the cool and the quiet.

Bzzt bzzt bzzt.

"Shit."

A host of nearby wedge-tail shearwaters howled their irritation and fussed their wings.

Jet rubbed his hands together to brush off the sand, then dug into his satchel, searching for the sat phone.

Bzzt bzzt bzzt.

"Yeah, yeah. Hold your horses. Got it!" He didn't take the time to check the screen. HQ had only messaged Malone on the heavy-duty satellite phone the previous day, asking for a radio check in. An actual call had to mean something serious was going on.

"Hello?"

"Hi, Jet. How soon can you get to the radio?" Shaz's voice came through tinnier than he was used to.

"Now?"

"ASAP."

"Shit. Okay. On my way."

"Sorry 'bout the alarming call." Sharon said once he got back to the radio shack and secured a connection. "You guys sure are drama-philic."

"I don't think that's a word, Shaz, but okay. What's going on this time? Not another call from that lawyer?"

"That'd be good news. No. A low is forming east of Tallon. It could come to nothing, but the modelling team seems to think it'll intensify. And if that does happen, it'll happen fast. HQ wants you to take extra measures."

"Extra measures? You mean more frequent than synoptic time?" Neither of them would get much sleep if they had to check the gauges more often.

"No, sorry. Bad choice of words. They mean you need to batten down the hatches. Shutter all the windows. Secure anything that could fly. Loose furniture. Tools. Stuff like that."

"Isn't all that what you do for a hurricane?"

"Cyclone, dear. We're in the southern hemisphere."

"Right. Sure." He ought to know things like that. Jet leaned toward the open doorway for a better view of the morning sky. "It's a bit blustery, but no clouds."

"Calm before the storm?" Her voice rose as though she was asking a question. "You two are significantly more secure on Tallon than you would be on a ship at sea, but the island is super exposed, and you're far from help. Follow Protocol F and you'll be alright. It's outlined in the manual. Step by step. Nothing either of you can't handle. We'll let you know if you need to upgrade from that."

"Batten down the hatches," Jet muttered.

"Exactly. Protocol F."

"And don't die," he added. If he'd learned anything from his work in health care, it was that things could almost always be worse.

"That's the spirit. The strongest structure is the cold storage, so stick anything essential that you can't otherwise secure in there."

"Yeah, okay. Good tip." What would Malone say if Jet insisted the cuc-scape go in the freezer? It would have good company, what with all of Malone's racked and stacked cuc guts in there. And what about the reef? Would Malone's real-life sea cucumbers be alright? What about Hilda? What about the island's birds? And the turtles that seemed to be on some kind of cosmic timetable, laying and burying their eggs? Would they be okay? "How long have we got to prepare?"

"Eighteen hours. Twenty-four if you're lucky. The system may even change direction or dissipate. Tallon is a tiny speck in a very large ocean. It may pass you by completely."

"But that isn't the prediction."

There was a short pause, then Shaz said, "No. This is real, Jet."

Damn you and your brilliant ideas, Dad.

"Why do disasters always happen at Christmas time? If it's not bushfires, it's floods, or storms...or all three."

"Catastrophising doesn't suit you, Jet. Where's all that brilliant sunshinyness I depend on first thing in the morning?"

"Not a word, Shaz."

"Not the point, Jet."

She had him there. "I don't know. Everything was just starting to feel good. Y'know."

"Too good to be true?"

"Maybe. No. I don't know. We, ah..." Shit, he almost told Shaz that he and Malone were getting it on. *Not professional, Jethro.* He and Shaz were friendly, but there was still a line. "I ought to get going. Thanks for the heads up."

"No prob."

"Will I hear your pearly voice for the ten o'clock measures?"

"Absolutely. Early shift for me, today and tomorrow. You take care of yourself, eh. And of that guy of yours."

"Will do." Jet resolved to have his act together by the time ten o'clock rolled around. "Over and out."

He flicked open the beast of a manual and it wasn't until he'd skimmed his finger all the way down the table of contents to *Appendix: Protocol F*, that Jet replayed Shaz's words.

That guy of yours, she'd said. And he hadn't refuted it.

Jet stared at the printed page, unseeing.

Who had given the game away? Him or Malone?

Was it still a game?

Or was it real?

Either way, 'what happens on Tallon, stays on Tallon' had flown the nest, and Jet couldn't bring himself to care.

"What did Sharon say? Exactly."

Jet added 'demanding' to his list of Malone's shortcomings. He'd found Malone in the mess, blind to anything that wasn't in the field of view of his microscope.

Don't be snippy, Jethro. Malone is just stressed. Same as you.

"The modelling guys, modeller people...modellers? Fuck. I don't know. Doesn't matter." Flustered, Jet took a steadying breath. "Shaz said they're monitoring a storm that's intensifying somewhere to the east and is likely to hit the island sometime late tonight, or early tomorrow. Since Tallon is vulnerable, we need to prepare. I have their instructions here." Jet slapped the back of his hand against the open page of the manual. "Protocol F. Looks pretty straight forward."

"Of course, Tallon's vulnerable. The highest point on the island is twelve feet elevation. A simple storm surge could wipe us out." Malone snatched the folder from Jet's hands. "Let me see."

"Hey, we're in this together. You and me. Adam and Adam. Remember?" It was near impossible not to snap back in return, and Malone didn't seem at all reassured by the reminder that it was just the two of them. "How about if you radio in our report at ten o'clock? That way, you can talk to them directly. Get the latest info."

"I can't do everything, Jet." He stabbed the to-do list in the manual. "All this, plus the bureau's measures? I need to protect my quadrats, and now I'll have to do two data sets today, either side of high tide, in case the worst happens and we are caught out by the storm."

He'd never heard Malone so wild. "It's not all on you. We'll need to work together to get some of this done, but I can deal with anything that's a one-man job." The frown line between Malone's brows deepened. Instinctively, Jet reached out to smooth it. "You do whatever you need to do out on the reef. Just help me out for a few hours through the peak of the tide. The lagoon's too rough for you to work then, anyway."

Malone took a shaky breath, then his wild eyes met Jet's. "Yeah. Okay. I can do that."

Jet smoothed both brows, then travelled down to still at his temples.

Malone blinked, and his hectic breathing slowed a little. "Sorry. I didn't mean to snap at you. I'm just concerned for my project. Everything's here. All of my equipment. The sea cucumbers. The samples. The data."

"And you." At Malone's quizzical look, Jet elaborated. "You're at risk, too."

Malone shook his head. "Now you're getting morbid. It's only a storm."

"Exactly. Only a storm. Not the fiery depths of doom. You go do your thing. I'll do mine. And we can meet up somewhere in the middle to get the joint stuff done. Deal?" It was stupid, but Jet stuck his hand out to shake.

"Deal."

Twelve hours later, under a leaden sky, Jet watched as Malone shot up through the surf-frothed surface of the lagoon, spat water from his snorkel, then duck-dived back down. Over and over. The only way Jet knew where to look was the bright flag attached to Malone's floating research station. When Malone came up and actually stayed up for more than the time it took to catch a breath, Jet clicked the 'speak' button on his walkie talkie. "You've done enough, Malone. Time to come in."

Truth be told, Jet didn't think Malone would ever think he'd done enough, but the light was waning, and, from his vantage point beside the shuttered mess building, Jet could see slanted sheets of rain bearing down from the north east.

Eventually, Malone staggered back to dry land, his face salt-crusted and sunburnt, every bit of him limp and exhausted.

According to Shaz's less personable colleague on the late shift, they'd get plenty of rain that night, but the real gales weren't expected to hit till midnight. Which meant they had a few precious hours to enjoy the calm before the storm.

Jet had no intention of wasting it.

CHAPTER TWENTY-THREE

Malone

The worst of the storm wasn't due to arrive for another few hours, but already squalls screamed around the rafters and drove stinging rain against the metal roof. It made Malone want to cover his ears and scream in return. "Sounds like a bad werewolf movie in here. Not that I watch werewolf movies. Good or bad. Well, not on purpose. That shits ridiculous."

"I don't understand. How do you accidentally watch a werewolf movie?"

"My friend Brady makes us suffer through movie nights. He has...eclectic taste." Malone squared the last of the tight-packed foam boxes in the cool room and took a micro-step back to appraise his work. Some of their gear could go in the secure freezer, but not everything would survive those super-low temperatures. "Is that everything?" Please, God, say yes.

"Where's your microscope?" Jet asked.

"It's in the heavy-duty box under that lot. The one with the fluoro orange 'UP' arrows." Obnoxious orange, but Malone didn't care. Bad enough that he'd lose a day, maybe more, to a bloody storm. The less he had to do to get back up and working afterward, the better. "I'll probably have to recalibrate it after all this, but if it gets tilted too far, or, God forbid, tipped all the way over, I might as well jump on the Titanic."

"You're so dramatic." Jet filled the tight space behind him and ran his fingertips across Malone's tight shoulders. If he wasn't already covered in goose bumps from the cold, Jet's touch would've made him shiver. Even through three t-shirt-material layers.

"Me?"

"Malone Archer, drama king."

"Compared to you?" That was a joke.

"Can't we both be drama kings? Not everything's a competition."

"Not in my experience. Academia is full of rivalries." Not unlike a pack of werewolves fighting over the funding spoils. "That's actually what I love about my friends."

"That you're rivals?"

"No. The opposite. None of us even works in the same arena. Lachlan's a teacher, so I guess our career paths are the most similar, but his students are all pre-pubescent. Dane thrives in corporate culture. Spencer's a pro athlete. And Brady writes and illustrates an amazing graphic novel series. I mean, it's god-awful dark, but amazing. You two would get along great." All the guys would like Jet. He was the sort of person to get along with everyone. Nothing like Malone.

A hand came around his waist, followed by another one, then Jet crammed in close, hugging him from behind. "You guys should form a band. Call yourselves The Spice Boys. You'd make a killing."

"Bzzt. Bad pop culture pun alert." Malone rested back on his heels a smidgen, letting Jet do some of the work of holding him up. Fuck, he was tired. And sore. Sore and tired. And it was barely eight o'clock. He covered Jet's hands with his own. "Jesus. You're like ice."

"Well, we are in a freezer."

"Refrigerator, actually."

Jet groaned and pulled away. "Cold is cold, Malone. Come on. We've done what we can. Not long before the hornet's nest lands. Let's grab some sleep while we can."

"Sleep." He doubted he'd get any. Not with his whole future on the line. Malone eyed the ceiling. One glorified tin can stood between his success and ruination.

Seriously, Archer? How about we upgrade your status to drama emperor?

The second Jet hauled open the external door, the wind and rain roared in, sucking all the air out and soaking the square metre of floor they'd left clear.

"Holy hell, Jet!" Malone had to brace his feet just to remain upright, and the fast change in pressure made his ears pop. How had the storm escalated so quickly? They been in the cool room for barely twenty minutes. No more.

"Come on! Let's go!" Jet yelled back to him, muscles straining with the effort of holding the door open.

Suddenly, 'ruination' didn't seem like such a drastic call. Only, it wasn't just Malone's research at risk.

Adrenaline surged at the realisation that it wasn't just their *things* on the line. He and Jet were isolated on a tiny pin-prick of an island, utterly exposed to the elements. It was one thing to know of the danger, in theory. Quite another to experience it, in reality. To feel it in his gut.

With one last glance back at the crate with the orange arrows, Malone sent a swift prayer to Mother Nature, asking for mercy, then raced out into the storm. As he came through, he caught Jet's hand and held on tight. He couldn't do much to control the weather or the tensile strength of the steel structure. But he could stick to Jet like glue. He could do his level best to ensure they got through the storm in one piece. Together.

One hand protecting his face from whatever the fuck might fly at him, and the other hand a death-grip around Jet's, Malone pushed through the driving rain. Since Jet's door was the closest, it made sense to aim for there, but it still took a breathless age to cross the courtyard and climb the few steps to the relative safety of their donga.

The second they were inside and the door securely shut, Jet barrelled into him and shoved him up against the far wall. Or, more specifically, Jet's mouth barrelled into him, followed by hands that seemed to be everywhere, all at once.

It didn't take long for Malone to figure out that Jet hadn't meant 'sleep' in the literal sense when he'd pressed him to leave the cool room. Not that Malone wasn't on board with the plan. The adrenaline that coursed through his arteries had to go somewhere, and if sex was Jet's chosen means of affirming that they were still alive and kicking, Malone wasn't about to argue. The battering storm provided a suitable soundtrack to the frantic way they went at each other. And slick heat soon replaced the chills that had leeched into their bones.

"Did you ever wish you were an octopus?" Jet asked.

Malone retracted his tongue from where it laved Jet's earlobe. Octopus? "What the hell?"

"With all those arms, and suckers, and...God, can you imagine? It'd be so hot." Jet gave a full-body wriggle that took Malone's cock from ninety degrees to one-eighty in zero-point-three-eight seconds. Or thereabouts.

Jet tried to swivel and tackle him to the bed, but he held Jet off. Before they got any further, Malone had to address the flaming monster in the corner.

"I'm not into tentacle sex, okay?" The words were a trip coming off his tongue.

Jet looked disappointed. "But two arms are just so restrictive. And I've only got one—"

"We are not discussing how many suckers you have."

"But, Malone—"

"No. That's a hard limit."

"What do you want, then?" Jet stripped off Malone's litany of rain-damp t-shirts in one fell swoop.

Jet didn't wait for an answer. He'd already turned his attention to divesting Malone of his shorts, and the sight of Jet on his knees made Malone aware of every bit of animal in his homo sapien soul.

Somehow, Jet was naked too, and they ended up on the bed in a classic sixty-nine. Jet's clever hands were all over him. Pulling. Pushing. Manipulating him. Rearranging him. Moulding him like clay. All to Jet's design, of course, but Malone didn't care about that. He was busy himself, tracing every jut and plane of Jet's body he could reach with the tip of his tongue.

He took a quick swipe at Jet's hard cock, lapping at the precum that beaded at the slit, because how could he not? But, as much as Malone found it hard to resist a sweet treat, he had a notion to start with savoury. He contorted Jet's upper leg into a foetal position, ran the tip of his tongue the length of Jet's perineum, and tasted the earthiness at his core.

"Ngh..."

Whatever else Jet said was lost on Malone because Jet's fingernails scoured down his treasure trail and paid back Malone's teasing tongue with a sharp tug at his pubes. A hive of tiny stings. "Mmgrph." It was almost too much.

Wet heat surrounded his length. Jet's tongue coaxed him. Jet's mouth consumed him. Such a simple thing. And yet, like a miracle cure, the pain was gone.

"Mmm," Malone rumbled.

So good.

Against the feral roar of the storm, he couldn't hear Jet's rasping breaths too well, but he could feel them—every exhalation a twin blast on his balls, sending shivers all the way to his toes. Was he hot or cold? Malone couldn't tell.

He wanted in on the action, too. To tease out every *mmm* and *aah* and *ohh*, like a linguist discovering a new language.

Of course, not all languages were verbal. He read Jet's body like it was the fucking Rosetta Stone. Every line and nick. Every nook and cranny told Malone something more about Jet and what might set him off into the stratosphere.

He nosed at Jet's tight sac, traced Jet's throbbing vein with the rough bristles of his chin, and worked his tongue around Jet's velveteen head. Malone couldn't get enough of the salty brine and musky sweat, and the sweet fullness whenever Jet's hips flexed with the instinctive drive to rut.

Short thrusts at first.

Careful.

But when Malone gripped Jet's arse and relaxed his throat, wordlessly agreeing to more, Jet took it as a signal to let loose.

Before, Malone would've guessed Jet was inclined to give messy head, but nothing could have been further from the truth. With rare head-tap-tummy-rub coordination, Jet sealed his lips, hollowed his cheeks, and slowly, incrementally, painstakingly sucked Malone all the way down.

Could he have lasted longer? Possibly. But the constancy of pressure was more than enough to take Malone to the edge.

Every base need surged to the surface, and he was no longer Malone, the scientist. Malone, the analyst. Malone, the brain. All rational sense flew away. Sex hormones barrelled through his bloodstream, taking over his mind and body. He shut his eyes, thinking to limit the sensory overload, but light flared behind his eyelids. It was as though Jet had flicked a switch inside him, firing every nerve ending.

By the time he felt the fireworks spark, it was too late.

His toes curled, foetal tight.

His jaw tensed, and it took every ounce of merciless control left to not snap it shut around Jet's most tender flesh.

None of it stopped the roar that tore from his gut as he came in great rushes, his seed hurtling out, seeking God knew what.

Survival of the fittest, perhaps? That was the law of nature. Twice, Malone thrust through it, coating Jet's throat. He revelled in the strength of Jet's milking tongue and the tight fit as Jet swallowed around his cock head. Drinking him down. Tapping him dry.

Mind blown, Malone didn't even realise his mouth had gone lax when Jet took himself in hand. The *thwick, thwick* sound came to him first, and he opened his eyes to the sight of Jet's angry one-eyed snake bearing down on him.

Mine.

Desire was a powerful thing.

Elemental.

Malone's brain was still mush, but he managed to bring himself back to the moment.

Back to Jet's taut body in his arms.

Back before it was too late.

Instinct took over. Malone brushed Jet's hand away, cradled his tongue along Jet's iron-hard length, sealed his lips, and sucked.

"You're staring at me like a specimen under a microscope." Malone reached up and tapped Jet's temple. "What are you thinking about so hard?"

Jet batted his hand away. "I can't quite figure out the colour of your eyes. They change from blue to green to grey, depending on the light. Like one of those spinning light gizmos."

"A kaleidoscope?"

"Yeah. Or like the sea. All the colours of all the depths."

"Depending on the light, huh?"

"Exactly. It's kinda infuriating, to be honest. What am I going to do when I paint your portrait?"

Malone firmed his hold, pulled Jet close, and rolled till Jet's delicious warmth was underneath him.

"Hey!"

Malone rolled his hips. Neither of them was hard anymore, but that didn't change the sweetness of the contact. "Problem?"

Jet huffed a breathy laugh. "Not a one."

Malone reached to flick off the lamp on the side table and the room went pitch black. "What colour are they now?"

Jet's breath ghosted across his cheek. Malone felt a single finger smooth from his temple to his cheekbone, across to the bridge of his nose. "Oh, I know exactly what colour they are now."

"Yeah? Tell me."

"The colour of smug."

"Hmm. Don't think there's a crayon for that."

Jet's laugh rumbled through Malone's chest, chased by Jet's arms that wrapped around him, like the whirling arms of a cyclone. Ever tightening. But he and Jet were safe in the centre of the emotional maelstrom—the calm eye of the storm.

It stunned him how comfortable he was in Jet's arms. The stirrings in his gut were as much about affection as they were about desire. And he fucking desired the man. Bear-in-heat level desire.

Undeniable.

He nosed the silk skin behind Jet's ear, taking in everything—the taste, the smell, the feel of him. "Mmm."

"Are you purring?"

"No."

"I think you were." Jet's arms loosened, and the tips of one set of fingers trailed down Malone's spine, light as a feather, vertebrae to vertebrae.

It was impossible not to rise into the touch. "M'not a cat," he protested.

"Agreed. You're all bear."

"M'not a bear."

"A huggly, cuddly, growly teddy bear."

"Grr."

"See?"

Equal opposite, Jet's fingers reversed course to skim up. Slowly. Eventually, they reached the point where spine met cranium, where they stopped and pressed. Hard.

Malone had been relaxed before. Orgasms generally had that effect on him. But Jet's firm touch in that singular spot transformed every atom in his exhausted body from solid lead to liquid mercury.

"Mmm." His eyes drooped shut, and all he knew was sweet peace.

Plop. Plop. Plop... Plop. Plop. Plop... Plop. Plop. Plop.

God. Malone needed to change his sleep alarm sound. Trouble was, his mate Lachlan had chosen it, and disappointing Lachlan always felt like a kick to the guts.

Plop. Plop. Plop... Plop. Plop. Plop.

"Make it stop." Jet slapped the bare sheets, pale-lit by the blue light of the phone.

"I would if you weren't lying on top of me." Malone stretched like a starfish, all the way down to the taut webbing between his toes. God, he felt good. Achy, but good.

Plop. Plop. Plop.

"M'v," Jet grumbled as he slid off enough that Malone could reach the phone on Jet's bedside table and swipe. "M'st'rly."

"Way too early," Malone agreed. But the measures wouldn't get done by magic, even if half the systems on the island were automatic.

"St'rm."

"Yeah." The storm wasn't over. Not by a long shot. Their donga might have been solid enough to withstand the battering, and insulated enough to be comfortable, but the thing was still essentially a tin can. No hiding from the maelstrom inside that.

A gale still tore around their donga, and the battering rain still fell in torrents, but the storm had reached its peak through the witching hour. By four in the morning, the intensity was definitely less than it had been when he and Jet finally drifted to sleep.

Unlike for the late ten o'clock measures, when they'd agreed it was far too hazardous to venture out, Malone could no longer justify the excuse to stay safely curled in Jet's arms. He levered himself out from under Jet's warmth and felt his way to the edge of the bed. He fished around for his headlamp and switched on the red-light filter that was less disturbing for the wildlife than bright white light. Not that too many birds would be out and about on such a wild night. Not the sane ones, anyway.

Malone pulled on his day-old shorts, checked to make sure he had all the necessary kit, and hooked a towel on the back of the door, convenient to dry off when he returned. Then he kneeled on the mussed bed and pressed a kiss into Jet's time-softened buzz cut. "Be right back," he whispered.

He didn't think Jet heard him. But as he forced the door open against the wind's resistance, Jet's quiet petition crossed the divide.

"Be careful," he said.

Malone turned back to face Jet. "Of course," he murmured low. He was always careful. Measured. Planned. A risk was fine, so long as it was calculated.

The moment he felt the full force of the gale beyond the protection of the compound, Malone was glad he'd had the foresight to volunteer for duty. He wasn't exactly a muscle-bound brute, but Jet, with his lankier frame, had a much higher centre of gravity. He would've struggled to stay upright against the lashing wind. Maybe even been swept out to sea.

Unable to deal with that horrible thought, Malone put it in a box and tucked it away.

Jet's safe, Archer. Focus on the job at hand.

From a distance, he could see that the windsock was shredded beyond repair. Replacing it would have to wait. He added it to the mental list of things to see to when the weather had come to rights. With any luck, the rest of the instruments had fared better. He pushed the last twenty metres through the swirling rain to the farthest point on the island, where the weather box sat, unmoved, like a silent sentinel.

He unlatched the louvered door and took a quick reading, logging the figures to memory, then turned his attention to the anemometer and pyranometer on top—built to be hardy, but far more exposed to the elements.

He thought about leaving them until daylight. Just like the windsock, he'd not be able to fix them if they were broken. But reporting the weather data was his responsibility. He couldn't put off taking care of the place, just because of a storm.

They usually kept a stepping stool conveniently placed to climb up to the top of the weather box, but Jet had stored it away with the rest of the loose equipment, leaving the only option a vertical metal ladder attached to the side of the box. Easy enough to scale on a fine day, but in the dark, with lashing rain stained ruby-red by the glow of his headlamp, it was more like navigating a slick ice ladder while travelling at hyper-speed through space under attack from a hail of blood diamonds.

Nope, not dramatic at all, Archer.

He hugged close to the box, gripped the thin metal railings, and stepped up from the first to the second rung. No problem. A gust caught him from the second to the third rung, but he clung on, locked his knees, and pressed his forehead to the top rim of the box, riding it out.

"Whoever determined the difference between a tropical low and a cyclone needs their head read." Malone voiced his frustration into the universe. Not that it'd make a difference. There wasn't some cosmic leader with a vested interested in his survival.

When he thought the wind might have died down a fraction, Malone braved another rung, high enough to get a semi-decent view of the instruments.

His left foot gripped fine. Rubber soles doing their job.

His right foot gripped fine, too.

At first.

He caught sight of the flying object way too late to duck. It clipped his right temple, then sheered across his face. Both hard and soft. He had no idea what it was. But it didn't matter. Instinct made him shield his face from God knew whatever else might fly at him. But one less hand hold on the ladder was one too little and his right foot slipped, the fierce wind collected his body as if it was a sail, and flung him into the night.

It wasn't a big fall. The soft sandy ground was a meter below him at most. He should have been fine. But as much as nature was full of predictable patterns, nobody had informed the island's burrowing birds that they had to dig their nests in an orderly arrangement away from human infrastructure.

When Malone landed, his right foot found semi-solid sand, and his left foot found...nothing.

His heel clipped something solid, but that was it. His toes dived deep into a burrow, momentum forcing him forward. He tried to catch his fall, but bushes stained red from his light rushed at him. Reflexively, Malone squeezed his eyes tight and rolled sideways, desperate to protect himself against the stiff branches. But his left foot, slotted toe-first into the burrow, didn't corkscrew with the rest of him, and pain, lightning sharp, shot from his ankle to his knee.

"Fuuuuck!" The guttural shout erupted from his lungs, taking with it every goddamn carbon, hydrogen, and oxygen atom necessary for his survival.

CHAPTER TWENTY-FOUR

Jet

It wasn't the deep ache in his balls that woke Jet. Although it should have been. That shit was delicious.

And it wasn't the eerie quiet on the donga roof. That was even more delicious.

Nor was it the sharp, silvery light that made a square halo around the curtains, hinting at the early hour.

No.

It was the solitude.

Jet felt the bed beside him. Cold. Which meant Malone had been out longer than it had been light.

Be right back, he'd said. Jet could still feel the ghost of the kiss on his crown.

Fuck, Jethro, whine a little more, why don't you? Malone's probably out there cleaning up after the storm, while you're in here doing your best impression of a sea cucumber.

He licked his dry lips.

A parched sea cucumber.

Jet threw off the sheet and rolled out of bed. Both walkie talkies were still on the bedside table, so Malone couldn't have gone far.

Piss. Slog of water. Get to work.

Hmm...not quite right.

Piss. Slog of water. Find Malone. Kiss Malone. *Then* get to work.

Better.

Jet visited the bathroom, slurped water from his cupped hands in the tiny sink, knotted a sarong around his waist, and headed out.

"Malone?" he called out.

It was early yet, and he had to shade his eyes from the blast of horizontal light that struck through the gap between the radio shack and the cold room. Above, the sky stretched out in cloudless, cerulean blue—a surreal sight after the tempestuous night.

"Malone!"

Everywhere he looked, there were signs of the battering storm. A rain gutter dangled from the dry-store roof. Clumps of uprooted saltbush clustered under the mess deck like tumbleweed. And, while the island would never be silent—not with the resident birdlife and constant ocean—there was an eerie stillness about the place. It took Jet an embarrassing amount of time to realise that the underlying hum of the generator was silent.

He climbed the steps to the mess and flipped a light switch.

Nope. Not even a flicker.

With the external shutters protecting the wide bank of windows from the worst of the wind, a shadowy gloom filled the large room. Still no sign of Malone.

Where was he?

Jet crossed to the radio shack and tried the usual dials and switches. Not even a hint of life. "Shit." If the radio was out, they were royally screwed.

Jet's pulse sped up. He dashed from building to building, then rushed back outside and through to the dune overlooking the lagoon.

"Malone!" he called out. "Mal!"

Where the fuck was he?

The beach was a mess of flotsam. A brief scan revealed tangles of rope and seaweed, soaked timber, plastic bottles, a couple of Malone's unmoored quadrats, and a long, wavering line of sea froth—like an ultra-long feather boa—beached from the storm swell that crashed over the encircling reef.

When Malone left him in the wee hours, the storm had still been raging. Which meant the seas would've been high, visibility low, and the chance of Malone being swept out on a freak wave, scarily possible.

Jet cupped his hands around his mouth and shouted out over the pounding ocean. "Malone!"

Nothing.

No sign of Malone in the churned lagoon or of the flag he'd anchored to indicate the location of his quadrats.

Surely, he wouldn't have gone out there. Not in such stormy seas. Not without giving Jet a heads-up.

But the man was obsessive about his sea cucumbers. They were his priority. If Malone had seen his flag was missing and the quadrats were washed up on the shore, he might not have thought twice about the risk before wading out to investigate what had happened to the rest of his research grid on the seabed.

"If you've gone and got yourself drowned, I'll..." Jet didn't know what he'd do. Probably turn right around and kill the man himself. "Stab you with my palette knife." That'd teach him.

Tallon was a tiny dot in the Pacific. There were only so many places where he could be. As Jet ran eastward along the beach, he held his hand up against the low rays, eyes madly scanning in every direction. "Malone!" He didn't know why he bothered calling out. Against nature's cacophony, Jet could barely hear his own raging heartbeat.

It made sense to circumnavigate the island first, then methodically work his way along the many sandy trails that rayed out from the compound to the beach, like a teardrop-shaped clockface. Since the original reason Malone had come out was to do the usual measures, Jet belatedly made for the weather box, stark white against the low green foliage and the deep blue sky.

His heart lifted as Jet got closer and saw the louvered door to the internal instruments swinging on its hinges. Malone had been there, for sure. He shut it and secured the latch, then turned a three-sixty, scanning the low brush for a sign. Any sign.

"Mal! Where the fuck are you?" He yelled, setting the usually docile birds that lived near the box all aflutter.

Feathery heads swivelled all his way, and Jet was sure their beady eyes were judging him for losing the one good thing that—

As one, their heads all swivelled the other way. Their attention caught by...something.

"What is it?" He stupidly asked, then snapped his mouth shut to listen.

The still-raging ocean covered just about every other noise. All he could hear was the roaring waves, the whop-whop of a bird taking off, and...

A moan.

The birds' heads all turned to look directly at the weather box.

Jet stilled. Didn't breathe. Waited.

There it was again. Low. Barely audible. Followed by a sharp-drawn breath.

"Mal?" It was a battle to keep his voice level.

Where the fuck was he?

Nobody was supposed to step on the native vegetation, but Jet didn't give a shit about that as he stomped through the knee-high foliage around the base of the white weather box.

The first thing he spied was the sole of Malone's shoe. Shit! Heart in his throat, he hustled further around and saw the rest of him, lying wedged between the dense bushes with a yellow-footed brown booby perched on his hip.

"Fuck, Malone! Shoo!" The idiot bird flapped its wings, but they weren't the best at taking off, and were notoriously hard to budge. It shat on Malone's leg as it tripped over its too-big feet.

At another pained cry, Jet waved his arms with greater gusto. "Shoo!"

The thing flapped its wings and stumbled clumsily across the brush till it, presumably, found a sturdy enough branch to take its weight. Jet had no idea. His attention was stuck on Malone and the unnatural angle of his left lower leg.

Bile rose, acid-sharp in Jet's throat, and blood thundered in his ears, adrenaline making him jittery as he crouched down, close as he could get, unsure what he could safely touch. "Bloody hell, Mal. What happened?"

Malone didn't answer. Nothing but a flutter of his eyelashes against his too-pale cheeks.

Think, Jethro. Emergency procedures. DR. ABCDE. He didn't give a shit about danger to himself. And he already knew Malone wasn't responding. But the rest? *Airway, breathing…*

Fuck. Was Malone breathing?

Don't be a fool, Jethro. People don't usually moan if they can't breathe.

Still, he hovered over Malone's face and watched his chest for a hot, drawn-out second. It seemed to last an age. When he saw it expand and contract with no sign of resistance, Jet blew out a relieved breath.

"Not dead." *Thank fuck.*

What's next?

"Circulation."

A quick feel of Malone's thumping carotid appeased his greatest concern, but the leg was definitely a worry. Malone had likely been lying there in significant pain in a questionable state of consciousness, while Jet had been…

Shit. Jet didn't want to think about how he'd lazed in bed, feeling hard-done-by to wake alone, so quick to assume Malone had prioritized his sea cucumbers over the island...*over me*.

"Fuck."

No time for that, Jethro. Beat yourself up another day. Malone needs you. Now.

It was the buck up Jet needed. He manoeuvred himself to feel Malone's scalp, checking for blood and any other external sign of head trauma. Then he made his way over Malone's body, from top to toe.

The closer he got to the break in Malone's left lower leg, the stronger the moans got. More insistent. "That's good, Mal. Tell me what hurts."

The leg looked bad. From the wacky angle, Jet guessed at least the tibia was broken. Maybe even the fibula. The skin was tight from the swelling, hot to the touch. But the most dangerous sign was the dusky colour of his foot. Broken bone could be repaired. Oxygen-starved soft tissue was a different story.

He pressed on the top of Malone's foot, searching for the pedal pulse.

Thready, at best.

And Malone hadn't even flinched at Jet's touch, which meant possible nerve injury too.

He could ice it to bring down the swelling. If they had any ice with the power down, that was.

And, he could try to reduce the fracture.

Shit. The thought turned Jet's stomach.

During his one and only visit to operating theatres in his student-nurse days, he'd fainted the first time he saw a scalpel blade slice through skin.

That was embarrassing.

This? This was terrifying.

He just wasn't cut out for the brutal side of medicine.

What was he going to do, though? Leave it? Leave Malone?

Fuck, no.

"Jet." It was barely a whisper.

"Thank fuck." He looked up to see Malone's hand reaching for him. "Yeah, Mal. It's me. I'm here."

CHAPTER TWENTY-FIVE

Malone

Malone gritted his teeth, but it did nothing to stop the scorching pain that seared up his leg. It was as if someone had hooked him up to electrodes, flipped the switch, then walked away.

"It's me. I'm here." Jet's voice was distant. Beyond the pain. "It's okay, Mal. I've got you."

He gripped Jet's hand and held on for dear life.

Fuck!

This was bad. So very bad.

"Jesus, Mal. What happened? Never mind. Doesn't matter."

"Hole," Malone gritted out. "Fell."

Bloody seabirds. Why couldn't they build nests above ground like all the other ninety-whatever percent of the Aves taxonomical class?

Bright light hammered his brain. Malone squeezed his eyes shut as tight as he could. Last he'd known, it had been full dark. Had he blacked out? How long had he been there? "What time?" He opened his eyes a bare millimetre. All he saw were fuzzy leaves, blazing sky, and Jet's distinctive silhouette leaning over him.

"Early yet." Jet squeezed his hand even tighter, then released it. "Stay here. Try not to move. I'll be back in a sec."

"No!" *Don't go.*

"I have to get the first aid kit. And something to use for a splint. Your leg is..."

"Wait!" *Stay with me.*

"Mal. Look at me."

He'd never seen Jet so serious.

"I will be back. Ten minutes. Tops."

And then he was gone. His absence was like a black hole, deep in Malone's gut.

He had no idea if it was five minutes or fifty, but, true to his word, Jet returned, cursing a blue streak. He dropped a pile of gear on the plants in front of Malone. "You'll never guess what I found in the first aid kit."

Twenty questions? Now? "What?" he bit out. Even his fucking jaw hurt.

"Con—" Jet stopped. "You know what? I'm not going to tell you. Not yet. Not till we get back to the compound. Give you some incentive to get there."

"If you think some fucking riddle is enough of a motivation to make me walk on a busted leg, you're deluded."

"I'll drag you if I need to. Throw you in the wheelbarrow." Jet popped a couple of pills out of a bubble pack and held out a bottle of water. "Here. Take these. Anti-inflammatories. They'll take the edge off."

"Not by much."

"Maybe not, but every bit counts. Right?"

Was the man serious? "Is this how you got Vic to cooperate? Sugar coat reality?"

"Is it working?"

"No." He did swallow the pills, though.

Jet gently placed a cold gel pack around his shin. The numbing sliver of relief was enough to feel that Malone could look without tossing the acid curdled in his stomach. He couldn't see under the gel pack, but the surrounding skin looked angry, and his ankle looked off. It wasn't where it ought to be, given the line of his leg.

Malone swallowed thickly. "How bad is it?"

"Bad."

Malone snorted at the distinct lack of sugar, immediately wishing it back.

Jet repositioned himself in a squat at Malone's ankle. "Can you find something solid to hang onto up there? I'm going to try to reduce the break. Bring the bones back in line."

"What!? No!" Jet might have the golden touch in some respects, but he was no trained doctor.

"Not gonna lie. It's risky. But leaving the break displaced is more of a risk. Look at it, Mal. The more your muscles contract, the more they'll pull the break out of alignment and expose your soft tissues to jagged bone. I have to try."

"Here?"

"Here."

"Fuck!"

"You said it." Jet didn't wait for further permission. He wrapped his hands around Malone's ankle, waited barely a second for Malone to grab for the sturdiest branch within reach, then pulled.

Never mind a simple electric shock, lightning shot up his leg and forced an unholy scream from deep in his lungs. Ink blots stole across his vision. He almost welcomed the darkness. The pain was so absolute, there was no centre to it.

The plant he held onto for dear life gave in the unstable sand, and he blindly scrambled for another to grip, then another, as the torture went on and on. Tearing flesh. Grinding bone. Was Jet going to pull his whole leg off? At full tension, Jet's firm hold slowly twisted, and suddenly, *pop*!

"Fuck!" The sickening sound triggered a cold sweat. Malone's gut cramped. Acid burned his throat. The ink blots blended, and darkness smothered his world.

When he finally got his breath back, Malone cursed, "Holy fuck, Jet. Stick a red-hot poker in my eye why don't you?"

"Sorry."

Jet still held his leg, but the pain was different. The lightning was gone. Thank God. But a bone-deep throb remained, and, weirdly, pins and needles tingled his toes. Was that normal? Couldn't be. Some kind of after-shock, maybe? It was a relief to shut his eyes and let himself drift—to distance himself from the horror.

"Mal? Stay with me. Mal!"

But nothing could stop the gathering darkness. Not even Jet's desperate voice, imploring him to stay.

Malone woke in the shade of the radar tower to a deep, throbbing pulse below his knee, and the sound of Jet's voice saying, "I've got a tourniquet, a blade, and a blow torch. I'm as ready as I'll ever be."

His head swam. What the fuck was happening? Was he delirious? Dreaming?

Dreams didn't usually hurt so bad.

Malone tried to lift his head, but it was heavy. Even his eyelids weighed a tonne.

Was he drugged?

God, he was tired. Nothing felt right. The only thing that didn't hurt was his foot. The pain made sense, but why couldn't he feel his foot?

He tried to wriggle his toes.

Nothing.

Blinking at the stark blue beyond the shade, Malone tucked in his chin and got a quick look down his body to see his leg elevated on some kind of contraption made out of one of their camp chairs. His five toes poked out above a makeshift splint made of sawn-off broomsticks, towels, and duct tape.

"Shit. I think he's awake. I don't know if I can do this, mate." Jet said to...someone. Malone didn't know who. Was someone else with them?

He closed his eyes to better listen.

Nothing but birds and waves and Jet saying, "Uh-huh, yep, sure thing."

All very agreeable.

Normal.

Peaceful.

Aside from the whole broken leg situation. Nothing normal about that.

Malone licked his dry lips. "Do what?" he asked belatedly. Voice like sand.

"Yeah. Okay. I know!" Jet's voice rose an octave, the way it only did when he was stressed.

"What's wrong?" Other than the broken leg, but that wasn't new.

A tourniquet, a blade, and a blowtorch.

The words filtered back into his sluggish mind. What could Jet possibly need with those? Other than... *Fuck! My leg! Is he going to cut it off?*

On a surge of adrenaline, Malone dug his elbows into the sand and tried to scramble backward. But Jet got a hand on his shoulder and, none too gently, pushed him back down to the ground.

"He's distressed. Tell me I don't need to do this," Jet said.

It was like struggling in quicksand. The bone-deep throb bloomed up to his groin. It took his breath away. "Don't do this! Of course, you don't need to do it!" Malone tried to say. His tongue was too thick in his mouth. Was he dreaming? Was this some kind of lucid nightmare?

"Shh, Malone. You'll hurt yourself." Jet's voice was tender and calm. Then it changed. Hardened. "Do I have your permission to begin?"

It was then that Malone realised Jet was speaking into the satellite phone, but Malone didn't care who Jet was talking to.

"No! No permission!"

Jet put the phone down on top of the first aid box, then leaned over him. His face was pale and drawn. He looked terrible. "I'm sorry, Malone. I'm so sorry. We need to do this."

"No, we don't. We don't need to do anything. It's just a broken bone. Look. It's splinted. It's fixed. It's fine."

Was this how soldiers felt, wounded on the battlefield? Your leg or your life?

"It's not fine. Elevation helps, but there's too much inflammation, and it's getting worse. Your skin's too tight. The soft tissues are so swollen they're cutting off your circulation. It's called compartment syndrome. I just need to cut the skin and fascia open. Just a tiny bit. Just enough to relieve the pressure."

Every bit of Malone rebelled at the thought. He madly scanned for escape. Instead, his gaze landed on the blowtorch planted upright in the soft sand. No way would he let that thing anywhere close to his flesh. He'd seen what burns could do.

"It's gonna hurt." Jet read his mind.

"No, it's fucking not, because you're going nowhere near me with a blade, or that...that blowtorch." He could barely spit out the word.

"The blowtorch is just for sterility. Malone, we *need* to do this," Jet repeated. "Now."

"*We* don't need to do anything. If *I* need surgery, then *I* need to get to a hospital, which means *I* need to get off this island. There's no *we* about that."

"Can you feel your foot, or is it numb?" Came Jet's blunt reply.

Malone bit down on his lip. He wasn't going to admit anything.

Jet took his silence as an admission. "Do you trust me?"

"About some things. Sure. But this? What the fuck, Jet? This isn't *M.A.S.H.*, and you're not Hawkeye. You're talking about cutting into me, in the open, where a fucking bird could fly overhead and shit all over me."

They both looked up. Sure enough, a pair of sooty terns swooped overhead.

"It's not ideal," Jet said.

Not ideal? "Understatement of the century."

"Believe me, I'd happily wait for a surgeon to do the job. A rescue boat is on its way, but we can't wait for them to get here. It'll take too long. Let me do this, Mal. Let me take care of you."

Malone could see the truth in Jet's eyes.

"Do you trust me?" Jet repeated the question.

"You're asking a lot."

"I know. I don't like this any more than you do."

"Doubt that."

Jet grabbed his hand and squeezed. "Let me take care of you."

All the wind went out of Malone's sails. "Are you sure?"

"I'm sure."

What could he say? Heaven help him, he did trust Jet. "Okay."

"Okay?"

"Don't ask me again. Just do it."

"Okay." Jet moved away.

Malone heard the click and hiss of the blowtorch flaring to life.

Fuck!

"Don't look," Jet said.

But Malone couldn't look away.

The scalpel blade caught the blue light of the blowtorch. Jet touched the sharp edge to his shin and the taut skin split, like an overripe fruit, bright red blood oozing in its wake.

Nothing could hold back his scream.

CHAPTER TWENTY-SIX

Jet

Jet was starting to feel a bit like a jinx.

What were the chances that both of his co-volunteers would suffer a broken bone and have to be evacuated?

The irony was, he felt healed by his weeks on the island. He didn't know if it was due to the healthy distance from Eloise's 'rightful' family, the natural wonder that was Tallon, or the recent uptick in orgasms...or, all three. It sure as shit wasn't Malone's sparkling personality. The ungrateful grump of a bastard could walk the plank, far as Jet was concerned.

You'd save his leg, then make him walk the plank?

Yep. That about summed it up.

"That is the ugliest wall hanging," Malone grumbled from his doorjamb leaning post. "How can you stand to look at it while you sleep?"

"First, it's a dreamcatcher. Second, you're supposed to sleep under it, not look up at it." Jet piled up all but one of their pillows on the bed to support Malone's leg. He was starting to wish he'd left Malone unconscious in the bushes.

Malone had no comprehension of the bravery and fortitude it had taken to slice through his skin. Real human skin, for fuck's sake. Never mind Malone's concern about a bird shitting in the wound. Jet had just about hurled all over Malone's leg when he'd made the first cut. God knew how he'd held himself together for the rest of that horror show. He never wanted to think of it again.

At the first sign of a pedal pulse, Jet had breathed a sigh of relief. It wasn't till he'd packed the open wound with loose gauze and wrapped the whole thing in bandages, raw flesh safely out of sight, that the whirligig in Jet's gut finally calmed.

The tarpaulin he'd rigged up to drag Malone from where he'd fallen to the rear of the radio shack got them to the base of the stairs to Jet's donga, but Malone was too heavy to carry up the stairs. Especially dead weight.

Scratch that, Jethro. Not dead. Don't say that. Don't even think it.

Hop after slow, agonising hop, Jet bore almost all of Malone's weight up the few stairs, leaned him up against the doorjamb, then unhitched himself from under Malone's arm to scoot through and sort the bedding.

"Ready?" Jet asked.

"As I'll ever be," Malone snipped, testing Jet's patience.

"I get it. This whole situation sucks balls. But it's not my fault. You could be a little grateful." The second the words were out of his mouth, Jet wished them back.

Malone was in significant pain. He shouldn't be held responsible for anything he did or said.

Hell, Jet was stressed half out of his own mind. How must Malone feel?

"It's just...my specimens. I'm..."

"Worried they'll defrost. I know." God, how Jet wished he hadn't told Malone about the power outage.

He hooked his shoulder back under Malone's right arm, bore his weight, and they shuffled together across to the bed. "That freezer has amazing insulation. If I don't open the door—which I don't plan to do—it ought to stay below freezing for at least twenty-four hours. Cross fingers Captain Thompson and his rescue crew get here by then, and that there's someone mechanical-minded on board the Opportune who can fix the power systems. Water in the generator fuel line, loose wire connection in the solar array...whatever the problem is." Not that Jet gave a crap about the fucking power systems. Compartment syndrome was the greatest risk, but it wasn't the only one. If he didn't get Malone to a hospital fast, the man could still lose his limb.

Jet got Malone securely situated in bed, shin blanketed by a bag of peas from the smaller kitchen freezer, checked his pulses for the hundred-billionth time, then took himself off to the bathroom for a shower. He'd worn gloves for the ghastly fasciotomy procedure, but every bit of him felt coated in blood and sweat and desperation, and it took every available litre of sun-warmed water to smooth the ragged edges of his soul.

When he finished, Malone was fast asleep.

With the radio down, Jet wouldn't be able to report the mid-morning synoptic measures, so he made quick notes of the data, then moved on to inspect the other changes the storm had made to the island.

Metric tonnes of sand had been swept away, revealing clutches of leathery turtle eggs alongside weathered shells that probably hadn't seen the light of day for decades. Conversely, on the opposite side of the island, new dunes buried plants and extended the beach, covering the shallowest corals.

He made as many detailed notes on the condition of the island as he could, then raced back to his donga. Thirty minutes was more than enough time to be away from Malone.

The whole day felt like a race against time. In between checks to reassure himself that Malone was still alive, Jet cleaned up where he could, detailed a list of necessary repairs that were beyond his skill set, and prepped for departure.

Everywhere he went were reminders of their time together. The places where they'd flirted. The beach where they'd first kissed. The lagoon where Malone caught him skinny-dipping. Hell, even the couch where he'd lazed most evenings, half-reading *Hornblower*, half-watching Malone's oh-so-studious, bespectacled expression as he focused down his microscope or doodled while he pondered whatever he pondered in that big brain of his.

Oh, who was Jet kidding? Only a quarter of his attention had ever been on *Hornblower*.

He'd never noticed having a nerd fetish before, but Malone Archer sure pressed those buttons, and he wasn't ready for it to end.

He thought he'd have more time.

He thought *they'd* have more time together.

Not just for their sex-capades to play out. He thought they'd have more time to connect deeper. Which was stupid of him, Jet knew. Nothing about their 'when on Tallon' agreement spelled deep. Just as summer was finite, their arrangement had to end. Their Tallon-shaped bubble would burst and they'd head back to Brisbane. Back to their regular, separate lives.

And his sadness wasn't just about Malone. Despite the island's tiny footprint, it felt huge to Jet. Freeing. A place where he could stop being so vigilant—so aware of the needs of the people in his life.

The people he cared for.

The people he loved.

A place where, for a season, he could focus on his own healing, rather than everyone else's.

No. Jet wasn't ready to give any of it up.

Not Tallon.

Not Malone.

Not the burgeoning peace in his heart.

But fate hadn't given him a choice.

As the shadows lengthened on the afternoon, Jet made a simple meal to share from the remaining edible food in the mess fridge, gave Malone yet another round of anti-inflammatories that barely took the edge off, then stayed to watch the pain-wracked tension slowly dissipate from his face.

"Did you get the power going?" Malone asked, blinking against the golden rays that sliced through the window and across his elevated leg.

"Not yet." Jet hated to admit the failure. It brought a pinch back to Malone's face. "The manual gave a few troubleshooting tips, but no dice. One of the solar panels is dangling off the roof, which is the likeliest culprit. I almost wish Vic was here." *Almost.* Because nothing about their time on the island would have been the same if Vic had stayed. "He'd know how to fix it. Or divert around it."

"Without electrocuting himself." Malone threw in.

"Exactly. As for the generator, the casing was cracked and there's a swamp inside. I couldn't see any other problem, so it might just need to dry out." Jet shrugged. "Time will tell."

Time, they didn't have.

He shifted up on his side of the bed to sift his fingers through Malone's hair. The comforting touch was as much for him as it was for Malone. Eventually, Malone's lids started to droop, the furrow between his brows softened, and he started to drift.

"Be right back," Jet whispered.

He dashed to the mess to retrieve his sketch book and Malone's favourite doodling pen. And, as the last of the sun's rays turned Malone's curls from gold to bronze, Jet captured a simple likeness drawn in lines that could never be erased.

As though their words had imagined him into being, Vic was aboard the Opportune.

His forearm was in a cast, but that did nothing to slow the man down. "Only need one hand to carry a toolbox," was his curt response to Jet's query about his arm. Jet gladly pointed out the crack in the solar array, then left him to it. He had more than enough to do to supervise Malone's transfer off the island than babysit Vic.

He'd thought single-handedly dragging Malone halfway across Tallon on a tarp had been a challenge. Getting Malone from donga to shore, shore to skiff, skiff to catamaran deck, and deck to berth, took a small army. By the time he had Malone safely stowed in a narrow berth below decks, both of them poured with sweat. A fresh bloom of blood seeped through the bandage, and Malone's skin was ashen beneath his tan.

Jet squatted beside him. "You doing okay?" Without taking the bandages down, Jet didn't know exactly how much blood Malone had lost, but it had to be significant.

Before Malone could answer, Wallace, the medic, forced his way into the tight cabin.

"How's my patient doing?"

Jet just about slapped him. Malone wasn't Wallace's anything.

He knew Wallace was a good guy. They'd gotten on well on their original voyage. But the medic had been a menace ever since he'd landed on Tallon—trying to take over, dosing Malone with God knew what drugs, usurping Jet's place in Malone's care.

Wallace hmm'd. "Looks like those dressings need reinforcing."

No shit, Sherlock.

Before Jet could voice his derision, Malone said, "Thanks, Doc. That'd be great. I could do with some more pain relief, too."

"Sure, sure. Give me a sec."

The second Wallace was gone, Jet dropped his forehead to Malone's chest and growled his frustration.

At first, Jet thought the hitch in Malone's breath was because he'd caused him pain, so he started to pull away, but Malone's hand curled around his nape, drew him closer, and the hitched breath turned to a chuckle.

"Who's a bear now?"

"Glad you're amused," Jet grumbled.

"I seem to recall someone, who shall remain nameless, told me to be more grateful."

"Yeah?" The hand trailed up and over Jet's scalp, brushing against the grain of his short hair. It made him shiver.

"Yeah."

"Sounds like a wise guy."

"Sometimes."

He lifted his head at that. "Hey! Try always."

"Gentlemen." The captain's voice interrupted them from the open doorway. "Good to see you in one piece, Malone."

"Good to be in one piece, Captain."

"Jethro. Sorry to make it so quick, but it's time to say your goodbyes. We need you above."

Jet sat back on his heels. "Above? Why?"

"The skiff's ready for the last trip to shore."

"So?"

"So, you'll need to be on it."

"Why?" Numb from exhaustion, Jet struggled to make sense of the captain's words. "I've got our things." He pointed to the backpack he'd stuffed with their clothes, toothbrushes, laptops, and a few other odds and ends he wasn't ready to part with. Once Malone was okay, they could return for the rest.

The captain looked puzzled. "We only came to pick up Malone. You're to stay here with Vic."

"What the hell? No way!"

Malone's hand came back down on his neck to soothe him.

"That's not happening," Jet said. Plain and simple.

"Vic can't be alone on the island."

"Then you'd better figure out a plan B, because I'm not staying."

"Vic got the solar power back up and running, and he's working on the generator. You don't have to worry. It's safe."

"This has nothing to do with the electricity on the island or my safety."

"Jet." Malone squeezed his nape. "It's okay. I'll be fine. You can stay."

"No." Jet glared at Captain Thompson, then at Wallace over the captain's shoulder. "I'm not leaving him."

CHAPTER TWENTY-SEVEN

Malone

Half-asleep, Malone swotted at the insect, or the bird, or whatever was making that godawful trilling sound.

It didn't stop.

He swotted at it again, to no effect.

He was just pondering opening his eyes when he heard a muffled sigh and footsteps. Then the trilling stopped.

Thank God.

"Hello?"

Jet.

Sexy Jet.

Sweet Jet.

Jet, who'd dropped everything to take care of him.

It was...a lot.

Too much for Malone to think about when he was barely awake. Barely conscious.

"He's asleep, sorry. I'm Jet, his, ah..." A pause. "Yeah, yeah, sure. We're at the hospital in Cairns. He's okay. A little beat up, but okay. The doctors said the surgery went well. They had to use an intramedullary nail and cross-screws to fix his tibia, but the fibula only needed a couple of pins. And they managed to close the fasciotomy, thank God. The stitches should come out in a week or so, but he'll be in a walking boot till the end of January. Nothing too dramatic. Nothing like it could have been, if..." A pause, then, "No prob. See you in a sec." More footsteps and the silly mm-bop tone of a video call. "Hi. Shit, you look... God, I'm sorry. I didn't mean to be an arsehole. It's just a shock to see someone who looks so much like him, and yet...not. Shit. I'm so, so sorry. Foot meet mouth. Let me put you on speaker. Here he is."

Jet's shadow fell over him.

"Bro?"

Myles?

God, how long since he'd heard his twin's voice? Barely a month, but it felt like years.

"Jesus. You okay? Since you told me you'd be out of range, we were going to leave an off-key sing-a-thon wishing you a merry Christmas. Surprised me to hear some other guy pick up. Thought for a sec you'd absconded from duty. AWOL with a sweet treat." Myles chuckled at his own joke.

"Mmm." Malone rolled his neck, seeking the source of Myles' voice. He tried to open his eyes, but his lids were so fucking heavy. He licked his lips. Everything felt as dry as if he'd swum in the dead sea, then air dried. Crusted with salt. "Myles?"

"Hang on. Let me just..." Jet's shadow disappeared, and the glow of daylight seared through his eyelids. He tracked the sound of Jet's footsteps till the shadow returned and a sliver of ice caressed his lips. "Open up, Malone."

"Mmm." He let it melt on his tongue. *So good.* "More."

"Jesus, Malone. You sound pornish." Myles chuckled.

Pornish? "Not a word." He blinked at his brother's familiar face, a soft blur on the small mobile phone screen Jet held a foot or so from his face. If he wasn't so out of it, he'd have gone cross-eyed. Or, maybe he already was and just couldn't tell.

"Is now," Myles insisted.

"Is not."

"Is."

"Boys. Behave." Jet pulled the phone back and raised a brow at Myles, then placed the screen back where Malone could see it.

"Bossy." Myles did a piss-poor job of holding back his amusement. His easy grin turning the silvery burn scar paler than usual.

Was Jet bossy? "Not usually."

"Or you've stressed him out. What did you do to him?" Myles lifted his brow.

"Me? I didn't do anything." Aside from falling off the weather box, breaking a leg, losing a fuck-tonne of blood, and having to desert all his research on the island. If anything, Malone was the one who deserved to be Olympic-level stressed. Except, he wasn't.

Nothing hurt.

His brain swam.

Floating on and on and...

"Mal." A touch brought him back, and his glasses slid into place, bringing Jet's gorgeous face into focus. *He's so beautiful.*

Like, not just regular beautiful. Hot beautiful. Sexy beautiful. Jizz my pants beautiful.

Someone snorted, and Malone shifted his bleary focus from the planes of Jet's gorgeous face to his brother on the tiny screen. "Did I say that out loud?"

"Yes, you did," Myles said.

Embarrassed, he side-eyed Jet. From the pink in Jet's cheeks, it was likely he'd heard Malone's comments. Belatedly, he tried to lift his finger to his lips to shush Myles, but it wouldn't move. A peg was stuck on it. "Silly finger." Not like Jet's fingers. They were resting there too, clutching a thick wad of blankets beside Malone's hip. It made him think of how they felt on his skin. Around his cock. The friction. The tension. The devotion to their task.

Ignoring the idiot peg, Malone made a clumsy ring with his thumb and middle finger around Jet's pointer finger. Jacking a finger wasn't nearly as much fun as jacking a cock, but it still felt good. "Mmmmmmmmmm."

"What's he doing?" Myles asked.

"Nothing." Jet shook him off.

Spoilsport.

Jet made a production of moving the peg to Malone's second finger, then planted a phallic-shaped gadget into the palm of his hand. "That's your PCA. Press the button on the end when you need pain relief."

"Hmm." He pressed the button because he was an experimenter. It beeped. "It beeped," Malone reported.

"Excellent. Good job."

"Goooood job." Malone preened. He fist-pumped. Or, at least, he tried to. For some reason, there was a slight lack of coordination between his brain and his fist.

"Oh, wow." Myles chuckled. "You've enthralled him, Jet."

"Nothing to do with me. It's the drugs. The anaesthetist gave him happy juice. It'll wear off over the next few hours. A good sleep, and he'll be close to normal."

"Mmm. Vic juice," Malone slurred.

"No. Not Vic juice. Different juice. Happy juice. Pain-free juice."

"Who's Vic?" Myles asked.

"Nobody," they both answered, then Jet added, "One of the employees at the weather station."

"Uh-huh. I remember when he had his appendix out. He was loopy, but nothing like this. Check out how he's looking at you all dopey-eyed. He's totally gone on you."

"No, he's not."

"Nope, nope, nope, nope, nope," Malone protested too. He was not gone on Jet. Not even a little bit. He had things to do. He had priorities. And Jet had priorities, too. Different priorities. Which were...

Nothing came to mind. Nothing but how beautiful Jet was, inside and out.

It was intimidating. Impossible to measure up.

Malone tried to make a true impact with his work, but he knew he didn't have Jet's knack with people. Malone was about as far from a man whisperer as it was possible to be. And yet, Jet had put up with him. Stuck by him.

I'm not leaving him.

Those had been Jet's words on the boat, when all Malone had wanted was to cling to him and whimper. Pathetic, really, how relieved he'd been when Jet had stayed by his side. Selfish, too. He'd not given any thought to what Jet might want or need.

"Hi," he said to Jet.

"Hi yourself. Myles is still with us on video chat."

"Myles?"

"Your twin."

Myles' snort was an audible work of art. "Definitely AWOL with something sweet. It's a good look on you, bro."

"More like away with the fishes," Jet grumbled.

Malone looked around. He didn't see any fish, just the usual pale walls of a hospital room, monitoring equipment with their squiggly lines and incessant bleeps. And Jet there, beside him, looking pinched and tired.

"You are not a fish." Malone reassured him.

"Cheers, mate. Good to know."

Myles cleared his throat, regaining Malone's attention. "You up for a chat with your favourite niece and nephew?"

Flo and Paris? "Heck, yes."

"They had a mountain of new toys under the tree, and they adore their Christmas present from Uncle Malone." Myles leaned in to whisper low, "FYI, you got them a worm farm."

"A worm farm?"

"Well, I couldn't exactly buy them a sea cucumber farm, so...it was the next best thing."

"Yeah. Okay." He probably would've got them salamanders, or frogs, or some other animal that lived in water, but worms weren't a terrible choice.

"Florence has already pulled the tail off one of the poor things, so Paris named the rest. He says if they've got names, they can't be killed."

"See!" Jet thwacked him in the arm. "I told you."

"Ow." Malone pouted.

"Sorry."

Myles grinned. "I'll go get them in a sec. What about you, Jet? Do you have any siblings?"

"He's got a double-decker Dick."

"Malone!"

"What? It's the truth."

Myles grinned. "I wasn't asking about his fun appendages, brother. Single or double."

"Oh my God!" Jet dropped his head down on their joined hands. It felt nice.

"His mum and dad are in Tanzania," Malone said.

"Tasmania," Jet muttered against his hand.

"Exactly. I bet they miss you." *I'd miss Jet if he was a whole country away.* "Have you talked to them? Family is important. You should go be with them. Why aren't you with them?"

Jet sat up. "Because I'm here with you, dickwad."

Rude. "That's no excuse. I don't need you. I'm fine here. It's Christmas. You ought to be with your family. Not Dick, of course. But with your folks. And Shane. People who love you. People who you love."

"I..." Jet stared at him for a long second, a flush rising up his neck. Then his eyes scuttled away.

Malone missed the connection instantaneously.

"You're not in this with me. Not fully," Jet muttered. "I don't know why I thought anything different."

Something in Malone's foggy brain was screaming at him, but he didn't know what else to say as Jet shoved back the chair, stood up, and yanked his phone from the charger on Malone's nightstand.

"Good to meet you, Myles."

"You too, Jet. Thanks for everything you did for my brother."

Jet shrugged. "It's what I do."

"What? Save idiots from themselves?"

"Care too much." A little quirk came to Jet's lips. If Malone could, he'd have chased it and kissed it before it was gone.

"Just enough, I reckon." Myles said. "He's drugged, you know. Doesn't know what he's saying."

"Maybe not right this second, but I've seen Malone under the influence. No filter. Only truth."

"Two truths." Malone reminded Jet. "One lie." He finally got his finger to work, holding it up to demonstrate. Not that he was telling a lie. Jet should be with his family. With the people who loved him. Who he loved in return.

It was just that Malone didn't fit any of those criteria, so he snapped his mouth shut and said nothing as Jet walked through the doorway, then disappeared from view.

"Bro, what the hell is wrong with you?"

Malone wrenched his attention from the empty doorway to the phone in his lap, where Myles glared at him. "What?"

"That guy left Tallon Island for you. He was there for you when you needed him the most. You don't dismiss someone who cares about you like that. Who you care about in return."

"I didn't dismiss him."

"Yeah, you did."

Had he? No. "What happens on Tallon, stays on Tallon." That was their deal. And nothing about Malone's situation—stuck in a hospital bed with a broken leg, barely able to think, let alone get his dick up for a hot shag—resembled the man Jet desired. "I gave him his freedom."

"He's not one of your test subjects. You can't pick him up, then put him down, and move on without leaving an impact. On him, or on you. Face it. You're pushing him away because he doesn't fit into your self-declared mission to heal humanity, one burn at a time. Trouble is, somewhere out on that reef, you caught a bad case of feelings. And so did he."

"Phtht."

"Don't be an idiot, brother. Admitting you have serious feelings won't limit your ability to succeed. After all, you wouldn't even be on this mission if you didn't love me so damn much."

Serious feelings for Jet? "Nonsense." Malone's attention strayed up to the pair of snowflakes taped to the opposite wall—a little bit of Christmas Jet had prized enough to bring with him from Tallon. Jet's was a chaotic mix of shapes and colour, while Malone's was a crisp white, precision-cut example of the holiday art form. Both were symmetrical, but they couldn't have been more different. "I'm just trying to be considerate. You said it yourself. He already gave up Tallon for me. He shouldn't have to give up Christmas with his family, too."

Myles threw up his hands. "He'd already given up a family Christmas to spend the summer on Tallon. You didn't choose that for him, Malone. He did."

"Huh. That..." made way too much sense.

Malone's hair crinkled on the pillow as he twisted his neck to stare at the empty doorway. "Do you think he'll come back?"

"Why would he?" Myles' sharp reply cut like a blade.

Why would he, indeed?

Chapter Twenty-eight

Jet

"Ungrateful sod." Jet huddled over the fifth-rate coffee he'd scored in the hospital cafeteria. Around him, the garish Christmas decorations flashed with far too much joy. Pretty soon, they'd throw him out. Then, technically, he'd be homeless.

Thirty-six hours after he'd found Malone at the base of the weather box, Jet was exhausted. Only, he wasn't the only one in Cairns seeking shelter and comfort. According to the rolling news streaming across the bottom edge of the muted television screen, the same fast-moving storm that had ripped across Tallon hit the coastal city a few hours later.

Cairns was used to cyclones, but the speed and timing of the tropical storm surge, coinciding with high tide, meant flooding was extensive. Add that to wind damage and widespread power outages, and the city was deep into disaster mode.

By rights, he ought to be out there helping with the clean-up. But all he wanted to do was find a safe place to lay his weary head and wallow in self-pity. Malone's words scrolled through his mind.

Why aren't you with them? You should go be with them.

And then the clincher.

I don't need you.

How dare Malone brush him off like that? After everything he'd done for the man. After everything he'd given up.

Go be with the people who love you, Jet.

AKA, not me.

If Jet ever needed a hint that the man felt nothing real for him, that'd be it.

Jet supposed he ought to be grateful that Malone was so keen on facts and figures. On telling the truth. Otherwise, Jet might've gone on believing that they had something special—a true connection worth risking his heart for. He might've gone on trusting that Malone was as invested as he was in a relationship beyond Tallon. But, no. Turned out, they barely knew each other. Seeing Myles' face—so like Malone's, and yet...not—was proof enough of that. Myles' visible scars were a punch-in-the-gut reminder of how Malone had reacted to the blowtorch. While Jet had honed in on the blood, Malone had blanched at the sight of the flames.

His heart ached at the memory of Malone's fear. At the time, he'd thought it natural. Nobody in their right mind would willingly be cut open. But, seeing Myles' face made Jet realise it was so much more. Malone carried scars, too. Internal scars. Invisible to the uncaring eye.

But Jet saw them.

He cared. God help him. He did.

But Malone didn't want his help. Didn't trust Jet enough to tell him the truth in his heart.

Which left Jet alone again. Discarded in a tourist town, with nobody and nothing to his name.

He swallowed the dregs of the crap coffee. The bitter taste slid down his gullet and swirled in his gut.

Fuck my life.

A woman in scrubs trundled around the cafeteria with a loaded trolley, handing out blankets, pillows and towels. When she got to him, she asked, "Do you have kin in the hospital, dear? Family? A significant other?"

"Oh, ah…" Jet desperately wanted to say yes. *Yes, I have kin here. Yes, he's significant. Yes, I need to stay close to him. Simply, yes.* But that clearly wasn't the truth. Not from Malone's end. Instead, Jet sidestepped the question and asked, "The hospital's letting us sleep here?"

"It's not terribly comfortable, but if you have kin in the hospital, and you're affected by the storm and unable to get home, you're free to sleep here tonight. Here you are, dear." She handed him a stack from her trolley. "If you don't mind me saying so, you look like you could use the rest."

Her kindness was the last straw. The final tendril of steel holding him together unravelled and Jet collapsed back into the stiff plastic seat. "Thank you. That's very generous."

"Thank the taxpayers, dear. Merry Christmas." She flashed him a tired smile and moved on to the next group of stranded souls.

Jet managed a few hours of broken sleep burrito-rolled in a cotton blanket on the inhospitable cafeteria floor, and woke feeling like death warmed over. As pre-breakfast clanging started up in the kitchen, he tidied up, visited the bathroom, and headed outside.

Originally built on the elevated end of the foreshore to take advantage of healing sea breezes, the hospital opened out onto a narrow ribbon of parkland that the storm had turned into a strip of debris and mud and sodden grass.

A hint of night cool still hung in the air, but it wouldn't last long. Jet didn't need access to any official weather instruments to tell him the relative humidity was fucking high. Within seconds, his t-shirt was stuck to his back, and he didn't even want to think about what was going on below the waist. Parboiled testicles, anyone?

Still, it was a relief to be out in the open air.

Jet yawned and stretched his arms overhead, doing his best to de-kink his spine and banish some of the tension that had taken up residence in his shoulders.

It made a microscopic difference.

He juggled his phone, debating whether to call his folks.

Malone was wrong about a lot of things, but he wasn't wrong about the importance of family. Especially around the holidays. Plus, his dad would love to hear about Tallon and the storm that had driven them off the island. Hell, his parents would even listen to him whine about Malone, so long as he kept it PG. But Jet hesitated. It'd be too hard to give them an honest update without mentioning the sticky situation with Eloise and her estate. How was he going to admit that he'd learned who his birth mother was, had secretly worked for her, had practically lived with her, all without a peep to them? No. That was a conversation best left for a day when he wasn't already feeling like an empty shell, battered and alone on a shore.

His second option was to call Shane. After all, why be a lonely island when he could call a friend? Shane was always up for a bitch session, and it wasn't like his best friend wouldn't eventually get the whole sorry story out of him.

Hand sweaty in the muggy heat, he searched for Shane's contact.

"Honey bunch! Merry Boxing Day! How goes it?"

"Hey, Flash. Got a sec?"

"Got a few for you. Wait, are you calling from your hammock? Bet you are. Jealous." Shane muffled his end of the phone. "Between you and me, my friend, you got the better deal. Hoo-aah, has it got wild around here. I need a nanny. Or maybe a manny. That'd be cool. Double up the testosterone in the house for Dillon. Poor little guy is swamped by chicks most days. Anyhoo...what can I do you for? Lay it on me. Dillon! I said two spoons of Milo. Not twelve, for frigg's sake! Sorry 'bout that, Jet. Kristy's in the hospital, and this place is a circus."

"Oh, fuck. I'm sorry. Is she alright? Is the baby alright?"

"We think so. I'm heading in as soon as Kristy's mum gets here. Might be early labour. We'll see. Kid's gotta come out eventually. Might as well be now. Am-I-right?"

"I guess." Jesus. And he'd been thinking *his* life was in chaos. No way was Jet going to lay his existential crisis at his best friend's door. He thought quickly. "Just wanted to let you know I'm back on the mainland."

"Already? What about that island gig?"

"Slight hiccup. Nothing to worry about." Shane was clearly far too occupied to hear about a little old storm.

"You coming back down here?"

"Don't know yet. It's...complicated." And nothing Shane needed to worry about on top of the birth of his third child. "Call me when the little alien arrives, will you?"

"Couldn't stop me, mate. You sure you're alright? If you need to talk, I'm here."

"I'm fine. I can take care of myself."

Always have.

A chime rang in the background.

"Fu-udge, there's the doorbell. Dillon, let in your grandma. Jet, I gotta go. People to see, babies to greet."

"Kiss Kristy for me, will you? Tell her she's one special lady."

"Always. See ya in a few."

"Yeah. See ya," Jet answered, but there was nobody on the other end to hear.

Deflated, Jet tucked his phone away.

He thought about heading back to the hospital to check in with the nurses on the ward. Make sure Malone was okay. But why go where he wasn't wanted? Wasn't needed?

He stood there, listless, for God knew how long, until a small group on clean-up duty, wearing fluoro vests, chunky gloves, and streaks of mud, flanked him as they passed by.

"Want some help?" he asked.

If Malone didn't need him, he'd make himself useful elsewhere.

They stopped, and the guy who seemed to be in charge said, "Cheers, mate. You got some gloves?"

"Nope. Sorry."

"No worries. We'll pair you up with Donatella. She's got some spares in the backpack."

Before long, Jet wasn't just dripping with sweat. Every bit of him was covered in grit and mud and disgusting slime. Donatella—six-foot-four in platform steel-toed boots—gleefully informed him that most of the muck had percolated up from the overloaded storm sewers.

"Lovely."

She grinned. "Just think how good a cold lager and a sausage sizzle will taste after this."

"Divine," he agreed, wholeheartedly. It was the shift in perspective that he needed. What man needed mutual love and affection when he could have a full stomach and a beer buzz instead?

Fuelled by donated sandwiches and energy drinks, Jet and the team worked together for the remainder of the day, roaming wherever they were needed. They helped clear out debris from parks and playgrounds, schools and homes, and stacked the wreckage on the nature strip for council trucks to remove.

It didn't take long for Donatella to get the whole sorry story of Tallon, and the storm, and his tangle with Malone, out of him. By the time they'd completed a full circuit of the neighbourhood, she'd spread the story of his and Malone's *daring escape from Hell Island* to anyone who'd listen, including a live news crew at their final, sausage-sizzle pit stop, who fell hook, line, and sinker for her overly dramatic retelling.

"And here he is! The hero of the hour!" She cried out as he made his way back to her, their second round of sausages in hand.

Jet would've beat a hasty retreat, except death-by-shoe was not on his wish list. Better to face a pesky journalist than a hangry Donatella.

He was so exhausted from their beast of a day, and the many beastly days before that, that all Jet did was stand there, glazy-eyed, doing his best to quell Donatella's more outlandish claims of his supposed heroics with, "It wasn't quite like that," and, "I was only doing my job," and, "yes, it was worth the risk," and, "It wasn't me who did the rescuing, that was Captain Thompson and his crew," and, "Of course we intend to return. Or, at least, I do."

Fuck my life.

When pushed to describe how he truly felt about his time on the island, Jet scrambled to think of a way to say 'life changing' without blurting out his heart and soul to the world. "It's a special place, with special memories," seemed the safest way to go.

"Did you have to?" he asked her when the TV crew finally left them to their cold sausages and warm lager.

"A juicy story like yours? How could I not?" She raised her greasy hand for a high-five. "Whoop! It's official. You're a true hero, Jet."

"God, no."

"Hell's, yes! A legend. And I get to say I knew you when."

"*You* created the legend. I only did what anyone with half a heart would do," Jet protested.

"Half a heart...half a brain...all the courage."

"Shush, you."

She ignored that. "Come here, love. We need a selfie together."

"Good idea." He stretched his arm up and around her broad shoulders and gave a cheesy peace sign to match her grin. "Send me a copy, will you? I need proof that I did time with the Queen of Cairns."

"Hey!" She thwacked him across the chest. "Be nice."

Jet rubbed the smarting ribs that encased his heart. "I'm always nice."

"And that's why you're a legend."

Jet rolled his eyes. He couldn't win.

"Come on. I need a third snag, and you need to go find that man of yours. Make happy with his sausage." She waggled her eyebrows. "Or his buns."

Just the thought of seeing Malone brought a fission of anticipation, but Jet quashed it with a slog of warm beer. "There will be no making happy with either. I told you. We're done." He was sure of it.

God, he was such a sad sack.

He'd told Donatella the truth. Personally, he and Malone were done. But technically, they were still colleagues. He couldn't just turn his back on the bastard. Not entirely. Not even if he'd wanted to. Which he did. He really, really did.

"Me thinks the man doth protest too much."

"Yeah, well, I just wish Malone would—" Jet stopped that thought in its tracks and sniffed his displeasure, inadvertently getting a whiff of himself.

Eww!

More like a sad sack of overripe sardines.

"I need a shower and a vat of antibiotics."

Both of which can be found in Malone's hospital room, Jethro.

"Grr."

"Who are you annoyed with now?" Donatella asked.

"Nobody. The universe." *Myself.*

"Sorry, love. Can't help you there."

"If wishes were horses, eh?" Donatella had called it right—Jet did protest too much. He might've been the one to come to Malone's rescue, but a secret, stupid, misguided part of him wanted Malone to be the one to ride in on his metaphorical white horse. To claim Jet and take him home. Forever.

You can want him all you like, Jethro. If he doesn't want you, then...

"I'm such an idiot."

"No, you're not. You're an idealist and a dreamer. There's a difference."

"He's a dreamer too, you know. I can see it."

"Mm-hmm." Donatella patted his arm, probably spelling 'poor, deluded soul' in morse code. "You take care, love. I'll look you up if I'm ever in Brisbane."

"You better."

"Meanwhile, I'll be seeing you on the TV." She walked backwards with her hands clutched to her chest, and put on the most god-awful high falsetto. "My hero."

Jet groaned.

Fuck my life.

By the time he got back to the hospital's main entrance, a mini-swarm of media awaited him. The reporters wanted more of the hottest good news story to hit storm-ravaged Far North Queensland, but Jet was having none of it. He ducked his head and scooted through the entrance unseen, then hurried to the elevator that would take him to the surgical ward on the upper floor. Its slow rise gave him way too much time to dwell on the irony that he was seeking out Malone for a safe port from the media storm.

"All I want is a shower," he told the judgmental ding of the elevator as it reached the right floor. "Nothing else."

Liar, liar, pants on fire.

"Yeah, well…" He paused at the sink outside Malone's closed hospital room to scrub his hands properly. Good hand hygiene was crucial in acute care settings. That was a fact. And he wasn't going to be the one to mess up Malone's recovery. Never mind that six minutes of scrubbing might've been a touch too long. It wouldn't hurt. And nobody was there to judge his healthy choice of a delay tactic.

He eyed the closed door. What was Malone doing on the other side? Regretting his choices? Wishing Jet was there?

"The legend returns."

"Ah! Fuck!" He spun around, heart tripping at the sight of Malone in a wheelchair, left leg outstretched in a thigh-to-toe brace, pushed by some young guy with a look in his eye that Jet didn't like. "Jesus Christ. Warn a guy."

"You came back," Malone said, his voice stiff.

Stiff with pain, with anger, with what? Jet hated that he didn't know. "Just for a shower," he bit out as the guy put his hand on Malone's shoulder, and Malone didn't shrug him off.

"Everything alright, Malone?" The guy asked.

"It's fine, Chris. This is Jet, my..." Malone tilted his head, searching for the right word.

"Colleague," Jet filled in the blank with the most innocuous term he could think of. It hardly did their complicated relationship justice.

Malone's bottom lip twitched and the little divot underneath deepened into shadow, the only sign that he was bothered.

"Jet, this is Chris, my physio."

Duh, Jethro. The polo shirt with the hospital logo ought to have clued him into that. "Hi." He gave an idiotic wave and shifted his weight to the other foot.

Seeing Malone again, especially seeing him up and sparking, was a shock. Not because Jet didn't want him to recover from his injury. That was fucking awesome. But it hadn't even been twenty-four hours since he'd stomped out of the hospital room, and Jet felt pulverized, while Malone looked fresh as a daisy. The change was remarkable. Of course, Jet didn't want Malone to be in pain, or stressed, or traumatised by the events that had slingshot them back to the mainland, but the erasure of those stress markers seemed to erase the good with the bad. As if none of it had happened. As if Jet hadn't happened. As if they were nothing.

It was galling.

"Can you get the door, please?" Chris asked.

"Oh, yeah. Sure, mate. Sorry." Jet gladly took the distraction.

He followed Malone and Chris inside and stood awkwardly in the corner while the physio helped Malone back into bed, checked he was okay, then left.

And then they were alone.

Jet looked anywhere but at Malone. His eyes skittered from the half-empty backpack hung over the visitor's chair, containing all their worldly goods. Next, to the two snowflakes still taped to the wall, reminding him of what they'd created together...and what they'd lost. Then, to the gathering darkness outside that turned the windows to mirrors, and revealed Malone, silently staring back at him.

Those cold eyes gave Jet the jolt he needed. "Do you need anything? No? Good." He didn't give Malone a chance to answer before he grabbed the backpack and swept into the bathroom, locking himself inside.

Time to focus on what you need, Jethro.

He didn't quite know what that was, but it sure wasn't Malone Archer adding to his future uncertainty.

CHAPTER TWENTY-NINE

Malone

How had it all gone so terribly wrong?

Malone knew it was a stupid question to ask himself.

He was at fault. Zero doubt about that.

He didn't blame Jet for finding every excuse under the sun to be anywhere other than in his hospital room, talking to him, sharing air with him. Malone probably would have done the same if their circumstances were reversed.

But the situation wasn't reversed, and all Malone wanted to do was reach out from his hospital bed and touch—to smooth his thumb along Jet's sun kissed jaw, shiny with lotion, and tweak Jet's sweet earlobe, with all the subtlety of a kid with a crush, craving attention.

Look at me!

But Jet wouldn't look. In fact, Jet was doing a brilliant job of ignoring him. That was, until visitor hours finished and the ward nurses demanded Jet stop pacing the corridors while other patients were trying to rest. Much to Jet's chagrin, they shooed him back into Malone's room with a stack of pink paper pathology forms and a dangerously sharp pair of scissors.

"You forgot to wear your hat," Malone said when there was a short lull in the snipping.

That was a stupid thing to say. It was his fault Jet had left his ridiculous yellow hat on Tallon. His fault Jet had left Tallon at all. His fault Jet had stormed out, slept God knew where, and wound up on a storm-recovery crew making a hero of himself with the locals.

Correction—lending his already heroic self to the locals. If Malone had needed any more proof of Jet's true worth to humanity, which he didn't, that effort for the people of Cairns would've done it.

The only negative Malone wasn't willing to take responsibility for was the pink paper blizzard surrounding Jet's chair. He just hoped that when Jet got to the bottom of the stack, the arts and crafts therapy would have done its job, Jet would speak to him, and all would go back to normal. In other words, Jet would roll his eyes and call Malone a jerk. Then they could move on, together...

Snip, snip, snip, went the scissors.

...maybe just not quite yet.

Malone pressed the button on his PCA and waited for the pain relief to take effect. His leg didn't need it. Everything was feeling fine and dandy down there. Thank fuck. But his heart? That was a whole different story.

Snip.

Malone closed his eyes and willed the drugs to take him under.

He woke from his drug-induced nap to Jet's hushed voice, taut with tension.

"Are you sure? Like, one-hundred percent su—? Okay... Yeah. No, I wish you'd asked me before contacting them. They have no idea that I found her... No. I don't know. I'm up here in... You saw me on the national news? ... Wow. Okay. Umm..."

Malone wanted to throttle whoever was on the other end, not letting Jet finish a fucking sentence.

"I could get on a plane, I guess, but... A week from today? Isn't that New Year's Day? ... Of course..." Jet's face hardened. "If he wants it, he can buy it off me... No, I don't know if Malone is—" Jet looked at him and saw he was awake. "Sorry, I have to go. No, I have your number. I'll call you back. Bye."

Malone is what? Malone wanted to ask, but he didn't. Last time he'd spoken to Jet, he'd made a royal arse-hat of himself.

Malone licked his dry lips.

Stay with me.

We belong together.

He had neither concrete proof nor objective data to back up his claim. But somehow, he knew it was true. He couldn't say either wish aloud after his idiocy on Christmas day, spouting lies that he thought Jet ought to be anywhere other than by Malone's side.

'Go be with the people you love, people who love you.'

Ugh. I'm such an idiot.

He shifted uncomfortably against the sweaty, wrinkled sheets. Dozens of pink snowflakes speckled the wall in front of him, overwhelming the original pair. Not all the pink sheets were cut like snowflakes. Some were square. Some were curvy. Some were jagged polyhedrons that defied classification. And one was a heart. A wonky, spiky, pink heart, with a giant, frowning gash in the middle.

Malone's hope plummeted.

He braved another glance at Jet, who stared back at him with eyes wide, cheeks drawn, wavering on his feet as though a soft breeze might blow him over. Was he shocked? Tired? Hurt?

Malone couldn't remain silent. Not forever. But every word seemed like a risk. What if he said something else wrong and made it worse?

I'm sorry.

Please stay.

"Are you okay?" It seemed like the safest option.

"I don't know." Jet swallowed thickly. "That was the lawyer. Eloise's lawyer. He saw me on the news."

"What did he want?" Malone's words came out rough at the reminder of seeing Jet on the news, ever so humble in his selfless care for others, being championed by some stranger.

That should've been you, Archer.

"Dick pushed to have the will read on Christmas Eve. I missed it because of the storm and.... all this." Jet waved over the hospital bed and Malone.

Malone didn't know much about legal wrangles, but he doubted Jet's absence from the reading of the will would give anyone licence to change it. "What happened?"

"Eloise. She...she gave me her house. Her home."

"Are you serious?" Malone grabbed the bed controls and sat himself up.

The haunted look turned to anger. "He talked to my parents. Got scanned images of my passport from them. He said that was enough to affirm who I am, which is total bullshit. The only reason I've inherited anything at all is because of Jebediah—who she gave away. Not me—Jethro. Richard already thought I was a mooch, and that was just from staying on Eloise's property for a few days after she died. Can you imagine what he'll be calling me now? Everyone will be wondering why I, Jethro Crane, have inherited a small fortune in property from the woman who died in my care. It sounds like some overly dramatic made-for-television movie. Nurse cares for an old woman. Nurse gets in her good graces. Nurse takes the old woman for everything she's worth. God. If I was Richard, I'd be contesting too."

"Wow."

"Yeah. Big wow. The lawyer says he needs me down there by next week."

A sharp knock made them both jump. The door swung wide open and his surgeon barged inside. The doctor looked from him to Jet and back again. "Evening, Malone. How are we today? Hope I haven't disturbed."

Too bad if you had.

Into their continued silence, the doctor clapped his hands. "Excellent. We've got good news and good news. Which do you want to hear first?" He laughed at his own lame joke.

Malone folded his arms across his chest and waited. Belligerence probably wasn't the smartest way to go, but he was all out of fucks to give. His leg was either fixed, or it wasn't. Jet, on the other hand, needed his attention, and he couldn't give it while another soul invaded their space.

"Okey-dokey. As we discussed last night, the surgery went very well. No problem with reducing your fractures, and the nurses tell me the fasciotomy wound we managed to close looked clean when they dressed it earlier this afternoon. A bit of oozing, which is normal, and some residual inflammation, but there's no sign of infection, and we're confident the risk of compartment syndrome is past. You'll be in that fixed-angle brace while we watch to make sure the fasciotomy wound is healing. After that, it's a walking boot, then rigorous physio to get your leg muscles back to full strength. You seem to be tolerating oral opioids, so we'll remove the PCA and IV line after you've had your last dose of antibiotics. You're otherwise fit and healthy, so, if everything's a-okay by tomorrow morning, you'll be free to discharge." He rolled back on his heels, clearly chuffed with himself.

What do you want? A trophy for doing your job?

"That's great. A huge relief. Right, Malone?" Jet tapped his good foot, and Malone felt himself soften.

"Yeah. Thanks, doc." At Jet's raised eyebrow, he added, "Appreciate it."

"Right. Well. You're welcome. We'll book you into the orthopaedic clinic in a week to get those sutures out and review your care—"

"Do I have to be here for that?" Malone interrupted. "In Cairns, I mean? It's only a few sutures. Any nurse or GP can take those out, right?"

"Oh, ah, well..." The doctor's attention swivelled between them. "It's more than a few sutures. It was an extensive wound. You'll need repeat x-rays and a surgical review, followed by an extended period of physio treatment. If you're thinking of going back to that island, I can't give you clearance for—"

"No. Not back to Tallon. Not yet. I meant Brisbane." Malone met Jet's eyes. "We need to get home within the week. Jet needs to be in Brisbane. And I need to be with Jet."

Simple.

"Flying is contraindicated after an injury such as yours. For starters, there's a risk of developing a DVT."

"Jet can drive us." A few days stuck in a car together should provide ample time for him to prove his commitment. That, or die trying. "Plus, he's a nurse. He knows what he's doing. He's one-hundred percent capable of taking care of me. Right Jet?"

"Malone." Jet's frown deepened. But Malone wasn't going to be discouraged.

For days he'd been at the mercy of stormy weather, of excruciating pain, of conflicting emotions.

No more.

His vision had cleared. Jet wasn't a distraction. He wasn't flighty or superficial. He was creative and insightful—a counterbalance to Malone's meticulous, analytical nature. Jet was what he needed and what he wanted. All he had to do was stop fighting it...and convince Jet that he was in it for real, beyond the summer. Beyond Tallon.

"You know orthopaedic surgeons in Brisbane, right doc?" Malone pushed again. "You could hook me up with a clinic down there. Send down my records. X-rays and such."

"Oh, well...I don't know."

"Isn't that all digital these days?" He pressed.

"Well, yes, but—"

"Great. Done."

And it was.

CHAPTER THIRTY

Jet

Jet needs to be in Brisbane, and I need to be with Jet.

Malone's words were a tender new shoot, slowly unfurling in Jet's heart, but confusion still swam in his mind.

He didn't know what to think. One minute Malone was telling him to go, the next begging him to stay. Jet was more at sea on solid ground than he'd ever been on the shifting sands of Tallon. He was tired and cranky, and he'd spent most of the evening pacing the hospital corridors for fear of snapping at Malone. Of saying something he'd forever regret.

Not that his uncertainty stopped him from cozying up to the man's side in the middle of the night when Malone's short, "for fuck's sake, Jet. Get in here with me," drove Jet out of the hospital visitor's chair and into Malone's bed. The space was tight. Two full-grown men squeezed into a single bed, with Malone lying flat and Jet on his side. But Jet was beyond exhausted, and it was such a relief to stretch out. He wordlessly pulled up the side rails to hold them in, rested his head on the free corner of Malone's pillow, stuck his thumb into the waistband of his briefs so he wouldn't accidentally pull Malone into his arms, and fell fast asleep.

The real trouble didn't begin till the morning when Jet woke to monster morning wood and a middle-aged nurse hovering over them with a temperature probe, saying, "Sorry to disturb, but if you'd just turn a little so I can get to your ear, Mr. Archer." And Malone, the bastard, doing exactly as requested, making out like he was a model patient, turning his face so that he and Jet were a bare inch from each other on the pillow. "Lovely. Thank you," she said.

No. Not lovely.

"Jerk," Jet muttered beneath his breath.

With a knowing smirk, Malone ever so slightly shifted his hip against Jet's rabid cock. It wasn't a bold move, but Jet felt it down to his toes. Malone blew him the subtlest of air kisses. "Morning, beautiful."

"I'm going to kill you," Jet replied, loud and clear.

The nurse jerked back. Malone's smirk deepened. And Jet rolled his eyes in frustration. "I didn't mean it literally."

"That's a relief," they both said, meaning completely different things.

Jet groaned and, for lack of a better option, hid his face in the hollow of Malone's neck.

Fuck my life.

After the nurse finally finished her routine observations and delivered the promised last dose of IV antibiotics, she made haste out of the room, shutting the door firmly behind her.

Malone tracked her movements. "Clever one, she is."

"Do you think she knew?"

"That you're packing a salami in your sarong? Yes. I think she knew."

"Fuck off." Jet didn't care if he hurt Malone as he contorted himself to reach for the bed rail latch, released himself from imprisonment, and dashed to the bathroom for a cold shower and blessed relief.

It took a while.

When Jet got out, he found Malone in a wheelchair, his leg outstretched, dressed in his university polo and Jet's second-favourite sarong, with a sheaf of papers on his lap and a satisfied grin spread across his face. "Ready for the road, dear?"

Jet grimaced. "I'm not your 'dear' anything."

"Surely, that's up for me to decide. If you're dear to me, then you're my dear."

"You and your twisted logic."

"There's nothing twisted about that. Simple cause and effect."

Unbelievable. "Whatever you need to tell yourself, *Sweetness*."

"Oh, I like that." Malone swivelled the chair, aiming for the doorway. "Grab my crutches for me, would you? I've called a taxi to take us to the marina, but we need to drop by the hospital pharmacy on the way out. Come on. Chop. Chop. The road's awaiting."

Jet blinked, flummoxed by the turnaround in Malone's demeanour. "Who are you? And who stole my surly Malone?" he asked, but the room was vacant—not an answer in sight.

As per Malone's plan, the trip to the marina to collect his SUV from the long-term parking lot went like clock-work. They cleared Cairns' light industry and commercial sprawl and were out on the open highway south within the hour, with Jet in the driver's seat and Malone, literally, back-seat-driving.

"I do know how to read a map, you know," Jet eventually snapped. "*And* I have this whiz-bang navigator you had installed in your own car."

"Sorry. It's just I..."

"Think you're always right. I know."

"That's not true. I can be wrong."

"Oh, really? When?"

Malone put down his phone and met Jet's gaze in the rear-view mirror. "Yesterday. And the day before that. And a dozen-dozen times in the days before that. I make mistakes all the time. If I wasn't prepared to admit that, I wouldn't be a scientist."

Stumped, there was a beat of silence before Jet had to look away. Back to the road. For safety's sake, he told himself. No other reason.

"I am sorry, Jet. For the stress. For the push away. But I'm not sorry for asking you to stay. That wasn't a mistake."

As far as grovels went, it was semi-decent, but Jet wasn't ready to hear it. He flicked off the air-conditioner, pressed the buttons to roll down every window, low as they'd go, and slung his elbow out into the hot, buffeting air that drowned out any chance of conversation.

Jet needs to be in Brisbane, and I need to be with Jet.

Eventually, he'd give Malone the time of day again. Forgive him. But not yet. Not till Jet could trust himself not to fall face-first into a wallow the way he had on Christmas day. He needed to be more self-sufficient than that. Safe within the bounds of his own skin.

Zen, Jethro. Zen.

The pep talk didn't do much good.

Late morning at the height of summer, the highway was a shimmery heat haze. Jet reached to flip the sun visor down and let his thoughts drift as the wheels ate up the miles. It wasn't just Malone that had thrown Jet for a loop, it was Eloise too. More specifically, what Eloise had left in her wake.

Over and over, Jet heard echoes of the lawyer's voice.

"Eloise Price left her house to you...."

...to you...to you...to you....

She'd knowingly, willingly left him her home. Him. Her secret son.

Jet couldn't get his head around it.

For weeks, he'd kicked himself for not confronting Eloise while she was alive. He should have told her who he was. He should have demanded an explanation. But he'd let fear win—the fear of facing yet another rejection.

If only he'd known that, all along, she'd known who he was and stayed silent...asking for nothing but his care and companionship.

Her reticence was unfathomable. And yet, he'd done the same. Like mother, like son; he'd held onto his fear and settled for a quasi-sense of belonging.

They could have been a loving family for each other. If only she, or he, had been brave enough to speak up.

Jet flicked a quick glance in the rear-view mirror.

Was he making the same mistake with Malone?

Was he resisting voicing his hurt and anger all to protect his heart? To prevent more hurt? To stave off the inevitable rejection?

What kind of sense did that make?

The realistic kind, Jethro.

Fuck that.

Wasn't he just caging the hurt in? Pushing away any chance at love? Fearful of accepting true affection?

Jet squeezed the leather steering wheel, fingers itching to squish a ball of clay—to make something positive out of the knot of tension he held inside.

"You okay?" Came Malone's low voice from the back seat. Serious as heartbreak.

His hand warmed Jet's shoulder. Gave him a gentle squeeze.

It wasn't much, but it felt real.

"Is this real?" Jet asked before he could stop the words from tripping off of his tongue. Flinging him out of his comfort zone.

Immediately, Jet wished them back.

Reverse! Reverse!

Beep, beep, beep!

Had Malone heard him?

Please, no.

"Yes."

Fuck!

It was all getting away from him.

Jet's mouth went dry.

What he needed was a sounding board. A chance to purge all his angst. To get it off his chest. Without consequence. And the only way Jet knew to do that was to talk to Shane—his go-to advisor. Shane would give him the fresh perspective he needed.

"I need to make a call." Jet said as he searched for a decent place on the rough gravel shoulder to pull the SUV over.

"Whatever you need," Malone said with irritating reasonableness.

For a country so large, the roads sure were narrow. In the distance, Jet saw a turn off to a farm gate. He flicked on the indicator, squeezed the brakes, then diverted off the tarmac. The wheels cracked and popped on the rough gravel as he brought the SUV to a stop, then shut off the engine.

To get any privacy he'd have to talk outside. So, Jet unclicked his seat belt and detached his phone from the charger. As he pulled up Shane's contact, however, memory made him hesitate.

"What's wrong?" Malone asked.

"Nothing. It's just...the last time I spoke to Shane, he was headed to the hospital for his baby's birth. He promised he'd call when he has news. Until then, though..."

"He hasn't called?"

"No. Not yet."

Malone was dead quiet in the back.

"I probably shouldn't call." Jet pulled his door shut again and buckled himself in. "Dammit."

After the silence had stretched out too long, Malone said, "You could talk to me. We could talk out...whatever you wanted to talk out with him."

"We aren't exactly that for each other, Malone." Jet's voice was dry as dust.

"People who talk? What about all those nights in the mess on the couch? All of those siestas in bed?"

"I don't recall much talking."

"True...but we can talk now. Pretend I'm Shane. What's the problem? Tell me. I'm excellent at finding solutions. It's what I do."

Jet eyed him in the rear-view mirror. "You know most of it already." And what Malone didn't know was about him.

"Even better. Lay the rest on me."

"Fair enough." *You asked for it.* Jet restarted the engine and pulled out onto the hot tarmac. No way could he stay still for this...or look Malone in the eye. "See, there's this guy..."

Chapter Thirty-one

Malone

"...there's this guy." The angle of Jet's jaw sharpened.

Oh, fuck. Jet was talking about him.

"He's super smart, intensely driven, ridiculously sexy."

Malone held his breath, waiting for the 'but'.

"But he and I aren't forever."

His heart squeezed. "Why?"

"Because that wasn't the arrangement."

Memory tickled Malone's mind—pleasure mixed with pain. "When in Rome?"

"Yeah. What's done is done."

What happens on Tallon stays on Tallon.

"Fuck that." Why'd he ever dug that hole for himself?

Because you thought Jet was a good-for-not-much peacock, Archer.

Not anymore, he didn't. Jet was the best of men—kind, caring, and fiercely protective of those he loved.

Jet's fingers squeaked on the steering wheel. "Everything he and I are is tied to an isolated place..."

True.

"...and an isolated time frame."

Also, true.

"Beyond that, he and I nothing. A wisp of cirrus cloud."

Oh, now. That's not true.

"I call BS. *You* and *I*," Malone emphasised the pronouns. He was done with the whole objective perspective bullshit. How he felt about Jet was entirely subjective—deeply personal. "*We* are whatever we say we are. On or off Tallon. What's the real reason?" *Calm down, Archer. If you push too hard, you'll drive him even further away.*

Jet's hands squeaked on the leather steering wheel. "On Tallon, we were in a bubble. Inside the bubble, everything was simple. The boundaries were clear. Outside the bubble, you have so many more options. Practically unlimited."

"As do you. Doesn't mean we can't still choose each other. If you don't believe me, then..." He held his palms up. Open. At a loss for how else to convince Jet that he was telling the truth.

"I don't."

"Ah." There was the true rub.

Show him you know him.

Show him you want him.

Show him you can be what he needs.

A kernel of an idea in mind, Malone refreshed the map on his phone then grabbed the headrest of the front passenger seat to get a better view of the road ahead. "Turn left at the next intersection. Follow the signs to Mission Beach. When you see the sea, turn left."

"Bossy." Jet grumbled, but turned off the highway as requested and fell in behind a caravan of RVs, then followed Malone's directions through the touristy town.

A few kilometres north they came to a road-side rest area between the lush rainforest and the rocky end of Bingil Bay. Malone said, "Pull the car over there, in the shade."

Jet cut the engine, bonnet facing the shimmering blue water and a dare-you-to-ignore-it yellow sign that screamed 'Achtung!' in giant black letters over cartoon symbols of a shark, a crocodile, and a jellyfish.

"Don't think you'll be wanting to swim here."

"Shame I left my stinger suit at home." Even if he didn't have a broken leg that couldn't be submerged till February, Malone wouldn't have ventured out in the hot pink monstrosity his friends had gifted him. Not when he had an audience that delighted in taking him down a peg or two. "Besides, that's not why we're here."

"Why are we here, then?" Jet asked. "It's pretty, but…"

Malone hefted Jet's backpack from the footwell beside him, unzipped the bigger section, and pulled out his data notebook, forever thankful Jet had thought to grab it before leaving the island. He flipped to an unused section and carefully ripped out an inner leaf of paper. "The graph lines might be a bit bothersome, but I trust you can make do. Here." He handed the sheet over with the box of crayons Jet took everywhere. "I figured you could do with some creative therapy after releasing all that angst." At least, he hoped Jet had released it. The alternative didn't bode well for him.

That gave him a thought. "Remind me to buy us a pink tree when we get home."

"Why would you want a pink tree? Not that I've got anything against trees. I'm a fan of photosynthesis. Love oxygen. Bring on the oh-two. But, why pink?"

"Because I made you need to do pink paper art therapy. I regret that."

"Your regret is for the tree?"

"No, for you, and for the reasons behind it. I can be insensitive, and stubborn, and obsessive, and oblivious to everything around me...including the needs of the people I care about the most." *Including you.*

"You're not that bad."

"I'm not that good, either. I'll never be perfect. Nothing in nature is. That's part of what makes it so interesting."

"So...you want to grow a pink tree to offset my future anguish?"

"Offset? I guess so. Anguish? I hope not. I can try to be what you need, but sometimes I'll fail. It's inevitable. To pretend otherwise would be a lie, and I already used up my quota."

Jet's expression softened, and he released his stranglehold on the paper. "Mr. Romantic," he muttered under his breath.

Progress, Malone thought, and he blew out a relieved breath. "Go ahead. Draw anything. Whatever catches your eye," he said, then turned his focus to the low waves that lapped the shore. Tallon was way too far away to see, but he scanned the horizon anyway, thinking back to their last moment of peace standing under Jet's seaweed mistletoe.

What he wouldn't give to go back to that day.

Undo all the damage.

Start again.

"Here you go." Jet held up the art work. "What do you think? Recognise anyone?"

"That's, ah..." *Me.* Only, Jet had given him blue skin, pink hair, and a golden yellow crown. He looked like a human nudibranch, vibrant cousin to his plain sea cucumbers. "A fair likeness. Except you forgot my ruby eyes."

"Oops. Sorry." Jet added a matching gemstone to the crown.

"Nice. It'll fit very well in my private collection."

"Hmm. That's a shame. I thought I'd offer it to the National Gallery of Art. They've been clamouring for my work."

Dry wit—nice. "Not MOMA?" Malone joked back.

"No. I don't think so." Jet put a finger to his lips, doing a piss-poor job of containing his smirk. "They can have my next masterpiece. This one is for you."

The smirk broke into a grin, and Malone knew right then that he wouldn't turn back time for anything. Without all the chaos and the pain, what happened on Tallon would have stayed on Tallon, and he wouldn't know the true depth of his feelings for Jet.

Fingers tingling with the need to touch Malone patted the front edge of the back seat. "Come here."

Please. Please.

"Why?" Jet asked, eyes dancing.

Pretty please.

"Come here," he repeated, conveying his true wish with a double pat to his chest, in rhythm with the beat of his heart.

Choose us.

The levity in Jet's eyes turned to warmth and, bypassing the doors, he threaded his lithe body through the gap between the two front seats to crouch in the foot well. Then he placed one hand on the seat beside Malone's hip, and the other on the backrest, caging him in.

"Hi." Jet's gaze slid down Malone's torso to the needy bulge at his groin.

Malone could barely breathe, uncertain what would happen next.

"Hi yourself." Malone let out a breathy laugh, feeling in his bones the never-ending tides of their relationship, drawing them together, apart, together. "Déjà vu," he explained when Jet quirked a brow in enquiry. "We've said those words before. Been here before. Done this before."

"Not this, exactly." Jet moved up and over to kneel either side of Malone's good leg, carefully forcing his way in. "Or am I wrong?"

"No." Jet was exactly right.

Malone smoothed his hands up Jet's back, the wide-open window behind him offering no resistance as he tilted his head back and lifted his chin suggestively.

It came as a surprise when Jet didn't take the bait. Instead, he asked, "Did you find anything else of interest in my backpack?"

"Umm...what?"

Jet skimmed a knuckle across the logo on Malone's shirt and hooked a finger into the pocket, giving it an idle tug. "Any other helpful supplies?"

"Supplies?" None of Jet's words computed. Unlike his deeds. Malone's body computed those just fine.

He bit his lip against the deep throb in his left leg and tented his right knee. Pressing up into Jet's heat. Persuading him closer in a move their bodies knew well.

Jet's moan vibrated between them. Their desire was in sync, even if nothing else was...yet.

Pliant, Jet rounded his back to fit into the cramped space and dropped his head to connect, forehead to forehead. Eye to eye.

"We need a whiteboard," Malone said.

"The fuck?" Jet jerked back. "You and your bloody whiteboards. I am not doing a pro and con list for our relationship."

"Don't need a list for that. The pro side wins. Hands down." Clearly, Jet knew that too, otherwise he wouldn't use the word 'relationship' to describe them.

"How do you figure?"

"One, we work well together."

"Not when you're being a grumpy arsehole. And a working relationship isn't exactly personal."

"Me being able to work alongside somebody *is* personal. Believe me. Two, we're compatible in bed."

A hum was all the response Jet gave to that. So, clearly, he agreed.

"Three, you drive me crazy."

"*I* drive *you* crazy?" If sarcasm was sugar, Jet's tone would've given Malone diabetes.

"Every bit of me is aware of you. I notice what you do, where you are, how you feel. I can't switch that off. It's kind of aggravating, to be honest."

"That's it?" Jet asked, incredulous. "Those are your three reasons?"

"The only conclusion I've been able to reach is that we belong together." Equal opposites. Magnetic poles. "Any further analysis would be superfluous." And Malone could think of far more interesting ways to spend their time.

"That's so simplistic."

"Truth doesn't always need to be complex."

"Then why the need for a whiteboard?"

"To list all the best spots to stop at for our trip. Things to do. Places to stay."

"We don't have time for random side-trips, Malone."

"Yes, we do. And our whole lives are random. If they weren't, we wouldn't have met." *And I wouldn't have fallen for you.*

Jet didn't look convinced, but Malone was determined. "We need time together. Just you and me. And the drive back to Brisbane will provide it." Time to convince Jet to give him a chance. Time for Jet to see the error of his ways.

"You think a few days on the road will be enough to prove we're a match made in heaven?"

"More like a match made on Tallon. And, yes, I do."

Jet shook his head. Disbelieving. "Didn't take you for such a romantic, Malone Archer."

"There's a lot you don't know about me, Jethro Crane."

"Now that's something we can absolutely agree on. One hundred percent." Jet shuffled his knees higher, delicious pressure against Malone's balls. "Right Mr. Romantic. What's next in this grand plan of yours to win me over?"

Malone brushed a butterfly kiss over Jet's nose, then nudged under to lift, using the tip of his nose much like his knee. Their unsteady breaths combined till finally... *Finally!...* Malone caught Jet's lips and dipped his tongue inside. "Mmm," he rumbled his pleasure at the sweetness within. "Perfect."

Jet gave a breathy laugh. "What happened to there being no such thing as perfect?"

"Pure bullshit." He nipped at Jet's lower lip. "You're perfect for me."

Jet pulled back an inch. His expression was serious. No...wary. "Are you sure? Like, one-hundred percent sure?"

"A thousand percent sure."

"There's no such thing."

"Yes, there is. A million percent sure."

Jet tensed. "No take backs. No changing your mind. No half-arsed, gone-tomorrow certainty."

"I'm infinity sure." Malone pressed his fingers into the tight swell of Jet's arse and circled his sharp hip bones with the pads of his thumbs. As though he could massage the truth in.

"Well..." The tweak of Jet's lips let Malone know he'd finally gotten through. "If you're sure."

"I'm—"

Jet cut Malone off with a hushing finger to his mouth, then he bent sideways and reached down one-handed into the backpack in the foot well. He rustled around, a frown of concentration on his face.

"What are you looking for?" Malone mumbled.

"Remember how I found something in Tallon's first aid kit?"

Jet's question stirred a memory, only he couldn't quite catch it. "Vaguely."

"Guess what it was."

"Um." It had to be something good. Something funny, given the way Jet was biting his lip, bursting to tell. "Sparkly crayons?" He guessed. Jet would get a kick out of that.

"Nope." Jet's eyes danced. "It relates to a different kind of therapeutic activity." He waggled his eyebrows.

"Rum?" Malone guessed. The last time he'd indulged, they'd gotten up to all kinds of eyebrow-waggling action.

"Warmer." Jet sat back up with something small hidden in the palm of his hand, fingers wrapped tightly around it. His voice lowered. "Something we both like. Something we've both missed."

Something small.

Something they'd both enjoy a whole hell of a lot—if Malone was to believe Jet's impish smile.

Something...

A memory snagged his mind.

It can't be.

It must have been written on his face, because Jet nodded, urging him to voice the delicious thought. "Condoms?"

"Ta-da!" Jet's grin was blistering as he revealed the foil square. "Pre-lubed."

"Fuck, yeah."

"Ha! There's the poetic Poseidon I know and love."

Love.

It could've been a slip of the tongue, but Malone quickly overrode the fresh caution in Jet's eyes and reiterated the rule Jet had demanded of him, "No take backs."

Jet's mouth pursed, then he slowly nodded. "No take backs."

"I love you too." Malone didn't see any sense in holding back that fact. "No bullshit."

Since the rest was only details, and hardly of the highest priority, Malone grabbed for the foil square and held it up between his thumb and first finger. "Now, can we please make use of this first aid remedy? I'm dying over here." He slipped it into his shirt pocket for temporary safe-keeping

"Really? Well...we wouldn't want that."

CHAPTER THIRTY-TWO

Jet

The first touch felt like stars colliding.

It shouldn't have. They'd touched a hundred times...a thousand times...nothing mysterious about it. But when Malone's fingers snuck under his t-shirt and skimmed up the tender sides of his ribs, Jet knew they'd entered new territory.

It was like being a virgin all over again.

Jet's nerves jangled as he raised his arms and Malone lifted the cotton higher. It was a relief for the material to cover his face for a few seconds—to have a moment to himself to experience the flutter of emotion that caught in his throat. Only, when the tight neckline released from his chin, stripping the blind away, and he saw Malone's desire in full technicolour, his nerves dissolved away.

Hands freed, Jet brought them down to cup Malone's scruffy jaw. "My dear," he said, echoing Malone's ridiculous endearment.

Malone dropped the t-shirt into the back of the SUV. "Sweetness," he countered with a quirk of a smile as he skimmed the tip of his finger slowly across Jet's lower lip.

Jet followed it with his tongue, then caught it with a snap of his teeth before it could disappear.

"Oi." The light in Malone's eyes flared. "None of that."

Jet circled the tip with his tongue, then let it go. "Why?"

"Because we're having a moment here."

Oh, serious Malone is seriously sexy.

"Hmm. I'd say we've *had* a moment. And I'm hoping we're about to have *another* moment." Jet waggled his eyebrows, just in case Malone didn't get it. "Not sure about this interval right now, though. Seems a bit dull." Jet squeezed his arse cheeks together against the meat of Malone's thigh, teasing them both. "Boring."

He felt the answering tightness in Malone's quad muscles.

"Cheeky arsehole."

"Whatever could you mean, Mr. Archer?" Jet squeezed again. "Ho hum."

"Get up here." Malone wrapped an arm around his waist, dug Jet's knee out from the hot cave between his legs, and lifted Jet's weight over to fully straddle both thighs.

Careful not to drop onto Malone's injured leg, Jet braced himself with his hands on Malone's shoulders. Concern must have shown on his face, though, because Malone said, "I'm fine."

"But, your leg. Let me turn around." Logistically, Jet didn't see how they could fuck face-to-face. Not without doing more damage.

"It's not a problem," Malone said.

"Oh?" He eyed the rigid outline of Malone's cock, and his hole pulsed, greedy for it. "Did your penis grow ten inches overnight? If not, docking procedures are going to be tricky."

"Fuck, no." Malone took his own turn waggling his eyebrows. "I have other things in mind."

"Other things?" Jet couldn't believe what he was hearing. "We finally have a condom, and you want to do *other things*?"

"Mm-hmm. For starters." The arm at his lower back drew Jet higher, till his shoulder blades pressed against the felt surface of the roof, and all he could see of Malone were cupid curls and the taper of broad shoulders hidden beneath his polo shirt.

Jet was about to insist he strip off said polo when Malone wrapped his other arm around the back of Jet's thighs and pulled him higher, closer, till Jet's head hung half out the window, spooking a seagull off of its 'Achtung!' perch.

"Um...Mal? I'm not too sure about this." It wasn't how he'd foreseen events progressing, but before Jet could protest further wet heat landed on his stomach, then on the peak of his hip-bone, then on the place below the knot of his sarong where the material split apart, then Malone hooked Jet's underwear below his sac, and— "Ngah!" —swallowed him down.

"Mmm," Malone hummed around him, sending micro-shudders to his balls.

Jet scoured at Malone's back. Tugging at the stretchy material of his polo. Scrambling for purchase. "Don't stop," he said, breathlessly. Not that Malone showed any sign of stopping. If anything, he ramped up a gear, doubling the suction just as he ran his free hand up the back of Jet's thigh to burrow under the leg of his stretched-taut underwear. In its wake, a rash of prickly heat spread all the way to Jet's crack, where the pads of Malone's devious fingers pressed against his hole, demanding entry.

Jet would have welcomed them.

Come on in. The more the merrier.

But right then a car whizzed by on the road.

And then another one neared. A hippy surfer-dude van, wallpapered with peace stickers.

Jet would have paid it no mind, but it slowed down.

"Malone?" Jet tapped his shoulder.

It veered off the road, tyres crunching on the gravel of the rest area.

"Malone." Jet instinctively curled tighter over Malone's head, inadvertently shoving his cock deeper into Malone's hot-as-hell volcano of a mouth. They both groaned, and it was all Jet could do to stop himself from rutting like a wild boar.

A single fingertip slipped in.

The van steered closer to their SUV. Sun glinting off the front window.

"Mal!" Jet clenched his cheeks and tapped frantically at Malone's shoulder. Didn't he know that was the universal signal for 'stop before people see my bare arse!'?

Seems not, Jethro.

"Malone! There are people!" Desperate to preserve at least some dignity, Jet gathered his strength to push up on the window opening, wrench his aching cock out of Malone's mouth, and duck back into the relative safety of the SUV, thereby impaling himself even further onto Malone's finger. "Gah!"

"Didn't factor that in, huh?" Malone eased another knuckle deeper and hooked the tip of his finger to press against Jet's sensitive bundle of nerves.

"Oh, God." Shivers ran up his spine and he rode Malone's finger twice...make that thrice...before he could control himself enough to stop. He hung in the air like a debaucherous still-life, his spit-shined dick wavering around, homeless, and Malone's finger still deep in his arse.

So undignified.

It didn't help that Malone looked wrecked, too. In fact, it was the only reason Jet didn't slap the wicked digit away.

Sure. Tell yourself that, Jethro.

"Bloody hell." Jet gripped the front and back seats and hauled in a breath to steady himself. "When we were on Tallon, I didn't care if the astronauts on the International Space Station could see my moon of a bare arse, but it's different here. I refuse to flash my wet dick to some random on the road." If he said it firmly enough, maybe his willpower would kick in.

"They won't see it if it's in my mouth."

"That's not..." The vision alone was enough to send Jet's mind spinning. "Fuck, Mal. Why do you have to be so logical?" It wasn't fair. Especially when the only coherent thought filling Jet's mind was 'cock, mouth, now'.

Malone just shrugged and leaned in to lick a pearly drop of precum off the tip. "Mmm. You taste like the sea."

"Gah!"

"You want me to stop?" Malone's tongue did a fancy little loop around his cock head before Jet could gather enough sense to grab at the man's wild hair and push him away.

"Yes! No! God, I don't know." Heart racing, he couldn't catch his breath, his lungs strung as tight as his balls.

"That's clear."

"Yeah, well, this *moment* we're having isn't exactly how I pictured it."

"Are they still there?"

Confused, Jet asked, "Who?"

"The people."

"Oh, ah…" He ducked and weaved as much as he could in his precarious position to look outside. The hippy surfer-dude van was nowhere to be seen. "No. They've gone."

"Good."

The word 'suction' did nothing to describe the sweet torture that Malone's lips and tongue and throat then put him through. There was nothing fast and furious about it. Malone's intense gaze seared into him as his clever tongue spiralled down Jet's length. He nosed Jet's black pubes, clamped his lips tight, hollowed his cheeks, and drew back…slow as molasses.

The urge to thrust was strong, but Jet held himself still, taut as a bowstring. Sensitive to every minute sensation, Jet swore he could feel the nubs of Malone's taste buds. He palmed the side of Malone's neck and ran a thumb along his jaw, feeling the muscles strain as he worked.

It wasn't a regular blowjob.

It was a loving.

The realisation made Jet's mind spin, knowing he'd almost thrown a relationship with Malone away. Missed out on everything they could be together.

A second finger slipped in and warmth flooded Jet's core. The rush as much emotional as it was physical. Impossible to contain.

"Malone!" he cried out. "Mal, Mal, Mal!"

Gawd, I sound like a fucking seagull.

Just as he was about to blow, Malone popped off of him. "I changed my mind."

"What?!" Jet squawked as the ghosts of rejections past came back to haunt. He tried to pull away, but Malone's left arm was a steel rod across the back of his thighs, holding him in place.

None of the intensity had disappeared from Malone's expression, either, and the way he rubbed his bristled cheek across Jet's raging cock was contrary to every fear in Jet's heart.

It made no sense.

Malone was the one who had run after Jet. Why was he suddenly having second thoughts?

What had Jet missed?

A puzzled frown appeared on Malone's forehead, then cleared. "No. Not that. Not us. Fuck. Sorry, Jet. I haven't changed my mind about us. Not that at all."

"Then...what?" he asked, lost.

"I meant my name."

It was Jet's turn to frown. "What about your name?"

"You keep calling me Mal."

"Oh. Fuck. I'm sorry. I know you don't like it."

"No. I do like it. I loved it."

"Oh, well..." Relief made Jet's heart race to a different beat.

"You can call me Mal. Only you, though. Nobody else."

"Just me?" Jet waited with bated breath.

"Just you."

Jet drew a finger up the side of Malone's face. He took his time, coasting up over the throbbing pulse at Malone's temple, collecting a bead of sweat that threatened to fall. "Mal," Jet tested the feel of it on his tongue...the sound of it out loud. And the last vestiges of chill burned away from his soul.

"Jet?"

It wasn't clear what Malone was asking, but Jet had his own answer.

"I'm ready." He plucked the condom from Malone's polo shirt pocket and ripped it open. "More than ready."

He backed away to glove Mal's hot and heavy cock, making him hiss.

"It's okay." Jet brushed a kiss to Malone's cock-swollen lips. "Let me take care of you." Cautious of Malone's injured leg, Jet contorted himself like a pretzel till he was repositioned, his back to Malone's front. One foot planted in the footwell, the other tucked up tight beside Malone's right hip. "Jesus. What is it with us and close quarters?" Jet muttered, huffing out a nervous laugh. Though God knew why he was nervous. It wasn't like it was their first rodeo.

Oh, wait. It is.

"Easy." Malone held Jet either side of his waist, guiding him down.

The two fingers had done a semi-decent job of opening him up, but it was still a strain—the pressure on his ring almost too much to take. "Go slow," he said on a hot breath, then bore down, and slowly, determinedly, took Mal deep within. "God, Mal. So full."

"So tight," came Malone's gruff, breathy reply. And for a long beat, Malone held him there, not letting Jet move despite the mad itch to do so.

Wandering at the lengthy pause, Jet scanned Malone's leg, searching for any hint of discomfort. "You okay?" he asked.

"More than okay." The grip at Jet's waist softened, and Malone's hands slid around him. Palms flat to his stomach.

It wasn't quite a hug, but the warmth of it brought a lump to Jet's throat. What he wouldn't give to be in their donga back on Tallon. Just them, a few thousand birds, and the vast horizon to witness them finally coming together. So close, and yet... "I can't believe our first time is in a car on the side of a road. I can't even see you." It wasn't fair.

"Close your eyes."

"What? Why?" Jet tried to twist at the waist, but Malone wouldn't allow it.

"Close your eyes," Mal repeated, his voice firm.

"If you insist." Daylight sparked tie-died gold through his eyelids. "Okay. They're closed. Now what?"

"Imagine us."

That was easy. Jet didn't need sight to envisage them together. He'd already captured in his memory every square inch of Malone's body.

"Imagine me behind you."

He felt Malone's forehead drop to the space between his shoulder blades. His hair tickling Jet's nape.

"Imagine me touching you."

One of Malone's hands travelled lower, encircling the base of Jet's throbbing cock.

"Imagine me filling you up."

Jet reflexively jerked his hips, thrusting an inch into Malone's fist and, consequently, an inch off of Malone's cock. "Fu-uck." So good. Jet wrapped his hand around Malone's grip and demanded, "More."

"Too dry. I'll hurt you." Malone released his hold, but Jet didn't let the hand go. He raised it to his mouth and licked a wide swathe across Malone's palm, then returned it to where it belonged.

"More," Jet repeated his demand as he gave in to his own need to move, but it wasn't until he heard Malone's breath catch by his ear that Jet really let go, rolling his hips to a thunderous beat. Between the rough stranglehold on his cock, and the sparks firing from every stroke of his gland, Jet didn't know in from out, up from down. All he knew was pressure and friction and the driving need to get closer, go further, feel more. "God, Mal."

"I know."

"This is so, so…" Jet's chest heaved, sheened pink with arousal.

"Perfect."

"Hell, yeah." It was. Truly. If he could, he would've ridden Malone into the sunset.

Jet arched his back and reached for Malone's sweaty nape, angling for a messy kiss that tasted of sunshine and salt and sweet promises.

Malone gave as good as he got—sucking on Jet's tongue, stealing every breath, matching him stroke for stroke. And when the inevitable release came, surging from the place deep in Jet's soul where hope lived, Malone was right there with him, holding him close.

Safe in his arms.

Home.

CHAPTER THIRTY-THREE

Malone

Five days later...

As Jet threw the SUV into gear and accelerated away from the red light, the momentum pressed Malone's shoulder into the back seat and made him wince as a flare of pain broke through the dull ache in his leg.

"Are you okay?" Jet asked.

"Yeah." Before he could explain to Jet for the umpteenth time that the pain was nothing new, and that, no, he wouldn't rather be coddled by nurses in a hospital bed than stuck in the SUV with Jet, Malone's phone chimed.

He tapped the notification, and the screen lit up, coating him in blue light.

Where are you? Thirteen mins till midnight!!!!!!!!!!!!!!

Malone looked around to figure out how far they still had to drive before they'd get home to Tennyson Bend. "Damn. We'll never make it to Brady's New Year's Eve party. Not before midnight."

The whites of Jet's eyes glinted at him in the rear-view mirror. "And whose fault is that?"

"Yours."

Jet sputtered. "How do you figure that?"

"You're in the driver's seat."

"Yeah, right. You were the one who insisted we stop at every bloody big thing in the state."

"I did not."

Jet snorted. "Whose idea was it to visit the big cassowary at Mission Beach?"

"That's different. We sealed the deal at Mission Beach. How else were we supposed to mark the occasion?"

"I'm thinking we marked it pretty well with *your* big thing." The dim light of the dash caught the prod of Jet's tongue in his cheek.

Malone did absolutely nothing to hide his grin. It was infantile of him, but he didn't care. If Jet wanted to classify his cock as a big thing, Malone wasn't going to argue.

"That doesn't explain why we had to stop at the big cane toad."

"Uh, yeah. That was a little underwhelming," Malone had to concede. "But it's not like it slowed us down much. It was right there, smack dab in the middle of the highway."

"And the big bull?" Jet gave an overly dramatic, put-upon sigh, which Malone didn't take seriously for one second. Jet had enjoyed the meandering drive south just as much as he had.

"Bulls. Plural," Malone corrected.

"Uh-huh. And we had to read *aaall* about each and every one of them. Fun times."

"Rockhampton has a proud agricultural history." *Truth.*

"Ri-iight. It had nothing do to with you wanting to prolong the trip so that we could have more..." Jet let go of the wheel just long enough to give air quotes, "'quality time' together?"

"No." *Lie.* Why did Jet have to be so insightful? It wasn't fair.

The main arterial road into Brisbane was one long strip mall of burger joints and petrol stations and car dealerships. Their fluorescent lights in every colour of the rainbow blurred into racing stripes as the SUV sped along the near-deserted road toward the city centre.

Too fast, Malone thought, wishing he could pump the brakes. To slow down. Just a little.

Aside from the fun of bringing in the new year with his mates, there were a lot of pros to returning home. Number one being he could stretch out flat on his bed and point at his blank bedroom wall and say, "that'd be a perfect spot to hang the cuc-scape, don't you think?", after which they'd sixty-nine blowjobs, and he'd fall asleep with Jet in his arms and a smile in his heart.

Or something like that.

The problem was, getting home meant letting the world in, and Malone wasn't ready to share Jet. Not yet.

"I have to admit, the big bottle of rum was pretty cool. If we ever get back to Tallon, Vic will love us for replacing the stock we drank," Jet said.

"I have no interest in the stuff," Malone sniffed.

"Uh-huh. Sure, birthday boy."

"You're the one who plied me with boozy lava cake and Vic juice."

"Oi! I'll concede to the cake, but the amount of truth juice you drank is all on you."

"I regret nothing." Especially not that choice. Without it, he wouldn't be with Jet, and they wouldn't be planning their future together. "Nothing," Malone quietly reasserted, because that was the biggest truth of them all.

"Our biggest mistake was going to the big pineapple today. That took hours."

"Buttermilk macadamia praline chunk ice-cream." Was more than enough explanation, as far as Malone was concerned. When he'd Googled the place and discovered they made his favourite flavour from local-sourced milk and fresh nuts, grown on site, no way was Malone not stopping for a cone of the good stuff. "And if my memory serves me correctly, you did enjoy that mocha fudge sundae."

"Details." Jet waved that off. "I liked the big whale better. Majestic."

Oh, now...that was a whole different kettle of fish. "Bloody whale," Malone grumbled.

"What's wrong with the whale?"

"Too shiny."

"Ri-ight. I think you're jealous. Disappointed there isn't a big sea cucumber."

"Don't be ridiculous."

"It's not ridiculous to want to celebrate the thing you're most passionate about. And, FYI, if someone did erect a giant cucumber—animal or vegetable—I guarantee it'd be on Australia's tourism must-see list. I mean, if you're looking to make a cultural impact..."

"That's not the sort of impact I'm trying to make," Malone protested. "Besides, sea cucumbers aren't the thing I'm most passionate about. Not anymore."

"Oh? Do tell."

God, he was adorable.

"Still fishing, Mr. Crane?"

"Still cagey, Mr. Archer?" Jet flashed back.

"Always." Not that it mattered. Jet had a knack for seeing through his bullshit. Still, it rarely hurt to speak the truth. "Your arse is my number one passion."

"Yesss!" Jet fist-pumped the air. "Numero uno."

"Oh, God. You're going to be insufferable now, aren't you?"

"I reserve the right to be lovable any damn way I please."

"Grr."

Jet laughed. And, God, that sound. It made Malone's heart so light. He felt for the car seat to make sure he didn't levitate.

As Jet flipped on the lane indicator and steered the SUV down into the toll-road tunnel, Malone's phone chimed for the fourth time in as many minutes.

"Is that Brady again?"

"They've all messaged me. Brady's pissed that we're going to be late. He says if we don't get to his place by the time the clock strikes midnight, he'll tell the reporters where we really are. Sic them on us. His words."

"Bastard."

"He's just kidding. Brady would never sell us out. According to his social feed, we're currently cruising back to Brisbane."

"As in, on-the-high-seas type cruising? Hornblower style?"

"More like in one of those floating cities with bingo and can-can dancers. But, yes."

"Huh. Clever."

"I'll tell him you said so."

"And the others?"

"Dane says he's run out of scotch."

"Is that bad?" Jet asked.

"Tragic."

"Oo-kay."

"Spencer sent car park instructions. He says we should use his space because Lachlan's is occupied with a papier mâché project, and the kayaks are clogging up mine."

"Ohhh! Papier mâché. Ooey gooey deliciousness. And you get art out of it. What's not to love?"

"Mm-hmm." Managing to keep a straight face, Malone nodded. "That's what I always say."

"Droll, Mal. So droll."

"I try."

"So, that's Brady, Dane, and Spencer. What about Lachlan?"

"Lucky last. He sent a picture of a cocktail topped with every tropical fruit imaginable and a canary yellow umbrella. The inscription reads, 'missing out'."

"Subtle."

"That's our Lachlan. I should tell him it's perfect for you. The umbrella looks just like your hat, only about a thousand times smaller."

"What would he say if I told him my drink of choice is a flaming sambuca?"

"He'd call you a retro weirdo, then run out to buy some sambuca and matches."

Jet sighed a happy sigh. "I can't wait to meet them all."

They emerged from the tunnel to crest the rise over Spring Hill, and the gleaming river city came into view. Strobe lights skated across the sky, illuminating the winding river and thousands of revellers lining the bank, eager for the stroke of midnight.

Malone hitched himself as far forward as he could and laid a hand on Jet's shoulder, needing to connect. "It feels odd to be back. Don't you think? Like worlds colliding."

"Mal, my sweet, our worlds already collided. And I can't wait to see what comes next for us. Together."

The last word barely left Jet's mouth before the sky exploded with star-bright fireworks.

"Me too," Malone said, and shimmers of light rained down upon them.

Together.

EPILOGUE

Jet

One month later...

"Stay in me," Jet said, breathless. He arched his back, not wanting to lose the close hold he had on Malone's softening cock, but the inevitable post-orgasm lethargy couldn't be denied. He just managed to swipe his still warm cum from Malone's stomach with a corner of the wrinkled sheet before flopping down flush on his glorious chest.

Thank the lord of the seas for narrow bunks.

"Comfy?" Malone asked, one broad hand resting on Jet's sweaty lower back.

"Mm-hmm." The stickiness between them wasn't delightful, but Jet wouldn't want to be anywhere else. He eased his knees out from their cramped position beside Malone's ribs and splayed his long legs down either side of Malone's, hugging them gently. In another week or so, when Malone's leg was fully healed, Jet would be able to stretch out from top to toe. "My own personal surfboard."

"Oi." Malone squeezed his arse cheek in retaliation.

It wasn't a terribly effective protest, since Jet couldn't get enough of having Malone's paws all over him. "You love me," he said.

"I do." Malone sighed, the great rise of his chest making Jet feel like he was suspended on cloud nine. Or, it would have, if cloud nine had a beating heart and if it swayed and swooped like a twin-hulled catamaran at sea.

Jet shifted a little to the stern side of their shared berth, his left shoulder squeezing into the small space between Malone and the fibreglass cabin wall. "We'll be there soon." He combed his fingers through Malone's sweaty chest hair. Zero urgency.

Malone slid his left hand along Jet's forearm and laced their fingers together. "Captain Thompson said we'd arrive at about sunrise."

"Mmm." Hazy dawn light filled their tiny cabin, which meant they didn't have much longer to relax together in total privacy.

The month since they'd driven home to Tennyson Bend had been a tangled mess of caring for his crotchety patient-slash-lover, passing the 'are you good enough?' test with their respective friends, welcoming Shane and Kristy's new little tyke to the fold, tackling legal bullshit with Dick and his dickish kin, and dealing with pesky journalists who still thought his and Malone's dramatic survival on Tallon was the love story of the season. Which it was, of course, but it was *their* story, and none of the journalist's business. In Dane's perfectly illustrative words, "They can all go fuck themselves."

Thank you, Dane.

Moving into Eloise's rambling old house by the river had been a weird but wonderful reprieve from the chaos, taking them one step closer to domestic bliss. In fact, the only thing he and Malone had argued about was where to hang the cuc-scape. As far as Jet was concerned, it was a good luck charm and deserved pride of place in the front entrance where visitors could see and appreciate it. Malone, for reasons Jet still couldn't get his head around, insisted it stay locked away in the privacy of their bedroom.

Go figure.

Boarding the Opportune to return to Tallon for the rest of the summer was the circuit-breaker they both needed. Eventually, they'd arrive on the island, but so long as the catamaran's engines roared, they could co-exist in their own perfect hideaway.

"I don't want to move," Jet said.

Malone squeezed their conjoined fingers in a brief clasp of agreement, then he loosened his hold, but he didn't quite let go. Instead, he played with Jet's fingers. Not so much weaving as crocheting—one hook, one thread, one knot at a time—smoothing along and around and between each finger at a mesmerising pace.

Jet's eyelids drooped at the dreaminess of it all. "We'll have to go on a hunt for washed up seaweed to macramé into a fresh dreamcatcher. You'd be good at it, what with your advanced attention to detail," Jet teased.

Malone's light huff barely registered, but his finger motions didn't stop.

Nerves firing, Jet's fingers twitched. "Or knitting. My mum tried to teach me when I was eleven, but I'm shit at following patterns." Was it his ring finger Malone was homing in on? Surely not. "The most fun craft Mum ever taught me was felting. There're no rules. Y'know? No matter what you create, it's never wrong. It's like crayons. Total freedom."

Stop prattling, Jethro.

He bit at his bottom lip. Worrying at a loose bit of skin. Trying to silence his mouth before he screwed up whatever Malone was working himself up to do. To say. To ask.

Please ask.

Malone's finger dipped and wove. Could he feel Jet's fluttering pulse? It was practically twerking, it was beating so fast. Normally, he prided himself on being a calm soul, patient and sensitive to others' needs. But there wasn't a single bit of patience or calm in Jet's soul as Malone spun an imaginary ring around his finger. It probably lasted only ten seconds, but to Jet it felt like an eternity. Nothing could stop him from blurting out, "We should make this our honeysun."

Malone's movements stopped. "What?"

Shit. It's too soon for declarations. Two months in each other's company, twenty-four-seven, is practically a year in dating time, but we barely know each other. Does he prefer fries or salad with his steak? Does he wear turtlenecks in winter? So many unknowns. Too many. I've seen him at his worst, and he's seen me at mine, but our life so far has been bright-shiny summer. He hasn't met my family. He doesn't know where I come from. He has no way of knowing if I'll turn into an ugly old queen, or a high-mainte-

nance nag, or an unlovable grouch. How could he possibly know if he'll still love me in five years, let alone fifty?

"Jet." Malone broke through his wild stream of consciousness. His gorgeous aquamarine eyes were like twin defibrillator paddles restarting Jet's heart.

"Yeah?"

"What's a honeysun?"

Shit. Why did I have to suggest that? So cheesy. But Jet couldn't not answer. Not when Malone was looking at him like...like... *Like what, Jethro?* Like he hung the sun and the moon.

Malone loved him. That much he knew for sure. So, why not dive in?

Be brave.

Jet steeled his heart. "It's like a honeymoon, only it happens before you get married instead of after."

Thankfully, the universe didn't implode.

Malone's movements started up again. Spinning around and around. Caught in an infinity loop. "You made that up," he said.

The mild accusation warmed Jet from the inside out. Maybe they didn't know absolutely everything about each other, but Malone knew enough to know Jet wasn't above a little creativity with the truth. Confidence bolstered, he said, "As though making stuff up ever stopped me. We can make a couple of froufrou cocktails out of Vic's rum. And I remembered to pack the hammock Shane gave me for our belated Christmas. We can hang it up and have wild monkey sex under the stars."

Malone huffed, amused. "A, Vic might have something to say about us drinking his rum again."

"Pshaw." A weak excuse. "Vic's a marshmallow."

"B, there aren't any trees on Tallon, so I don't see where you're planning to hang it."

"I'm sure I can find a couple of hooks somewhere in the supply shed. We can string it up between the dongas." He could see it so clearly. "You and me under the Milky Way, just like on your birthday." What felt like an eon ago.

The hand on Jet's arse spread out to cover one butt cheek. Proprietary. "Which brings me to C. Nakedness in a string hammock seems like a murderous mix."

Jet was about to take Malone to task for his not so sexy use of alliteration when the catamaran's engines shifted down a gear, the change in momentum pressed them together, and a fingertip dipped into Jet's crack, making him squirm. "Holy Poseidon." He stuck his nose into the warm nook of Malone's neck.

It wouldn't take much convincing to go again, but right then a familiar voice hollered an, "Ahoy there!" from somewhere far too close for comfort.

"Was that Vic?" Malone asked.

"I think so."

"Buzzkill," Malone muttered, making Jet snort.

Maybe Malone did have a point about wild monkey hammock sex within hearing range of their cranky team leader.

He lifted his torso a few inches to get a better view out the low porthole window. At first, all he could see was the wide blue ocean and the soft pink and purple of the dawn sky above, but then the catamaran changed direction and the island came into view. The familiar globe of the radar tower perched above the low-lying weather station was nothing but a dark shape, backlit

by a thin edge of gold on the horizon. "Sun's rising," Jet said as
a shard of light shot through their porthole and into his eyes.
"Ugh." He tilted his head down, blinking fast to wash away
the afterimage, then paused the battering, because that same
glow had turned Malone's curls to spun gold. "Oh, wow. You're
glowing like an angel."

"Me? An angel?" The fingertip in Jet's crack dipped lower,
proving Malone's incredulity well-founded.

"When I first saw you, I thought you looked like a cupid."

Malone's eyebrows scrunched together, expressing exactly
what he thought about that.

"A handsome, manly cupid," Jet expanded, memory sparking fresh heat in interesting places.

The eyebrows relaxed, and a half smile quirked Malone's
mouth. He reached up and caressed Jet's bottom lip. "And I
thought you looked like a bird of paradise."

"What? Like a rainbow lorikeet?" They were pretty, but Jet
didn't see the likeness. "I know you don't mean a cassowary.
Out of the two of us, you are the hard-headed one."

"No. A bird of paradise is a flower, with lush and spiky petals
of yellow and purple."

"Okay." That wasn't totally terrible. "I can get behind yellow
and purple. At least they're complementary colours."

Malone groaned. "Please tell me we don't have to consult the
colour wheel again."

Jet ignored that complaint. Malone loved sea cucumbers, for
fuck's sake—he couldn't help being aesthetically challenged.
"I'm not spiky, though." That part of the analogy was ridiculous.

"Beautiful," Malone said, with a hint of a smile.

"Better."

The smile spread. "Luscious."

"Even betterer." He rewarded Malone with a kiss that was, indeed, luscious.

"Mmm."

Jet chased Malone's satisfied groan it with a spiky nip to his lip.

"Oi."

"Serves you right."

"For what?"

"For teasing me with your cupid hair and your twirly fingers, promising forever."

Gawd, did I really say that?

Jet hid his face again. His heart racing in jagged spikes.

The hand at his lower back traced up Jet's spine and spread out at the base of his ribs, soothing Jet into misplaced comfort until Malone asked, "Does this mean I should have waited to ask Captain Thompson to marry us on the way back from Tallon?"

"Cap--" Record scratch. Jet lurched up. "You did what?"

A blush flared up Malone's neck, but his eyes were clear as Tallon's lagoon on a fine day as he met Jet's gaze. "I, ah, I had a little word with the captain last night."

"About?"

"About making us official."

"As in...?"

"As in you becoming my Mister Archer, and me becoming your Mister Crane. Turns out he's not just a ship's captain. He's a celebrant, too."

"Mal." Jet couldn't stop his mouth from falling open. "Are you serious?"

The blush raced up to his hairline. "I blame Kathy."

The Opportune's first officer? "How so?"

Malone grimaced. "She got all gushy over us. Made out like we're some kind of romantic fantasy. All rainbows and unicorns."

That didn't sound so bad. "I'm rather partial to rainbows and unicorns."

"Yes, but life isn't always like that. Love isn't always like that. It's gritty and real. It's about sticking together through thick and thin."

"Joy and pain," Jet agreed. They'd had enough of the latter to last them a lifetime.

"Exactly." Malone reached up and threaded his fingers through Jet's black-as-night hair. It'd grown another finger-width since New Year's Eve—just long enough for Malone to get a grip and hold on tight. "No matter the risk, you're not afraid to commit to what brings you joy."

"Including you."

Malone's smile was a work of beauty. "Including us."

Jet couldn't have said it any better himself. Unable to contain the love that welled up, he dropped down onto Malone's chest and pressed a kiss to his warm heart. "How wild are the winds of fate?"

"Is that a yes?"

Jet looked up, heart in his throat. "That's a hell yes."

Malone's tension subsided, and again Jet felt the rise to cloud nine.

Honeysun, here we come.

THANK YOU!

Thank you for reading *Thrall*!

Jet and Malone's story was always about rising to challenges.

Challenge #1: How to make stormy weather sexy.

Challenge #2: How to make sea-cucumber science sexy.

Challenge #3: How to make seaweed macramé sexy.

Hmm...

Challenge accepted!

If you enjoyed Jet and Malone's story and would like to help other readers discover it, please consider leaving a rating or review!

For quirky content and updates on future books, subscribe to my newsletter at https://ptambler.com/newsletter-sign-up/

ALSO BY PT AMBLER

Tennyson Bend:
Haven
Deuce
Thrall

———ℓℓ———

Duly Domesticated:
Where There's a Wil, There's a Way
I'll Make a Manny Out of You

———ℓℓ———

For an updated list, please visit:
ptambler.com/books

ABOUT PT AMBLER

PT Ambler is an Aussie MM romance author who gets a ridiculous amount of joy letting her guys run rampant on the page.

Other fun things include sing-along road trips, zoning out in nature, day dreaming, people-watching in cafes, and coffee...smooth, delicious coffee, covered in shavings of rich, dark chocolate...mmm.

One of these days, she's going to write a novel set in a café about a gorgeous barista, who... (PT drifts away into a caffeine-fuelled daydream).

To find out more, check out https://ptambler.com, sign up for my newsletter at https://ptambler.com/newsletter-sign-up/, or catch me (occasionally) on Instagram at https://www.instagram.com/pt_ambler/

www.ingramcontent.com/pod-product-compliance
Lightning Source LLC
Chambersburg PA
CBHW030634020726
47493CB00006B/1711